Written by

Nigel J Williams

Blood and Country

Volume Two in the Salt's War Series

1

Contents

3

Prologue. Invergordon.

By the end of 1917, HMS Invergordon's strategic setting on the banks of the Cromarty Forth was proving ideal for covert Naval submarine operations. The submarines would venture out at night under the cover of darkness and pass quietly into the North Sea and enter the Russian Baltic.

Of course, this was a long time before the advent of modern sonar and wireless detection. Back then covert spying missions carried out by submarine, were virtually undetectable.

But, right from the beginning, unknown to all but the current Prime Minister and a few choice fellows at the Admiralty, Invergordon had been designed for a duel role. Because HMS Invergordon was also home to the Royal Naval secret intelligence service. The elite. 'NIS.'

Invergordon was where Naval spies learnt their trade, honed their skills, and prepared for one day to go; `Deep cover. `

Formed just after the Russian Revolution in 1917 the *'Blue liners'* as they were affectionally known, the forerunner of our modern-day Naval intelligence service was set up to counter Russian spies entering Great Britain, posing as political or economic refugees

Czar Nicholas, and the whole of the Romanov family, first cousins to the monarch King George V had been brutally murdered by the ruling Soviet just after the Bolshevik revolution in October of that year, and Soviet Russia's relationship with the British Empire had deteriorated to the point where war, seemed all but inevitable.

So, the British Government of the time led by the staunch Liberalist Prime Minister *David Lloyd George* formed a Naval counter-intelligence division in order to infiltrate these self-proclaimed 'sleeper groups.' The government's concern at the time was that this 'Fifth Column' was becoming so entrenched in the higher echelons of British society that their communist ideology was spreading throughout the country like a pandemic. 'Leninism,' as it was referred, seemed an attractive prospect to those unfortunates that had been so sadly cast aside and left on the scrapheap at the end of the Great War. Soviet intentions were to drive an intelligence spike right through the very heart of the British Imperialists.

So, this is HMS Invergordon's story: But it's not only that, it also tells the story of the very brave men and women who work in our intelligence services, risking their lives every single day of every single year, vigilantly protecting our shores from all enemies either foreign or domestic. And ask only one thing in return. Absolute loyalty to our country. So, 'Blood and Country' is dedicated to them. Because this is their story as well.

Chapter 1. Salty Passes Out.

H.M.S. Invergordon: Deep water port and Naval Intelligence Base. 1964.

Following his discharge from TS Seaway in 1961, Salty was offered a regular commission in the Royal Navy by his friend and mentor, Captain Jack `Black` McPherson.

So, the following is Sam's part of that story.

"Attention! Officer of the guard ready to receive the salute. Sah!"

Newly promoted sub-Lieutenant Sam Salt placed his ceremonial sword to his nose then turned his head towards the Captains podium, as the Royal Marine band struck up; 'Hearts of Oak.'

At the same time, Captain Jack `Black` McPherson offered up his white gloved hand in a formal salute, and watched as his protégé, the young sub-Lieutenant Sam Salt marched smartly passed.

Fluent in French, Spanish, German, and two other separate Arab dialects, but more importantly Russian. Salty had finished top of every class and was passing out of HMS Invergordon as leading cadet and with flying colours.

The newly promoted sub-Lieutenant sensed his parents were watching him as the band played and he marched passed with the cold steel of the sword pressed hard against his nose. He thought he could see them standing next to Jack in the morning mist, he could even make out the outline of their smiling faces through the drizzle as they waved, and applauded. He wanted to wave back or even shout out, but their image just faded in the hoary grey, and once more they were gone. And gone forever.

As he entered the guards hangar at the end of the long parade ground, Salty and fourteen other young officers who had passed out that day stamped their boots to the damp concrete floor and marked time as four ratings pulled the heavy steel doors across and fourteen newly promoted sub-Lieutenant's hollered a loud cheer, lofting their white peaked caps high in the air. And in that glorious moment four long arduous years of back breaking training, were temporarily forgotten.

As the cheering quelled, Salty picked his cap up from the concrete floor, dusted it down and looked up to see Captain Jack `Black` McPherson standing just in front of him radiating a grin that could only be described as; 'the cat who'd found all the cream.' So, smartly replacing his cap and standing immediately to attention, Salty quickly raised his right hand up and offered a smart salute of his own as Jack walked towards him;

"Well done sub-Lieutenant Salt, you made it, I wasn't always sure you would, you know. A little touch and go at times. A bit touch and go my boy."

Jack's eyes tightened around his weather-beaten face as he realised his playful attempt at humour was utterly wasted on the young Salt, and the joke was actually on him. After all, Salty had won the leading cadet sword and passed out with flying colours. And Jack loved and respected him for it.

"I want you to pop in and see me in the morning Salt. Something is brewing make sure you're at my office, no later than say," Jack looked down at his watch. "O-eight hundred hours tomorrow, and I'll fill you in with all the details then."

"Do I assume there's a sortie being planned then Sir?" Salty happily enquired.

"Isn't that what I just said Salt! Yes, there's a sortie being planned."

"Sorry sir, it's all the noise in here, I couldn't quite hear you with all this commotion going on."

After four long years of tortuous back braking training Salty was desperate to hear Jack say those words, and he just had, so his first 'sortie' was in the offing.

Ignoring the din and clatter in the great hangar, Salty replied and shouted out the sharpest. "Yes Sir," he was able to muster as Jack stroked his beard like he always did when he was deep in thought. Then conscious that he may have been showing his protégé a little bit too much attention, Jack returned the gesture with a smart salute of his own and took his leave.

And as the saying went at Invergordon;

'Firm but fair is our Jack.'

It had been four long years since Salty had arrived at the Royal Navy's Top-Secret training academy, four years since Jack had rescued him from the orphanage hell that was TS Seaway in Anglesey and offered him a commission in the Royal Navy.

And, in all that time Salty hadn't received as much as a single letter, not even a card from his old friend's Blakey, Asker, and Guns. Last, he'd heard Guns and Asker were aboard the mighty aircraft carrier HMS Eagle basking somewhere down in the Mediterranean, and Blakey his closest friend by far, had simply dissapeared off the planet. Vanished, gone.

In fact, the only contact he'd had in all that time from anyone even remotely connected with Seaway, was from the lovely, *Nurse Louise Taylor,* the stunning uniformed beauty who'd helped nurse him back to health after his well-deserved, but impromptu knock on the head by the burly Royal Marine, Sergeant Steiner.

A letter had arrived by Air mail Avion from a Royal Naval hospital called *'Bighi'* located somewhere on the island of Malta, and writing back was top of his to-do list. But he'd decided to wait until he could write and pen her the good news himself, namely his promotion from lowly midshipman to a sub-Lieutenant, and a serving Royal Naval Officer.

As he was about to turn around and celebrate the rest of the day with his fellow officers, something completely unexpected happened. Something he just wasn't prepared for. Loud shouting was emanating from the other side of the hangar. So, he looked across to see what all the commotion was about.

"Sub-Lieutenant Salt! Is that you over their Sir?" Came the voice as two junior ratings marched straight towards him, and as they approached, the front one bellowed out again.

"Yes Sir! We mean you Sir!"

Startled, a little taken back and holding his finger to his chest, Salty mouthed the word *"me"* under his breath as he looked towards the two matelots that were now marching line abreast and in perfect step towards him. Then stopping just a few yards in front of him, they brought themselves smartly to attention and offered him a sharp salute, and Salty still wondered who the hell they were. Naval protocol demanded an acknowledgement, so he returned the formality with a smart salute of his own, and the taller of the two was the first to say something;

"Ordinary seaman Anstey offering my heartiest congratulations on your passing out today. Sir!"

Salty instantly recognised the singularly distinctive and unmistakeable Birkenhead twang, then not sure whether to laugh, cry, or maybe even dance on the spot. He decided to do the next best thing and launched himself towards them seizing both their broad shoulders tightly in his. And Asker and Guns had arrived.

Biting his bottom lip, struggling to find the right words Guns was the next to say something.

"Able seaman Fred Ballard reporting Sir, also wishing you my heartiest congratulations on your passing out today, Sir!"

"Forget the bloody Sir's you Seaway mutts, where've you been? Where the hell is Blakey? What happened to…...?" Salty asked, but before he could complete his sentence, all three white caps were lofted skywards this time. And the celebrations were about to begin.

Later that evening sat in the relative comfort of the officer's mess Asker borrowed three shillings from Guns and walked over to the bar to order the first round.

"Three pints of Watney's please Gov."

Civilian attired, and temporary bar staff for the night, chief petty officer *'Dinghy'* Smith didn't like being addressed as *'Gov,'* certainly not by a junior rating! And an ordinary seaman no less. But he decided he'd let it go this time because he liked the newly promoted sub-Lieutenant Salt, so offering nothing more than a frown, he placed the three pints on the bar, and let it go.

To Salty, Asker still seemed as daft and as playful as ever, he'd filled out a bit maybe grown an inch or two, but Asker was still Asker. And the same went for Guns, who was busy eyeing up the Wren officer sat down on the table opposite. Salty thoughts were; *her first mistake was to offer Guns even the slightest hint of a glance the moment she walked in.*

"Sir, sorry I mean Salty." Asker said leaning across the table as he looked sheepishly around the room. "Now just hear me out for a minute and pretend you knew somebody with a load of knock off fags he wanted to get rid of, would you be able to put that person in touch with somebody who might just want to buy them? I mean they're dead legit, aren't they Guns?"

"Oh yeah dead legit these are, me and Asker knicked 'em out of the quartermaster's stores on Eagle, these are proper fags' mate, they're kosher, make no mistake."

Salty, sat quite still for a moment considering his reply before he leant across the table and asked them both to move a little closer.

"Now listen you two we're all good mates, right? But, if I get caught with as much as a knock off rice bloody pudding in my locker, they'll kick my ass straight out of the Navy, and I'll lose my commission so don't go asking me again! And I'll pretend I didn't hear you. Okay."

"Yeah, sorry mate, just forget we ever said anything." Guns replied as Asker remained quiet, clearly shocked at Salty's outburst. But Salty was far from finished.

"Good, and just so you both know, don't try and sell them around here either. Asker get your ass up there and order three more pints and put them on my mess account. Oh, and don't call Chief Petty Officer Smith *'Gov,'* he bloody hates that!"

Asker and Guns had never heard him talk like that before, he'd changed he was a different person somehow. They'd always looked up to him. But there was something different about him now and they both wondered if the hours and hours of physical and physiological training, may have altered him somehow?

Either way, Salty now possessed a self-assured confident tone that neither of them recognised. But they were certain of one thing. They wouldn't ask him again.

So, with his tail placed firmly between his legs, Asker stood up picked up the three empty beer mugs and sloped off to the bar, as Guns who was quickly trying to change the subject tentatively asked;

"Have you heard anything from Blakey? The last me and Asker heard he'd moved to a place called *Javea* down in southern Spain. We got postcard from him a few months ago saying Fiona was working in a bar called Sandra's and he was doing some part time work on the fishing trawlers."

Salty sat instantly upright as he heard Blakey's name being mentioned remembering the time they'd spent together at Seaway and the hell they'd shared, they'd fought together, ate together, even cried together, sometimes in stomach splitting laughter, and other times in pain. And Salty missed his friend. So, he stroked his chin and without uttering a word picked his glass up and gulped down a large measure of the lukewarm Watney's.

In four long years he hadn't heard Blakey's name mentioned once, he'd heard nothing from him since their final days at Seaway. Memories like those transcended time, and they'd been right by his side throughout all the arduous training and everything else Invergordon had thrown at him. They had moulded him, removed the boy somehow, changed him forever.

After a few moments spent deep in thought Salty started to relay his own version of events and looked squarely across the table at his two friends.

"Well once you two were packed off to HMS Raleigh, I only saw him the once. Blakey told me that Jack offered him the same choice as the rest of us, you know entry into the Royal Navy, but Jack said Blakey had turned him down flat and went off to live with Fiona at the Holyhead Arms."

"It must have been about a month after that, that Frank her dad was found dead in the hobby room with a bullet in his head. Killed himself, apparently? Well that was the official story anyway, after that they stayed at the Holyhead for about a month or two and the next thing, I knew was an estate agents *Sold* sign suddenly appeared outside, and they'd buggered off somewhere? And until you just told me it was Spain, or Javea, I didn't have a clue where? I mean, you know Blakey he loved the sea, didn't he? So, it's no surprise to me that he's working on the trawler's, and Fiona loved bar work, so it all makes sense really." Ordering the sixth round, and the alcohol beginning to have the desired effect; Salty eventually asked the question he'd been burning to ask the whole night.

"Did you know Medhev escaped?"

"Noooo." Replied a shocked Guns and Asker in perfect unison.

"Well apparently he escaped while he was being transported up to Wakefield nick from a holding cell in London. The two prison officers escorting him were both shot and killed by an assassin on the side of the road. One of the poor buggers was up for retirement a few days later. I've since heard he's gone back to Russia, but I'll tell you this if it takes me a whole lifetime to track him down, I'll get him you just mark my words."

Salty's hatred for Medhev was as fresh as the day he'd tried to kill him on the beach at Seaway, his father's untimely death still haunted him. He couldn't work out if it was the manner in which he'd been killed, drowning in a thousand feet of filthy seawater with seventy-five brave men, or the fact that Medhev, his killer was still alive and walking around. Either way it still riled him, and the mere mention of his name was like a piece of sandpaper being drawn across his bare skin.

Guns sat for a moment reflecting on what Salty had just told him as Asker who'd overheard the conversation interrupted the silence by saying.

"Well just remember what you used to say at Seaway Salty." Asker said as he placed the three fresh pints on the table. "Good goes to good and bad goes to bad, and Medhev's time will come, he'll get his make no mistake."

"Oh, he'll get his all right, you can bank on that."
Salty replied, as all three clinked their glasses together.

The very next day up bright and early, and despite the previous night's heavy drinking Salty was sat all alone in his room reading Louise's letter.
For the third time…...

Dear Sam,

You've probably forgotten all about me by now, but I haven't you. I'm the girl who nursed you get back to health at TS Seaway. I know that it was a long time ago and it must be getting on for nearly four years now, but you're not the easiest person in the world to track down, and if I didn't know better, it's almost like the Navy doesn't want you to be found.

Anyway, that aside I'm now a petty officer nurse in the 'Quarns' the 'Queen Alexandra's Royal Nursing Service' and I'm based in Malta, and I'd love to hear from you, so please write back, but If you don't, I will understand (sort of).

*In the meantime; Sam or Salty as I knew you back then,
good luck, and a big kiss from.*

Louise Taylor

J122 234G. Petty Officer Wren: Louise Taylor:
The Queen Alexandra's Royal Naval Nursing Service
Royal Naval Hospital, Bighi. Kalkara: Malta Garrison.

Salty read it and decided he'd write back that night…...He
hadn't forgotten her at all. Far from it….

Dear Louise,

*Thank you so much for your letter, and my apologies for
the delay in replying, you see I've been rather busy getting ready
for my passing out of officer cadet school, and I can now
officially inform you that I am writing to you as the newly
promoted sub-Lieutenant Sam Salt. I must admit I often
wondered what had become of you, and if I'm perfectly honest,
that thought crossed my mind, almost daily.*

*So, when I received your letter a few weeks ago I was to
say the least, absolutely delighted. You'll have to tell me more*

about Malta, I've heard it's beautiful, so you must describe it to me in your next letter.

Maybe when I'm next due some leave. "I'll hop on a tug" and turn up and surprise you. If you don't hear from me for a while it's nothing to worry about, you see I'm about to be posted to God only knows where, but please keep writing Louise, the letter's always get to me, and as soon as I'm able, I'll write back. I know it's early days, but you won't be far from my thoughts. As you never were.

Signing off with a kiss and a hug.

Salty

D161876X sub-Lieutenant Sam Salt.

HMS Invergordon. Ross and Cromarty Highland. Scotland.

Chapter 2. His First Sortie

Captain Jack `Black` McPherson was sat his desk studying the latest intelligence reports coming out of the port of Tangiers, the recent photographs taken by his field agent showed a Soviet submarine berthed at the back of the harbour with its fin markings painted out.

As he was looking down through his magnifying glass trying to establish exactly what type of submarine it was, the door knocked and his assistant at Invergordon Commander Terry Walker walked in and stood at attention in front of his large desk.

"Sub-Lieutenant Salt is here to see you Sir; Shall I show him in?"

"Yes, Walker show him in, oh and ask Jean to fetch me two nice cups of tea on your way out, will you Walker? Thank you. Come in Salt pick up a chair my boy, sit down, sit down." Jack said as Walker ushered Salty over to his chair in front of his big mahogany desk before quietly closing the large glass door behind him.

Salty was trying to make himself comfortable in the upright wooden backed chair as Jack glanced over the top of his brand-new pair of gold spectacles and wondered if he might be being a little bit too ambitious and maybe it was too soon to be placing his young agent in harm's way.

Jack had already decided which mission he was sending him on, he'd picked a particularly interesting sortie, one that his newly promoted sub-Lieutenant might just have a vested interest in.

"Well, jolly good day yesterday Salt don't you think? Was that you I saw drinking with two ratings in the officers mess last night?"

"Yes Sir, it was, you probably remember them from TS Seaway, Seaman's Anstey and Guns."

"Yes, yes of course I remember them, nice lads, but you mustn't make a habit of that my boy, wouldn't do you know, you're an officer now so make sure you behave like one, well anyway that aside for the moment, let's get back to the sortie."

Jack coughed as he always did after making a point, then looked down at the file and pushed his gold rimmed glasses further up the bridge of his nose.

"I'm now going to read you the mission statement, it will give you some insight as to what you're up against. Okay."

"Thank you, Sir."

Jack had a unique way of injecting his subordinates with just enough fear to demand their respect, and Jack certainly had Salty's. So, gently stroking his beard, Jack started to read.

"Well it says here that large shipments of pure un-cut cocaine and hashish, together with huge quantities of Soviet arms and ammunition are being smuggled across the Mediterranean Sea aboard a Soviet submarine from the Moroccan port of Tangiers. The shipments are then unloaded in the dead of night at our own Royal Naval shipyard in Gibraltar, then smuggled aboard Royal Naval warships and auxiliary vessels, before being brought back to the UK."

"The report then goes go on to say that the agent NIS dispatch should be aware that the investigation indicates an onward link to the provisional IRA has been established."

Jack paused for a moment, allowing Salty to consider the report. Before continuing.

"HMS Scorpion a weapons class destroyer is one of several Royal Naval warships being used to transport these illegal shipments back to the UK, the consignments are hidden deep in the ships hold, then unloaded in the dead of night upon arrival in Portsmouth harbour. To date no arrests have been made, and the shipments have been deliberately allowed to pass through British customs, unhindered."

"Now, you're probably sat there wondering why we haven't already seized these drugs or grabbed hold of the weapons when they're being unloaded, aren't you Salt? Well you see these shipments are just the tip of the iceberg, our main concern at this stage is to find out who is behind all this. We also need to find out who's in command of the submarine, and who the Soviet Captain is? But more importantly than any of that, we need to know who his IRA contacts are?"

"Think of this mission as a sort of giant sprawling *Hydra* with several heads flying around, and it's not until you chop the big one off that the whole bloody thing falls apart. It's a tight nasty little ring Salt, and there's no doubt in my mind somebody bloody high up in the Royal Navy is behind it all. The report goes on to say that NIS recommends the agent is dispatched with all speed to join HMS Scorpion at the earliest possible opportunity."

Jack removed the mission statement from the inside of his file stapled it to the cover, and passed it across the desk to Salty, but before he was able to resume the conversation he was interrupted by Jean as she knocked on the door and without invite wheeled her trolley in with two cups of English tea, served in his favourite bone china tea service. Two custard creams were displayed spread on a plate next to the big tea pot.

"Thank you, Jean, just put them down over there will you please." Said Jack with a wave of his hand.

"Yes, certainly Captain, couple of biscuits there for you as well your favourite, custard creams Sir."

"Yes, yes Jean, now forgive me but I have some very important business to attend to here, so can you just leave them over there and close the door quietly behind you, thank you again Jean."

Jack loved Jean and she him, but he hated being molly coddled, it irritated him got under his skin, but Jean was far from finished.

"You'll end up having a heart attack one day Captain McPherson, you will, you need to slow down you mark my words."

As she was closing the door behind her, Jean pointed her finger towards Jack and repeated herself:

"You mark my words Captain McPherson."

Jack huffed at the audacity of the woman as a brief smile formed in the corners of his eyes, and he said to Salty.

"Ballsy woman that Salt, don't mess around with her. Anyway, moving on sub-Lieutenant you can now speak four or five languages fluently, you have also finished top of the class in shooting, explosives, hand to hand combat, and field craft, but

I won't lie to you Salt, there were times when I wondered if you were a little bit too soft for this type of work, but you went on to prove me wrong didn't you? You knuckled down, hardened up, so well-done lad jolly well done."

Happy with his mentor's complimentary speech, Salty wondered if it might be the right moment to ask if his nemesis the infamous Kapitan Leonid Medhev just happened to be the Soviet submarine Captain? It was a long shot but as he started to open his mouth, and before he was able to utter a single word, Jack interrupted him with a wag of his finger, intermating further silence. So, reluctantly Salty sat upright in his chair and continued, to listen.

"Right Salt, that said and done what we have here is a clear case of drug smuggling and arms importation into our Royal Navy shipyard in Gibraltar, and it's going on right under our bloody noses. But do you know what really bloody riles me Salt, well do you?"

"No Sir." Salty replied, thinking he knew what Jack was about to say.

"Well I'll tell you then lad, it's our brave British soldiers who at this very minute are serving in Northern Ireland, putting their lives on the line each and every time they step out of their bloody barracks! Only to be maimed and killed by these sodding weapons. And to top it all the smugglers are our own British servicemen, so that's what really riles me Salt!"

Feeling rather ruffled by his sudden outburst and without offering Salty a biscuit, Jack dipped the first of the two custard creams into the strong cup of tea crunched it up in his mouth, and simply carried on.

"Take this file with you and make sure you read every part of it Salt, don't miss out a bloody word, not a comma, be prepared to meet all eventualities and cover every risk."

Salty sat forward in his chair. "I will, but there is one other thing I'd like to ask you Sir?"

But Jack pretended not to hear him and just carried munching away without comment as he picked up the second biscuit and dunked it into Salty's tea and before Salty had a chance to interrupt him again, he finally said.

"I want you to find out who these people are, so I can bring justice down on their bloody heads like a giant smithy's anvil!" Jack slammed his large fist down on the desk, but even then, he was far from finished.

"You will be leaving by RAF Britannia aircraft for Gibraltar first thing in the morning from Brize Norton, so I think that just about wraps things up around here rather, nicely don't you?"

"Yes Sir."

"Oh, and do take care of yourself my boy. I didn't invest all my time and the Queen's money training you just to see you go off and get yourself killed, now did I."

As he finished talking Jack could feel a strange paternal feeling sweeping over him, but he chose to ignore it and simply smiled at his young protégé across the desk as he picked up Salty's tea swallowed it down in one large gulp, then finally added.

"Oh, Salt, forgive me I nearly forgot after you leave here report to Commander Prosser in the *Den*. That's all for now, and jolly good luck and make sure you keep your bloody head down."

Salty quietly closed the office door behind him and Jack opened Salty's medical file as he always did when placing one of agents in harm's way fiddling with his beard as he sat there pondering to himself. It was then that he noticed Salty's extremely rare blood group, listed as *RH Null,* so he closed the file and decided he'd call Walker on the intercom.

The *Den`* as Jack described, wasn't a Den at all it was an old hiding place, a deep cave frequented by the infamous *Bonnie Prince Charlie* whilst hiding from his English pursuer's during the Jacobite uprising of 1745. And it was now being used by the Royal Navy for the storage of the Royal Air Force's nuclear tipped *Thor* intercontinental ballistic missiles and doubling up as a supply depot equipping all NIS agents with the new covert weapons, the expanding organisation was rapidly being equipped with. Presenting his security pass at the entrance to the den, the two Royal Marine sentries standing guard smartly shouldered arms, and Salty walked through the two steel sliding doors.

Commander Prosser was sat at his desk studying an open file with two Webley Mk IV's, and several rounds of ammunition loosely scattered on the filing cabinet behind him. As Salty walked up to the desk, the Commander immediately stood up, fearing it might be Jack on one of his unannounced walk arounds. Then realising it was only sub-Lieutenant Salt and looking slightly awkward, he quickly sat back down again, and offered him a chair.

"Oh, it's you Salt, do come in, pull up a chair my boy must say that sub-Lieutenants uniform looks rather dashing on you, glad you could make it, Captain McPherson said you were going to pay me a visit."

Although Salty liked and admired the Commander his authoritarian Victorian overbearing nature unnerved him, his plummy Cambridge accent and sarcastic satire made him feel a little uneasy. But Salty liked him all the same. Salty removed his peaked cap and placed it on the corner of the desk, drew back the chair and quietly sat down as the Commander closed the file.

"Okay Salt let's get down to the nitty gritty, shall we? I've read the file Captain McPherson gave you, as no doubt you have."

"I haven't Sir, he's only just given it to me, but he briefed on its contents."

"Good, well I must say it's a rather complicated sortie especially considering that this is your first time out, you know the best laid plans and all that. You see, this isn't just a simple case of drug smuggling as you may have been led to believe, the weapons and the IRA involvement really do complicate matters somewhat. So, it's an extremely dangerous sortie indeed, make no mistake about it these people are killers Salt. Killers!"

"I understand Sir."

Salty was already weighing up his options, he'd trained hard for four years and could kill a man with four inches of rope, but the IRA! Well nobody messed about with the IRA, and the Commander sensing his apprehension, noticed him swallowing hard as the reality of the mission began to sink in.

The Commander could recall his first time out when he'd been ordered to kill a man using a claw hammer on a river boat in Paris. And thought to himself; *You never forget the first one.*

"Anyway, these weapons aren't just your everyday revolvers and pea shooters like these."

The Commander picked up the Webley revolver and held it an inch from Salty's temple, but Salty didn't flinch, it was a test and Salty understood that, anyway he'd passed all the others.

So, the Commander feeling rather disappointed that his test had failed, simply placed the gun back down on the desk picked the file back up and carried on with the report.

"Yes Salt, it's worse than that, they're also smuggling in rocket launchers, land mines, and hand grenades and they're all destined for the ruddy IRA. Oh, and theirs more Salt, much more."

The Commander hadn't drawn breath in over five minutes and sensing he may have reached a sort of plateau, Salty took his chance to interrupt him.

"Sir, may I ask you something?"

Although like Jack the Commander Prosser hated interruptions, he decided to allow Salty's transgression this time.

"Go ahead Salt."

"Well Sir, if I may speak off the record?"

"Yes, you may these cave walls are quite impervious to all types of sound, so carry on."

"Well, it's about Medhev Sir, I know he's meant to be locked up somewhere in the U.S.S.R, but if there's a Soviet Captain in command of this submarine. Could it be..."

This time the Commander was the one to interrupt.

"Salt, I really don't have the foggiest, we haven't even established what type of Soviet submarine it is yet, let alone who is commanding it. In fact, the same as you the last I heard he was locked up in some frozen Siberian Gulag, so it's highly unlikely it's him."

Commander Prosser hoped that answered his question, as he rose from his chair and beckoned with his hand for the young sub-Lieutenant to follow him to the back of the dark cave.

"Follow me my boy I've got something to show you, I've a feeling you're going to like this."

As they entered the darkness at the back of the den, Cmdr. Prosser flicked the switch on, and a single fluorescent tube flickered to life revealing damp walls and ancient tribal markings that had been scribed centuries before. Armageddon slept only two metres away as huge grey 'Thor' missiles with yellow stamped markings were stacked three high and four across warning the user to *Remove end cone before use.*

Just above his head affixed to the stone concave ceiling were galvanised steel pipes connecting sprinkler heads that had never been designed to dispense water, instead they'd spray deadly *sarin* nerve gas throughout the Den instantly killing anyone within a seventy-metre vicinity of the cave in the event of enemy infiltration, or a terrorist attack. It was obvious to Salty that the Thor's would be protected at all costs.

Crates stacked high on metal racking filled with ammunition, bazookas and Sten guns lay all around, a cordite fuelled mustiness filled the cold damp air, as Salty adjusted his eyes to the dim yellowing light.

The Commander was the first to speak, breaking the deafening silence; "Right sub-Lieutenant, I'm going to put on a little demonstration for you, so put these on will you." The Commander instructed as he handed Salty a set of thick padded earphones with one hand holding a shiny *Parker* pen in the other. "Now this may look like an everyday Parker pen Salt, but it isn't, it's actually a noise penetration device or an NPD` for short, now make sure you're holding your earphones tightly against your ears and keep your mouth closed, nod when you're ready."

Salty pushed the earphones as tightly as he could against his ears and over accentuated the mouth closing part, before nodding in reply.

"Good, the Commander said, "then here we go… One…. Two…. Three."

Holding the earphones as tightly as he dared, Salty watched as the Commander depressed the top of the pen and it instantly discharged a high-frequency sound penetrating every inch of the dens stone walls, the oscillation frequency was so highly pitched it caused the loose ammunition on the metal racking to jump around inside its wooden crates.

Then as fast as it had started, it ended, and as calmly as one might hand a child an ice cream the Commander placed a brand-new Parker pen into the top of Salty's blazer pocket.

"My God Sir, what the hell was that? I've never heard anything like it, it's terrible how long does it last?"

"Well, let's discuss the drawbacks, first shall we. You see you only get one go on this little device, the sound it produces is set at such a high decibel level that exposure for longer than five or maybe six seconds will lead to permanent ear damage."

"The victim or victims are totally incapacitated, so you see my boy if you do find yourself in a tight spot, you must protect your ears using these tiny little ear plugs. They're a new invention made out of something the boffins are calling silicone. So, make sure you keep these little chappies with you at all times, and don't use your NPD pen without them. Okay."

Salty nodded his understanding his ears were hurting his teeth were vibrating, even his jaw ached. He'd be doubly sure to wear the ear plugs.

"Now moving on we need to talk about the weapons side of things, but I'm sorry to say very little has changed on that front. On top of my cabinet is your revolver and two boxes of live ammunition. Hopefully you won't be needing them, but make sure you pick them up before you leave. Okay."

"Yes Sir, I'm all ears." Salty replied sarcastically, shaking his head as he followed the Commander back to his desk through the dimly lit cave.

Sitting back down at his desk the Commander opened the mission file and started to chuckle to himself as his broad shoulders moved up and down, and his head rolled back as he wiped a laughter tear from his eye.

"Oh, dear Salt, according to this you're going to be temporarily demoted all the way back down to an ordinary seaman, didn't last very long in that pretty new uniform of yours, did you?"

"Oh, and it gets worse than that Salt, if I didn't know better, I'd say somebody at headquarters is playing a little joke on you. Your cover name is to be *Thomas Crabbe*, good God Salt intelligence do have a sense of humour after all, wouldn't you say?"

"Yes Sir, they must have." Salty replied, unsure whether he was unhappier about the demotion or the cover name. The still chuckling Commander then passed him his new identity card, and travel warrant.

"All joking aside you mustn't get too down hearted about this my boy, the reason for your temporary demotion is so that you blend in with the ships company. You see as a newly posted officer aboard a Royal Navy warship you'd stand out like a spare prick at…... Well never mind about that, you'd just stand out."

"As an officer, you would be expected to make decisions and give orders, and we don't want that do we, heh? So, your remit is to blend in and don't create any fuss or pass any opinions, just blend in."

Salty was feeling slightly uncomfortable as memories of washing decks and scrubbing heads at TS Seaway came flooding back.

"Now you're going to be posted to Gibraltar, where you'll board HMS Scorpion a weapons class destroyer. I must admit she's a tad tired, a bit rough around the edges but all told, Scorpion is still a good ship. We've made doubly sure that none of your old ship mates from Seaway are aboard, so you'll be totally unknown, in fact you'll be completely incognito, and that's exactly how you'll remain Salt. Incognito."

"Scorpion is about to go on a flag waving mission across the med to Tangiers, now I've already told you that over the last few months a Soviet submarine has been taking little moonlit trips from there to Gibraltar delivering these ruddy weapons and drugs. So, by going to Tangiers we not only get the chance to find out who is in command of this Soviet attempt at supplying the IRA with weapons, we might also find out who their contact is at our end."

Salty didn't wait to be invited to speak this time; "Sir, so that I understand you correctly, you want me to board a ship with an unknown crew some of whom may or may not be weapons and drug smugglers, nip across the med with them to Tangiers, arrest the perpetrators in a foreign port and bring them back to Gibraltar."

The Commander looked back at him across the desk hollow cheeked, his patience was clearly being strained, so he tried again.

"No Salt! That is not what I said now is it! Now listen lad, to coin a phrase used by our very own Captain McPherson you are to *remain under cover*, just as you've been trained. You are not to reveal yourself to anyone, you're there to simply, study, watch, listen, and report."

"The arrests if there are any will take place when you return with HMS Scorpion and you're safely back inside British waters in Gibraltar. Finally, so that you clearly understand me Salt, we haven't lost an agent in the field in over forty years! So, don't go putting your neck on the ruddy line, not on this one. Okay son!"

Unintentionally the Commanders fondness for Salty had revealed itself in the last word of his sentence, and Cmdr. Prosser abhorred sentimentality.

"I understand now Sir," Salty replied, "but I do have one last question if I may? Who is going to be my handler on this mission?"

"Well that pleasure falls to me Salt; I'll be aboard Scorpion acting as her foreign liaison officer while she's out in Tangiers."

Salty, felt like crying at that stage, but instead offered him a wry smile as the Commander sat quietly across the desk placing live rounds into the chamber of his Webley revolver…

Chapter 3. Medhev's in Tangiers

Kapitan Leonid Medhev was sat in the lobby bar of the 'Hotel Maroc,' as the pungent aroma from the local souk market filled the air inside the large marbled lounge.

Medhev hated Morocco, he hated the intense heat, the smell, the flies, the sickly mint tea, but more especially he hated the Moroccan's. To him they were offensive the way they openly begged in the streets was an utter disgrace. They were nothing but filth beneath his feet and he wouldn't tolerate them. He'd swat them like the flies invading his presence.

Following his capture two years before, he'd been offered another chance and been handed an extremely important mission by Stanislav Koralev his KGB handler, and he'd be sure not to let him down again. He'd fulfil his orders to the letter this time. Whatever the cost.

He'd spent his time in disgrace within the walls of the freezing hell of the infamous Sevvostlag Gulag` carefully planning his vengeance. But his time there hadn't been wasted, his hatred held no bounds. Salt and McPherson would pay, and he'd make sure they would die painfully and very slowly. And that was why Medhev had begged Koralev for Mikhail Kuznetsov to accompany him. So, that this time Medhev had his own torturer aboard. His very own 'Smithy.'

But today he was sat in the bar next to the infamous IRA leader Brigadier Patrick Daniel O'Hare, or simply Paddy as he preferred to be called, by his so-called friends.

"Where can a man get a bloody drink around here Captain?" Paddy asked in his southern Irish drawl. "I'm bloody parched I am."

Medhev, who could hardly understand Paddy at the best of times looked across the bar at him as he swatted another fly with his large Mongolian hand, before he replied; "Today is the last day of Ramadan my Irish friend, you'll not get a drink in all of Morocco today. So, come forget the drink we must leave now, let's get down to the submarine and see how the loading is going."

Medhev got up from the stool and threw three rolled up Dirham's at the waiter's tray as he breezed past, the waiter would have preferred Franc's, but it didn't matter either way as Abdul hated all Russian's.

Down at the harbour the loading was going well; Senior Lieutenant Boris Andropov was an expert planner, the off loading of the submarines newly acquired cruise missiles had been carried out during the night in record time. And they were now laid out neatly stacked in eight rows in the stifling heat on the harbourside.

Six Russian Spetsnav guards surrounded the horde with their PPSh-41 sub machine guns primed and ready watching five black hooded Berber's load the shiny boxes containing the very latest Mosin-Nagant rifles, grenade launchers, and heavy machine guns. The horde bound for Portsmouth, and the Provisional IRA.

Medhev smiled, he was pleased with the progress as he watched from the shade of his awning as the *Hashish* and *Cocaine* was carefully wrapped up in brown grease proof paper then stuffed into wooden cases and loaded deep down inside the subs hull.

"Bloody good guns these." Paddy remarked as he picked up a new grease covered rifle staring down its long wooden shaft pointing it directly at HMS Scorpion berthed the opposite side of the harbour.

"These will go down well with me mates in Dublin, tell you what wouldn't mind a bloody toke on that hashish meself Captain," said Paddy pointing at one of the brown packages, "let's roll up a smoke up shall we?"

Medhev considered Paddy's request a repugnance he despised drugs, his father had been a Mongolian goat herder and an addict. The deep scars on his back and his mother's untimely death at his father's hands, bore evidence of that.

"Stop acting like an idiot you Irish prick, now put that fucking rifle down and leave the hashish alone and let's get the sub loaded. I am hot, I am tired, and I am becoming impatient. That Royal Navy destroyer opposite is watching our every move and making me nervous, so the sooner this is done, the better."

The tent flap lifted, and senior Lieutenant Andropov was standing in the opening, Andropov smartly saluted Medhev and handed him the communication from Soviet Naval Headquarters.

Medhev read it.

Transmission: From Soviet Fleet Headquarters: Kronštádt

To: Kapitan Medhev: Submarine M418 Tangiers:
M418 to hold consignment in Tangiers until further notice. Stop.
Be informed that Agent Maria is on station and will arrive at 19.00 hrs G.M.T. Tomorrow night. Stop.
She will make contact at the Tangerine club. Stop.

Medhev looked quickly down at his watch noting the time it was 17.15 hours, before returning his attention to the message.

Agent Maria confirmed she also has information concerning Daniel……..

The message was abruptly terminated at 16.58 hrs G.M.T.

Medhev knew the British had the ability to intercept and sometimes corrupt messages so he held it in his hand for a second, before he turned around eyeing Paddy up and down suspiciously;

"Where did you say your hometown was again Paddy? You know I have always wanted to visit Ireland, maybe I will sneak a little run ashore the next time I pass your little emerald Isle."

The confines of the hot tent suddenly felt so much hotter to Paddy, a little claustrophobic even, but Paddy replied with his best Irish drawl without breaking sweat.

"Wicklow Captain. County Wicklow, it's beautiful and if it wasn't for those bastards the British over the border it would be bloody paradise."

Medhev wondered if Paddy's answer sounded a little rehearsed but decided to ignore it until he heard from Agent Maria later. He could wait…...after all, the loading was going well.

Suddenly there was a loud crashing sound from outside, and Medhev immediately screwed the communique up and threw it into the corner of the tent then lifted up the flap and started shouting at three black hooded Berber's who'd accidentally dropped a wooden case full of rifle ammunition onto the concrete quayside.

"Idiot's, idiot's, you pigs. Guard's! Guards! Place them under arrest."

Paddy could hear Medhev's ranting becoming a little more distant as he walked off, and the shouting started to subside, so he quickly picked up the communique from the tents dusty floor and read it.

Paddy, who was fluent in Russian looked up checking the tent flap every few seconds, then threw it back down in the same spot.

Outside, sweating in the forty-degree heat Medhev patted his Tokarev automatic as he lit another Turkish cigarette holding it between his new gold teeth as he drew the warm smoke deep into his lungs and looked across the warm crystal-clear waters at the grey shape of HMS Scorpion, berthed opposite.

Seconds later, two crisp rifle shots spoiled the early evening peace and Medhev smiled as two naked bodies, the offending Berber's were tossed into the Mediterranean. Just like the filthy pigs they were......

Chapter 4. Sebastien

Sebastien was converted from a fishing boat to a coastal patrol vessel back in 1938 when the Spanish Civil War was at its height. It was rumoured that *General Franco* himself had once stepped aboard. Bullet holed gunwale's long since painted, bore evidence to her previous role.

Sebastien now reconverted to a fishing trawler struggled through the tempestuous sea as giant rollers crashed against her taught wooden hull in tune with Sou` easterly winds and howling gales. The boat creaked and strained as it left the whitewashed villas of Javea far behind and headed to the open sea. Javea's red and green harbour lights disappeared in the mist as Sebastien left the safety enjoyed within the town's stone harbour walls, as Gonzalo manned the wheelhouse, steering her straight and true.

Gonzalo, Sebastien's Master looked upon Stephano Gomez his first mate as a brother, they'd sailed the route together a thousand times since they were children. But when Gonzalo's father, Gonzalo Senior was lost overboard one stormy night, everything had changed. Bankruptcy loomed, so the offer from the Royal Navy to use Sebastien as a *'Surveillance vessel'* was a godsend, and a life-changer. They now earnt more in one season, than five. And the money was regular. All they had to do was keep quiet allow the Royal Navy to board Sebastien far out at sea and rig up their wired antennas while they were happily left in peace, to catch fish.

What could be better. Who cared who they spied on? The money was good, and they were slowly becoming rich.

Chief Petty Officer William Blake signals and communications branch Royal Navy NIS, or simply *Blakey* to his friends rested his mornings brew on the galley table, as he listened to the Russian signals traffic coming out of Tangiers.

Intercepted radio traffic between the Soviet submarine, the M418 and her base on Kronštádt island weren't very good that day weather conditions were poor, humidity was high and at best communications could only be described as 'scratchy.'

Blakey's job was pure signal interception, translation and suppression. Suppression` was the most difficult skill by far, and suppression was Chief Petty Officer Blake's speciality. Suppression or '*blocking'* as the Navy referred, held the key to a successful sortie the ability to intercept, alter, and sometimes re-send a message could mean the difference between life or death for an agent in the field. And CPO Blake was extremely good at it.

"Message coming through CPO Blake on Soviet frequency. Intercept M418: Time recorded is 16.55 hours."

Transmission: From Soviet Fleet Headquarters: Kronštádt:

To: Kapitan Medhev: Submarine M418 Tangiers: Stop.

M418 to hold consignment in Tangiers until further notice. Stop.

Be informed that agent Maria is on station and will arrive at 19.00 hrs G.M.T. tomorrow night.

She will make contact at the Tangerine Club. Stop.

Agent Maria confirmed she also has information concerning Daniel…….

Blakey listened to the first part of the transmission, then quickly shouted. "Red flag, Johnson, block, block, block!"

"Aye. Aye CPO. Red flag activated message intercepted. Shall I relay to HMS Scorpion?"

"Yes, straight away Johnson, use 978.Megaherz in the ultra-high band, the Soviets can't interdict up there."

Able Seaman Johnson liked Blakey, the relaxed out of uniform regime suited them both, Johnson did his job and his CPO his, the intercepted message transmitted through the trawlers long whip antennae would be received in real time and, maybe, just maybe save an agent's life.

Blakey waited for the return three 'ping' signal to come back, acknowledging that Scorpion had received Sebastien's radio traffic, three pings would signal success. A few seconds later, and three loud pings reverberated around the trawlers wooden hull at the same time as Gonzalo who was manning the bridge spotted the fast approaching patrol boat and picked up the internal microphone.

"Blakey, Johnson, we have company. Looks like a Moroccan fast attack boat approaching a hundred metres off our port bow, pulling in the antennae now, dump, dump, dump!"

Those three words had been used only once in Blakey's two and a half years aboard Sebastien and that was now, so he pulled out the wires, as Johnson grabbed hold of the grey *Marconi 600 UHF Transmitter-Direction-Finder* and headed for the secret panel aft of the galley bulkhead. The rusty flap opened, and the expensive equipment was thrown out to the sea.

Then they raced up the ladder opened the hatch and watched as the fast patrol boat cut alongside with the barrel of its 50 mm calibre Browning machine gun pointing directly towards Sébastien's hull. Stephano and Gonzalo both instinctively raised their arms and Blakey ordered Johnson to raise his.

"Hands up Johnson, remember the drill we're fisherman," he said, as the boat heaved to on their port side, and Stephano switched the trawlers diesel engine to idle.

They all watched as an overweight Moorish Kapitan clambered aboard and pulled out his old German Luger pistol from its leather holster closely followed by his first officer holding a German Mauser WW2 rifle. The Kapitan pointed the pistol straight towards Stephano and angrily demanded.

"Who is Kapitan of dis boot? Answer me now! Who is Kapitan of dis boot?"

Squinting his eyes Gonzalo stubbed out his large Cuban cigar on the deck as he looked across at the ranting Kapitan and studied him, before offering his reply.

"It is me senor, I am the Kapitan. What is the meaning of this? We are a Spanish fishing trawler out of Javea, what your problem senor?"

"I am not the one with the problem Kapitan! You are! I am Kapitan Mohammed El Bouchtat of Royal Maroc Navy and you have entered Maroc waters, so I impound your ship for taxes, unless of course you pay in full." At that moment Bouchtat raised his hand behind his head offering a signal, and the lone sailor mounting the Browning machine gun on the patrol boat cocked the huge weapon twice in warning.

"You see my friend you must pay, or we take your ship to Maroc and you never see family again, never see ship again. Your ship *"puff"*, gone, blown sky high maybe if you lucky you still on it. If not, you will rot in my prison so pay now, and we will be gone."

Gonzalo, who had fished those same waters with his father and Stephano for over twenty years, and in that time had seen his father washed overboard and tended to Stephano miles from shore with fishhooks embedded in his groin was very, very angry. Someone he'd never even met or harmed in any way was standing in front of him threatening to blow his ship up and telling him he'd never see his family again.

And that was why Gonzalo Jose` Garcia threw the three-pronged shark hook that embedded itself deep into the skull of Kapitan Mohammed El Bouchtat. The long silver hooks struck just below his hairline, and just above the eyes. Mohammed didn't try to remove the hooks there wasn't any point by then, because he was dead anyway.

The serrated barbs wouldn't allow extraction once embedded. Not without tearing half of his forehead away. So, he fell to the deck quite dead as Blakey pulled his Webley revolver from his pocket and fired off two shots at the officer with the Mauser hitting him straight between the eyes killing him instantly, while a third just missed the sailor manning the machine gun, and all four instantly ducked down below the gunwale.

The machine gun rattled its deathly spray along Sebastien's hull, the high calibre rounds only just missing the top of

Blakey's head as the trawler rocked back and forth, under the impact.

"Gonzalo! Fetch me the flare gun, grab it from that locker over there," Blakey ordered, pushing Johnson's head further down into the wooden deck.

"Now listen you three, when I shout; *Now!* All of you go down the hatch, and shut it behind you, okay."

Blakey took a quick glance above the gunwale and could see the lone sailor hurriedly feeding a new ammunition belt into the machine gun, then shouted; *"Now"* allowing himself just enough time to point the flare gun at the six Jerry cans loaded on the back of the patrol boats deck. And just long enough for his three compatriots to disappear into the ships hold.

The red-hot flare exited the gun as the sailor fired his machine gun and shouted "Allahu Akbar," then a huge explosion ripped the patrol craft from bow to stern. Then a secondary explosion occurred a few seconds later as the heat ignited the patrol boats internal fuel tanks. And falling debris showered Sebastien's deck.

As the patrol craft started to sink, it pushed Sebastien's hull sideways and away and Blakey watched as the heat from the sinking craft gradually diminished, and only bubbles remained.

And the Royal Marocs Naval fast attack boat. *'Timsahe'* or *'Alligator,'* slowly disappeared beneath the heaving swell.

Gonzalo was the first to emerge from the hatch door and ran towards Blakey shouting; "Are you all right my friend, that was a very brave thing you do, you save my life, my boat, I am indebted we are all indebted."

"Where's Stephano?" Blakey quickly asked him, "the last time I saw him he was holding his side before he disappeared down the hatch." Gonzalo looked behind him and watched as Johnson pulled Stephano's body out of the hatch. Stephano hadn't quite made it inside as a 7.62mm high calibre round had entered his abdomen only a second before he managed to close the door, and blood was pouring from a stomach wound. And Stephano Gomez was quite dead.

At Sandra's bar Fiona looked out over the beautiful Arenal bay as she washed the days dishes, the sun was shining, there was a light westerly breeze and all was good in the world, she loved their life in Javea.

"They're nearly four hours late Julia, that's not like Gonzalo he's usually the first to moor up especially after three days out. Must have hit a westerly, Blakey always says those westerly's nearly make the boat stand still, never mind let's have a nice glass of Rose` shall we? It's gone five."

Julia, Stephano's wife and mother to his twin girls poured the pinkish wine out from the clay carafe as she looked towards the door. The mosquito netting was slightly obscuring Blakey's outline as he stood in the opening. Gonzalo and Johnson with their heads down, and their caps in hand were standing quietly behind. And it was at that very moment that Julia dropped the carafe onto the marble floor. And realised she'd just become a widow....

Chapter 5. Paddy O'Hare.

The thick mooring ropes creaked and strained as Scorpions large grey hull rocked gently in the harbour swell.

Paddy looked down at the illuminous phosphorous digits on his diver's watch…….. It was precisely 2.00 am and the guard on duty at the gangway failed to notice him removing his frogman's wet suit in the shadows.

Due to the close proximity of their Soviet neighbours across the harbour, Scorpion had been placed on a *Red Alert-Priority One* by Cmdr. Prosser. And able seaman Todd Baxter the guard on duty that night had been warned to expect trouble, so side arms and SLR`s with fixed bayonets had been issued.

As he looked through the darkness, Todd noticed a movement to the side of the ships bow line, so immediately raised his rifle and issued his challenge.

"Halt! Who goes there?"

Paddy immediately held both of his arms high up in the air, so Todd could see his outline against the ship's grey masse in the half moonlight.

"The password is Pelican!" Shouted Paddy just loud enough for Todd to hear, then holding his hands up he started to walk towards the gangway. And closer to Todd.

Todd automatically jerked his rifle up and shouted; "Just keep moving towards me and keep your arms up and no funny business."

Still moving forward, Paddy smiled to himself watching as Todd shouted out behind.

"Master at arms, Pelican is coming aboard, Sah!"

"I must say, Jolly good show able seaman." Paddy remarked in his best English accent as he looked up and saw the figure of Cmdr. Prosser running down the sloped gangway.

"That's okay Baxter, I'll take it from here" the Commander said gasping for breath before smartly saluting his superior officer standing a pace in front of Todd Baxter.

"Welcome aboard HMS Scorpion Captain Fox, this way please follow me Sir."

Able Seaman Todd Baxter shouldered his rifle, removed his tin helmet and scratched his head in disbelief as he watched the heavily bearded, wet, bedraggled Captain Fox follow the older Commander Prosser, his junior officer up the ship's gangway, as he mumbled to himself?

How the hell do they manage to get themselves into that state, bloody officers, they're all wankers.

The officer of the watch saluted them both as they reached the top, and Cmdr. Prosser asked him to; "Fetch ordinary seaman

Crabbe and ask him to report to my cabin immediately Lieutenant."

"Yes Sir, I'll pipe down for him straight away." The Lieutenant replied as Captain Fox unzipped the top of his rubber wet suit and passed him his Naval issue *HR10* serrated fish gutting knife.

Entering the cabin, Commander Prosser hung his hat up on the back of the door before closing it quietly behind him as Captain Fox sat down on the cot opposite and began his attempt at pulling on the wet suit's tight ankle restraints, as the hapless Commander looked on.

"Can I help you in some way Sir?" Cmdr. Prosser politely asked him.

"Yes, yes, pull this bloody thing off me will you Commander."

Cmdr. Prosser knelt down and started to yank the bottom of the wetsuit, maybe a little too vigorously for the unprepared Captain Fox, as the Commander fell backwards against the metal locker behind him only to reveal a pair of emerald green *Shamrock* embroidered underpants. Noticing the shocked expression on the Commanders face the half-naked Captain thought it might be prudent to try and explain.

"Oh, you've noticed the underpants Commander, well they were in case the Ruskie's decided to strip search me, you see I really like to get into the part."

Barely able to stifle a laugh as he looked down towards the deck, Cmdr. Prosser handed him a dry set of number eight uniforms from his bedside cabinet, then turned his back to face the bulkhead. A few seconds later, there were three loud knocks on the cabin door and the Commander looked over towards the Captain who was busily finishing buttoning up his flies and shouted, "enter."

The door opened and Salty, or ordinary seaman Thomas Crabbe as he was known aboard HMS Scorpion walked in removed his white cap, and crisply saluted his two superior officers. Immediately he recognised the seated Captain as the same Captain Roger Fox he'd first insulted, then apologised to during Narwhals memorial service all those years ago, in Portsmouth cathedral.

"Welcome aboard sub-Lieutenant Salt, jolly nice to see you again" the Captain remarked as he stood up and both officers exchanged glances shaking hands.

"It must be what? Five years or more isn't it? My God how you've changed Salt, mind you wasn't sure you'd recognise me sporting a full set young man."

Salty was taken back by the Captains unshaven appearance and stood there open mouthed for a moment before offering his reply.

"I had no idea you were a member of NIS Sir. I mean that day at the memorial you just seemed so ordinary, I mean, I don't mean that...... Sorry, I just meant, I wouldn't have had a clue Sir."

"Not something one would broadcast from the rooftops, is it Salt?"

"No of course not, sorry Sir."

"It's quite alright you don't have to apologise, you're one of us now. I've been following your career with a great deal of interest and I must say you've certainly done well for yourself young man especially considering all that dreadful business that took place at Seaway."

Following his last remark, the Captain stood with his hands behind his back, looking towards the deck for a moment deep in thought, before finally adding.

"I was so very sorry to hear about your mother Salt, she was an absolutely splendid lady, please accept my belated condolences."

"Thank you, Sir, I do. And yes, she was."

"Well time is of the essence so let's get down to the business in hand, but before I hand over to Commander Prosser here, there's something very important you both need to know. I can confirm that our old friend Kapitan Lenonid Medhev *is* in command of the Soviet submarine M418, moored just across the harbour from us."

Salty's throat tightened and his mouth instantly dried as he heard the news that his father's killer was just across the harbour, less than half a mile away from where he was standing.

Captain Fox allowed him a little time to absorb the news, understanding the hatred the young Lieutenant must feel towards Medhev, and quietly wondered to himself if Jack had been right to send him on this particular sortie in the first place.

"But there's much more to tell you gentlemen I'm afraid" he added scratching the top of his head "I've a feeling my cover is about to be blown. You see, at around seventeen hundred this afternoon, Medhev received a communique from his headquarters in Kronštádt. Now if my instincts serve me right, I think he may be about to discover my true identity."

"However, I did have a spot of luck, two Berber's dropped a case full of live ammunition on the quay at about the same time as he was reading the communique. Unfortunately, both of them paid with their lives a few minutes later."

"Medhev being Medhev must have assumed that a thick Irish Paddy like me wouldn't be able to read Russian; so, stupidly he threw the communique down on the tent floor, and of course I read it. According to the wording, another old friend from the past is about to visit us, our very own Agent Maria."

Anyone even remotely involved in the Seaway case wondered how a sweet middle-aged woman who'd happily washed their clothes, fed them, and saw to their everyday needs, was in reality the Soviets' top ranking Spetsnaz Agent in the whole of Europe. And a highly specialised killer to boot.

Cmdr. Prosser up until that stage hadn't spoken a word, decided to add to the report.

"Well, luckily for Captain Fox here, our spy trawler Sebastien was able to intercept the radio signal and shut it down before the message was completed. Since then we've managed to successfully scramble all of the signal traffic coming out of Kronštádt. We're not sure how long we can keep it up, but I'm reliably informed that it should take at least four or five days to restore full communications."

"So, it's up to you Roger but my advice would be to stay put, to not go back. Sorry Sir, please excuse my over-familiarity I did mean to address you as Captain."

"That's quite all right Commander, drop the formalities while we're here, call me Roger, you too Salt. Okay."

"Thank you, Sir, I mean Roger." Both Salty and the Commander replied in near perfect unison.

The two officers sat at the small cabin table awaiting Captain Fox's further update as Cmdr. Prosser unscrewed the top of his eleven-year old Navy Anchor rum, and poured out three exact measures, placing the thick glass tumblers down on the cabins shiny Formica fold-down table. Swallowing hard and allowing the liquors warmth to flow through his cold body, Captain Fox quickly returned to his report.

"Now the question is this, if we assume my cover is about to be blown, then I am of little, or of no use to the sortie going forward, correct? Therefore, that leaves us with just two choices gentlemen. Firstly, we either board the M418 at first light tomorrow morning and take them out there and then. Or, our second choice is we intercept Agent Maria and dispose of her before she's able to meet up with Medhev. Of course, the downside to that is we miss out on finding out who their British contacts are. As the Commander has already pointed out we can't keep blocking messages from Kronštádt forever, I'd say four maybe five-days tops, so for now Medhev won't be any the wiser to my true identity. Now this is where you come in Salt, you need to be at the *Tangerine Club* tomorrow night, sorry I actually meant tonight, excuse me my body clock is all over the place at the moment. My question is this Salt, are you up to it? I mean you do understand what I'm asking you to do, don't you? You need to take her out before she meets up with Medhev. I'm asking you to dispatch Agent Maria…....."

Salty knew the day would come when he'd be asked this question, four gruelling years of intensive training at HMS Invergordon hadn't been for nothing. It had prepared him and now it was payback time for all the money they'd invested. The dispatch order, or *'kill'* for short struck a deep chord as he tried to remain calm, and mentally prepare himself for his first dispatch order. So, swallowing hard, and hoping neither of them noticed his inward anxiety, he asked the question.

"Captain, we do have a problem though, she might recognise me from my time at Seaway, I know I've changed in size and appearance since then, but there is always that chance Sir."

Cmdr. Prosser who was sat patiently listening to the conversation, began to feel a little anxious at the thought of his young protégé being placed in harm's way so soon, and answered the question for him.

"That's a good point Salt, but we do have a contact at the Tangerine Club and quite by coincidence he's looking for a new waiter to assist him with the evening rush tonight. And that's exactly where you come in, you'll be dressed up in the local garb, your face will be stained just a few shades darker and like all good NIS Agents you'll simply fade into the background."

"What's the preferred method of dispatch Sir?" Salty asked swirling the remnants of the Commanders rum around in his mouth, as the Captain without uttering a word reached down and opened his cupboard drawer just underneath the small table and placed a small black and white capsule in his hand.

Straight away Salty recognised the shape and colour of the tiny pill as, *cyanide*, and without further dialogue, nodded his understanding and placed the tablet in his shirt pocket.

"That answers that then Sir," he confirmed, as his hands started to shake and the enormity of the task before him slowly started to sink in. Captain Fox felt for him and like all seasoned agents he could recall his first dispatch order like it all happened yesterday. It was a Chinese diplomat in Kowloon harbour in Hong Kong, and at the time the NIS *preferred method* as they liked to call it was hanging. Because in that particular case they needed it to look more like a suicide, than a murder. So, the Captain really felt for his young officer.

"Well gentlemen there lies the plan." Captain Fox remarked. "So, if we're all done here, I think its way past my bedtime, and

I need to slip back across the harbour and resume my role as good old Paddy O'Hare. How is Paddy doing locked up in Barlinnie prison anyway, Commander?"

"Not very good Sir I'm afraid, he's been on hunger strike ever since he got there, and he won't say a ruddy word to anyone, not a word, fanatical type you know the sort. Apart from Captain McPherson and us here, nobody knows we've got him."

Captain Fox got up and looked across the table before making his final point; "A few other things before I leave Salt, be sure to take your knife, revolver, and NPD pen, just in case you can't get close enough to pop her the pill, make no mistake she's an extremely dangerous adversary and has to be eliminated. If she meets up with Medhev and is able to reveal my true identity............Well I don't think I need to say anymore, do I?

"Oh, I nearly forgot Salt, apparently your contact at the Tangerine Club is an old friend of yours, his cover name is Ahmed, you probably know him better as Lieutenant David Buckley, do you remember him from your time at Invergordon? From memory I think he was a year above you. Short, dark, swarthy chap, sort of a Romany Gypsy look about him."

Salty certainly did remember Bucks` as they all called him in those days. Bucks had seen a ranting petty officer off at the pass, by feigning a stomach cramp when Salty had reported back to

Invergordon extremely drunk one night following his first liberty boat. Bucks` had saved his *career bacon* that day, and Salty hadn't forgotten.

"The codeword will be *Plentiful* Salt," the Captain confirmed, "only myself the Commander here, and of course Buckley or Ahmed` are privy to that. Finally, Commander Prosser here will kit you out with all the local garb and make sure you're ready. So, on that note gentlemen. I wish you both good hunting, and a very good night."

As Captain Fox departed the cabin and closed the door behind him the Commander unlocked the gun cabinet then placed a letter down on the formica table together with a shiny black revolver beside it and said.

"This letter arrived for you from overseas this morning and by the look of it looks like it's been floating around the system for a while, so I'm afraid it's a bit tattered and torn, the NIS sensors must have been all over it."

The red and blue striped edging of the envelope and the red Maltese star on the top righthand corner was the giveaway. The letter was from Louise, and Salty almost ripped it from the Commanders grasp as he wished him a very "goodnight" forgot to salute him and made his way back to his bunk, three decks below.

Dear Salty,

I received your letter last week, so congratulations are in order sub-Lieutenant Salt, you must send a photograph. I've attached one for you, I hope you like it, my friend Jack took it yesterday when we were on a day's leave in Valetta Harbour.

Salty, turned the page and sure enough sellotaped to the back was a picture of Louise, looking totally resplendent in her bright white nurses' uniform, her dark auburn hair, olive skin and dark brown eyes brought the colour image to life.

In the background was Valetta harbour and she looked stunning, but Salty couldn't help but wonder who the hell Jack was? Nevertheless, he read on anyway.

I might not recognise you now after all these years, but I bet you look splendid in your new uniform, so do send me a photograph as soon as you can.

When are you next due some leave? We should meet up as I can also "hop on a tug" as you put it in your letter and come to see you. I know you aren't able to discuss where you are, or what you're doing but whatever it is please stay safe. I feel we may be embarking on something rather special, you and I, and although we've yet to meet again after nearly four years, I really can't wait for that day to come.

I hope you don't find my words a little premature, but since the first day I saw you in that hospital bed at TS Seaway I knew somehow, that our time would come.

So, I'll sign off by using the same line as you.

With a hug and a kiss

Yours

Louise

Petty Officer Wren:

The Queen Alexandra's Royal Naval Nursing Service:

Royal Naval Hospital Bighi.

Kalkara: Malta Garrison.

Chapter 6. The Tangerine Club.

Tangiers. Northern Morocco.

"It's Witchcraft...... Witchcraft.... Strictly tabooooo." ......Frank Sinatra's mystical tune filled the smoky bar as Frank Abram's the Tangerine's local crooner serenaded European ladies boasting beehive hairstyles sat along the long marble bar.

Medhev was dressed in his formal dark blue Soviet Naval Kapitan's uniform and was puffing eagerly on his favourite Turkish cigarette as Paddy downed his second Whiskey, and thanked God Ramadan was finally over. Paddy held up two fingers shouting out as loud as he could above the music.

"Two more whiskies please," as Salty dressed in his white ankle length Muslim *Thobe* passed by holding a large brass tray in front of his face acknowledged Paddy's request with a sly nod as he slipped past Medhev without as much as a sideways glance.

"What time do you make it Kapitan?" Paddy asked as the Russian, looked down at his watch and was barely able to make out the Roman numerals in the clubs dingy light, "It is a quarter to seven Paddy, Agent Maria will be here any minute let me do all the talking, she's a very competent agent. We don't want someone like you scaring her off, now do we?"

Medhev's blunt guttural ignorance infuriated Paddy, but years of training automatically took over as he acknowledged his comment with a simple wink followed by a broad smile and thought.

That's exactly what you'd expect from a thick Irish paddy like me.

Paddy knew he had to get Medhev away from the bar, too many innocent people were milling around, and Salty was too exposed for a quick kill, so it had to be fast and discreet, but above all it had to be professional.

"Come on Kapitan let's move away from the bar, Paddy said pointing across the room. "I can't hear meself think in here there's a table over there, waiter, waiter!! Bring those two whiskies over to that table over there, will you?"

Salty acknowledged the order and walked towards the bar with the heavy brass tray balancing precariously on his shoulder. Behind the bar *Ahmed Boukali`* cast a brief smile towards him as he loaded the tray with the two whiskies. Despite his red fez and pencil thin moustache, Salty instantly recognised him as his old friend Bucks as he whispered *"Plentiful"* to him.

Paddy and Medhev were sat at the glass table on the other side of the smoke-filled room watching as a steaming hot lamb tagine was delivered in a clay bowl to a woman sat opposite with a hooded Berber sat next to her. Tension started to fill the club's atmosphere as the clock hands on the filthy whitewashed wall rapidly approached seven, and Salty placed the two glasses on the table as he listened to Medhev's conversation.

"Hey, Paddy that's her over there, that's Maria, she's sitting next to Andropov dressed in that Berber's robe, she must have slipped in quietly. My God what a disguise her own mother wouldn't recognise her, she looks more like an Arab than one of these stinking Arabs."

Paddy's whole body immediately tensed in his chair, as he listened to the news that discovery might be only a table away, and the closer she got to him, the closer he was to death. So, he reached into his right trouser pocket and fingered the outline of the barrel on his snub nosed thirty-eight special as Medhev who was temporarily distracted, smiled and waved across the room, towards Agent Maria, and Andropov.

Then suddenly without any warning, all hell erupted, as Salty recognising the impending danger purposely dropped the full tray of empty glasses onto the marble floor and shouted out in Arabic; "Mazerh, mazerh, sorry, sorry,"

Panicked, Agent Maria pulled out her Tokarev automatic and aimed it straight towards Paddy's head, at exactly the same time as Salty drew his serrated fishing knife launching it across the table at her. A shot then discharged the barrel of her Russian made Tokarev and embedded itself in the marbled ceiling.

Salty stood transfixed for a moment and watched as the sharp serrated blade entered her body just three inches below her abdomen, and a crimson stain instantly spread across her white burqa as she looked across at him staring wide eyed and holding her stomach.

For a moment she thought she recognised him, then bent forwards and collapsed onto the cold stone floor with her finger pointing at him, her last spoken words were. "I know you, don't I? you're…."

Then just as he'd been trained, Salty pulled his Webley revolver from his Thobe` and without saying a word he calmly pointed it towards Leonid Medhev, his father's killer and every instinct he possessed told him to end his miserable existence there and then, to just finish him off. But instead he decreased the pressure on his trigger finger, as another shot rang out.

And Salty's world turned black….

Chapter 7. Bucks`

Lieutenant David Buckley saluted Commander Prosser as he entered HMS Scorpions wardroom. The swirling fan on the low overhead was providing a little respite from the days intense heat, as he removed his cap and wiped the perspiration from his forehead.

Without looking up or saying anything, Commander Prosser who seemed a little distant and forlorn, slid the mission statement across the desk towards him, and said.

"Draw up a chair Lieutenant, now please tell me in your own words what happened. You were meant to be there as a back-up, a rear guard in case anything went wrong, well something did go wrong didn't its Lieutenant? Because I've got Captain Fox with a hole the size of a golf ball in his shoulder, and sub-Lieutenant Salt lying two beds down with a concussion. You could have killed him Lieutenant, lucky for him you've got a very light touch my boy, must say a light touch."

Cmdr. Prosser sat for a moment peering across his desk at him waiting for an answer, but before the young Lieutenant was able, the Commander did something he only did on very rare occasions, he said something nice.

"Its okay Lieutenant stand down, you can relax, I'm only playing with you, you did a damn fine job my boy so well done, good show. if you hadn't shot and killed Andropov when you did, then knocked Salt over the head with that gun of yours, he'd be wrapped in a union Jack in Scorpions ruddy freezer compartment by now."

"So well done you've earned yourself a mention in dispatches to Captain McPherson, it's the very least I can do for you. Now tell me your side of the story, will you? Then we can discuss how we intend to move forward with this."

Having knocked him down, then built him back up so quickly Bucks` sat for a moment and wondered how best to engage with the terrifying Commander, so, he placed his hat down on the desk and quickly decided when dealing with him honesty as always, was the best policy.

"Well Sir, I had to think on my feet, you see after Lieutenant Salt threw the knife at Agent Maria, Andropov trained his gun on Captain Fox, so I had to knock Lieutenant Salt out of the way to get my shot off. The bullet caught Andropov square in the forehead, but unfortunately for Captain Fox, I wasn't quite quick enough, and he was able to get his shot off first."

"If I'm perfectly honest Sir, my only issue is being ordered to let Medhev escape. But all said and done, I do think Lt. Salt played his part admirably, if he hadn't thrown the knife when he did, I think we would be sitting here looking at a very different outcome. He saved Captain Fox's life Sir."

Commander Prosser clearly admired the way Bucks` had reported the facts, he also liked the way he'd emphasised his last point and stuck firmly by his friend, but the Commander would always wonder if Salt might have pulled the trigger. But he'd never know. That aside, the deception had worked. Buckley had followed his orders to the letter, and allowed Medhev to escape, so there was still a good chance of uncovering who the top man was. The same man currently heading NIS's most wanted list.

It was a fact, Salty *had* saved the Captains life, he'd stopped Agent Maria from getting off another shot and now she was dead, so all in all, the mission could be deemed a success. And based on that information Commander Prosser's report would reflect just that, success, and nothing else needed to be said.

"Okay, Buckley you're quite right, quite right, you saw it all, we agree not to disagree, so we concur."

Cmdr. Prosser smiled across the desk at Bucks` who nodded in appreciation, and the file was now officially closed. Only five people were still alive and privy to the real story, one of those was an absent Russian, the other two were sitting opposite each other. And the last two were in sick bay.

"So, to bring you bang up to date Lieutenant you've probably noticed that the M418 slipped her moorings this morning, no doubt heading back to Gibraltar and to what Medhev hopes might be calmer waters. She reloaded her cruise missiles in the dead of night and buggered off with all the arms and drugs right under our bloody noses, just as we'd planned. So, you could say we've achieved our objective Buckley my boy."

"After all, the plan was always to allow Medhev to escape and make his delivery. But this time we'll be waiting for him. I must apologise for not letting you in on the finer details sooner, but we simply couldn't, you see the less people who knew the better. Security and all that. It's their top man we're after, and our intelligence suggests it's somebody very high up in the Royal Navy, so I don't want the ruddy *killicks* cat locked up, I want the treasonous rotten bastard hidden deep within our own ranks. So, now I need you to go away and find out who that person is, and that's why I'm placing you aboard our minesweeper HMS Cauldron, she's leaving for Gibraltar today. I want you to do whatever is necessary to find out who this man is, and report straight back to me."

"You are to apply for a job at the dockyard, that shouldn't be too difficult, they're crying out for English speaking loaders at the moment, so this is your cover story."

Cmdr. Prosser handed Bucks a typewritten reference from the department of works on the Island of Malta, with a Maltese Cross and Red Ensign on the heading, before finally adding.

"This letter will get you through the gates, your new identity and all of the other documents you'll need are in there as well, so off you, and get yourself aboard Cauldron she's pushing off in about an hour. And be sure to keep in contact, usual protocol and all that. Oh, and good luck Lieutenant."

Bucks` rose from his chair then looked across the desk at Cmdr. Prosser; "I do have one question if I may Sir? What's going to happen to sub-Lt. Salt? I mean he's the one who should be mentioned in dispatches, not me."

"Well sub-Lieutenant Salt will no doubt be pampered for a few days, then who knows he may well turn up in Gibraltar to assist you with this little sortie of yours. Captain McPherson is flying in today from Invergordon to take personal charge of everything, so depending on what happens in Gib, he may well turn up as well, now on your way my boy."

Efficiency his middle name, Cmdr. Prosser had covered every minute detail and Bucks` was now officially *Ted Kennedy* an Irish Stevedore from Belfast, at least that's what his papers said. And although the same as all NIS Agents on active service

worldwide he could speak four languages fluently, he thought
he might struggle with the protracted Northern Irish drawl.
But he'd do his best anyway…...

Chapter 8. Undercover.

Royal Naval Garrison: Gibraltar Harbour.
The afternoon of the next Day.

"Hello mate, my names Ted, that's Ted Kennedy who do I report to for work at the harbour? I'm a Stevedore just back from Malta, says on the sign this is the harbour office, so I was wondering if you were hiring?"

Billy Johnson, a native of his beloved Newcastle and now clerk of the works in Gibraltar harbour looked up from the ships manifest, ticked three boxes without checking and pushed his cap back on his balding head, as he looked out through the sheds dirty sliding window and said.

"You got any proper ID lad? You need special clearance to work here this isn't bloody Malta you know, and yes, we're hiring, the moneys crap, the hours are shite, but the weathers good."

Bucks` straight away knew the type, so playing him like a professional he was he smiled at him before he replied;

"Sounds good to me mate, when can I start? Got me references and me security clearance papers here from Valetta. I just need a start, you could say, I'm a bit down on me luck at the moment."

Within the time it had taken Bucks` to complete his answer and pass him his papers, Billy had stamped his security clearance, and was telling him to; "Report to this office in the morning, and make sure you're here no later than 07.00 hours young man, bad timekeepers really piss me off. We're loading first thing in the morning, clock machines over there, my names Billy Johnson, I'm the head ganger round here. So, don't forget that and keep your nose clean, there's no drinking while you're working. I know what you Paddies are like, okay."

"Thanks Billy that's great, I'll be seeing you tomorrow morning bright and early, thanks for the start Billy, I really appreciate it."

As Bucks` made his way along the quay, he couldn't believe the harbour security or rather the lack of it, it was virtually non-existent. Over a dozen of the Royal Navy's latest warships were moored with only four sentries standing guard each end of the harbour entrances. Un-supervised and left virtually to their own devices the night shift crews were busily loading boxes and pallets, as crane jibs and derricks loaded with everything that could be loaded swung to and fro. Pallets were stacked ten high crowding the busy quayside at each of the ship's gangways.

The next morning, after spending a restless night and enjoying a greasy English breakfast at the Royal Naval hostel just below the rock, Bucks` arrived at the main gate at exactly ten to seven. And the Naval guard on duty casually checked his pass waved him though without looking at his face.

The quayside on all three sides of the vast harbour was thronging with welders, fitters, and painters, all busily refitting and repairing the Royal Navy's best. Bucks counted just four guards posted at each entrance that morning. The number a clue to when the arms were being loaded. With eight guards posted during the day, and only two at night, it was glaringly obvious that he needed to get himself on the night shift.

Billy Johnson was in his clerking shed filling out the ship manifests, and seemed pleasantly surprised to see him, fifty per cent of all the new Stevedores arriving in Gib tended to be late on their first morning after a night out binge drinking in the countless bars, and clubs that surrounded the dock. Some didn't even bother to turn up at all. So, he smiled as he handed Bucks` his clock card and told him. "Right Ted, you always clock in here, got that? You'll be loading HMS Cassandra, she's a destroyer, and she sails tonight so your job is to make bloody sure that everything on that manifest is loaded."

"Here's a carbon copy, don't lose it. Okay. Apparently, some big wig from the Royal Navy is paying us a visit later today, so make sure you stay sharp and keep your wits about you."

"Thanks Billy, I'll make my way over to her now, one thing though, I'm a bit of a night owl meself, I work better on nights, so what's the chance of getting me fixed up Billy?"

"Well I haven't got a problem with that lad, but I must admit, it's a first, but if that's what you want, leave it to me and I'll see what I can do. The moneys better, but I'm still a bit shocked, it's usually the other way around, we gotta grab hold of `em kicking and screaming, but I'm sure some married bugger will be bloody glad to swap with you. I'll let you know later lad."

Billy liked the newcomer, he seemed keen, the reliable type, but he'd rather just wait and see, never can tell these days. So, he simply returned to checking HMS Cassandras manifest and licked his pencil as he muttered to himself. "Never can tell."

That same morning Bucks` reported the imminent arrival of some *'Big wig'* by radio to Cmdr. Prosser, as the rest of the day passed without incident. Then a little after the sixteen-hundred-hour tea break the Royal Navy's all-important visitor arrived.

The shiny black Rover Ninety with four motorcycle escorts drew up fifty yards from HMS Cassandra's mooring just behind the light cruiser HMS Belfast. Then, an immaculately turned out Royal Naval Commander stepped out from the front of the car, and opened the cars reverse opening door, and a fully-fledged

Rear Admiral emerged into the bright sunshine of Gibraltar harbour, and quickly yomped up the gangway.

Bucks` was sure he'd seen what looked like a camera flash going off by the metal workshop as the Admiral got out but wondered if it might be the sunlight reflecting against the car's shiny black bodywork, so turning towards his newly acquired Stevedore's mate, he asked. "Who is the big wig then Taff?"

"Apparently, it's some Rear bloody Admiral from Portsmouth don't know his name, looked a right fat bastard, didn't he? Somebody important no doubt, that's why the whole place is crawling with bloody Naval guards."

The shift ended as the Klaxon echoed throughout the harbour's white stone walls, and Bucks` walked over to clock out. Billy was waiting for him by the clerking shed.

"Right Ted I've got you fixed up on nights, you can start tomorrow night. Okay lad?"

"Can't I start tonight Billy? I'm, here aren't I? It seems a bit daft to be going back to that bloody hostel when I could be earning, I could really do with the double shift, I need the extra money Billy."

"Well there's no bloody stopping you is there lad. It's fine by me, so you might as well get loading now and climb aboard Pelican she's berthed just in front of Belfast over there. Oh, and report to the Chief Ganger his names Frank, or Franz as he likes being called, he's a nosy old bugger is Franz, Polish, I think? Been here a long time, permanent nights, so don't tell him your life story or the whole bloody harbour will know your mother's middle name by midnight."

"Thanks Billy, appreciate that, I owe you a pint."

"Aye they all say that lad." Billy laughed, hoping Ted meant it. Billy liked Ted.

Salty replaced the *Kodak Brownie* and the *Schneider* optical lens back in its leather case, the weather was beyond hot, and the trip across the Med on Cauldron's sister ship, HMS Amethyst, had worn him out, so he decided to get some shut eye. He'd contact Bucks` once the nightshift ended.

Completely unaware of Salty's presence Bucks` lifted the sacks of flour passing them along a line of seven loaders deep down in Pelican's hold, seventy bags a pallet, five pallets to go, he was tired, it was six in the morning, and his shift ran till seven, and he was beginning to wonder if he'd make it.

With five years under his belt in Adolf Hitler's elite; *Gross Deutschland Division,* and another eighteen spent in the shipyard, Frank, or Franz as he was called knew every trick and every scam in the book, Franz also knew a Stevedore when he saw one, and he knew Bucks` was no Stevedore.

"Bin at zis long lad?" He said. "It's just ze way you handle the sacks, all skew-whiff and the like, look, use your hook then grab zem like this, hook the sack by ze strap, lift then balance it on your shoulder, and you're off."

"Sorry Franz I'm bit out of practice I guess, been out of work for a year since leaving Valetta."

"Oh, you were in Valetta, were you lad? You must know my old mate ze Chief Ganger their Tommy Stiles, goot bloke old Tommy, how'z his legs? Still playing up are ze?"

Bucks` had a choice and could play this one, one way or the other, the way he saw it, his chances of answering Franz correctly were fifty-fifty, so trying to avoid arousing any suspicion he rushed through his reply. "Yes, I remember Tommy, Franz, yeah both his legs are fine now."

Then he tried to let the conversation drop as he lifted another sack and Franz watched and wondered if Bucks` might be a chancer who simply needed a job, and if so, that was fine, or was he a bloody plant? After all Tommy Stiles only had one leg and he'd retired Valetta back in fifty-six, so which one was he? He'd ask up the line.

Can't be too careful, not with another load coming in tonight.

Salty crept along the harbourside, it reminded him of his time spent with Blakey at Seaway. Sometimes a stroll, other times a dash, lift a sack here and there, look natural, blend in, avoid eye contact that's how he remembered it. Inhaling the sweet morning air, he reached HMS Pelican, and watched men lowering themselves on top of pallets deep into the hold, while others dashed around barking orders. The noise was deafening. The partially lit hold reminded him of a scene from Dante's Inferno.

As Salty stared down into the dark hold, Franz emerged balancing his heavy frame on an empty pallet being pulled up, so he quickly turned away to face the quayside, then with a backward glance, watched as the big man walked along the quayside towards Belfast and boarded the big grey cruiser.

Salty shouted down the hold; "Ted, Ted Kennedy, you their Ted? If you can hear me you've got a telephone call at the office, it's urgent."

Bucks` heard the shout and looked up through the labyrinth of men, cables and pulleys and was relieved to see his old friend standing above. "I'll be right up, give us two minutes mate."

As Bucks` emerged from the dark hold gripping hold of the two ropes and balancing on the empty pallet, he couldn't help but wonder.

Was Franz testing me? Was that the right answer? Was there really a bloke called Tommy Stiles in Valetta? Either way he knew he was working in the ideal environment for a murder. His murder perhaps? He could almost picture Franz telling Billy;

It was an accident Billy, he fell straight down into the hold, must have smashed his head in on the way down, poor sod.

And no one would be any the wiser.

As the wind picked up, Pelican's mooring ropes creaked and strained in the harbour swell as Salty looked around to check their exit route and stretched out his right hand helping him to gain a footing. "Glad to see you Salty" whispered Bucks as Salty acknowledged him with a warm smile replying. "Cmdr. Prosser put me aboard the next sweeper leaving Tangiers, he said you might enjoy a bit of company. Anyway, I've got a lot to tell you, so keep your head down and follow me."

Both darted between the pallets along the slippery quayside, as they made their way towards the yard's engine repair workshop, and the loft area above, Salty's new hide. As they scaled the wooden ladder both of them looked down between the wooden rafters watching men in oily blue overalls forge parts, and weld steel girders, as eager young apprentices greased massive engine blocks. The smoggy air was filled with an acrid smell of grease and diesel fumes. The loft was the safest place in the yard. Nobody ever went up there, not unless they had to.

"Right Bucks,` after you left Tangiers Cmdr. Prosser visited me in sick bay, and ordered me to get my ass aboard HMS Amethyst, he told me to take a couple of photographs of the Admiral as he got out of the car, funny thing though, he kept his head down and his collar up the whole time and literally ran up the bloody gangway"

"No one at NIS knows anything about it. So, who the hell is he? And what's he doing here? The M418 slipped her moorings the night before last so I've a feeling the delivery's going to be tonight. But Medhev won't be able to stay out in the straits for long, not with all our anti-submarine netting, mines, and all the other stuff we've got out there."

"My guess is they'll unload at sea stick it aboard a couple of tenders' and bring it ashore somewhere near *Catalan Bay* the most secluded beach on the whole of Gib and only two miles from here by road. Once it's ashore they'll transport it by lorry to the harbour, pay off the guards and stick it aboard Belfast."

"What makes you so sure it's Belfast?" Bucks` asked him.

"Because that's why that fat Admirals gone aboard. It all adds up, he has to be their top man the Soviet contact."

Bucks` was knackered, and Salty watched as his eyes started to droop, not sure if his sudden tiredness was brought on by the diesel fumes from below, or the straight twenty-two hours he'd just worked. So, he reached into his pocket and pulled out a single white tablet.

"Look you've been up for a whole day and night, so go and get your head down over there for a couple of hours, when you wake up take this, it'll keep you awake, just take the one though, strong stuff this, it can send you a bit doo-dally if you take too much."

"You know what Salty, I read something about these somewhere." Bucks` replied staring at the small white tablet in his palm. "Apparently the Germans used to take these on the eastern front when they were fighting the Russian's."

Salty hadn't heard Bucks' because he wasn't listening. He was too busy thinking about how they could climb aboard Belfast without arousing suspicion. So, he turned around and said;

"Right, I'll take the first watch, I'll give you a nudge in a couple of hours, all right mate."

But Bucks` hadn't heard him either as he was sound asleep by then.

As the night shift started to arrive at O-Six hundred hours, he nudged Bucks` and they watched as shipyard workers with metal lunchboxes tucked neatly under their arms trudged along the quayside towards the clocking machine in Billy's office. And Billy began to wonder where his new Stevedore, the reliable, smiley Ted Kennedy was?

The Admirals car parked alongside Belfast hadn't moved all day, security was tight and four armed guards had been posted fore and aft of her brightly lit gangways.

As ordinary civilians or even shipyard workers they wouldn't stand a chance of climbing aboard, they'd be challenged before they reached the bottom of the first gangway, and that was why Commander Prosser had provided them with two fake I. D's and insisted that Salty took both of their number one uniforms with him.

"Right Bucks` let's get into uniform, keep hold of this pass, and tape your Webley to the bottom of your right leg, make sure the safety's on. They're bound to search our upper bodies and we don't want you losing any toes. Now do we?"

At times it was convenient for Salty to forget Bucks` out ranked him, but neither cared who led, or indeed who followed, as long as they got aboard Belfast.

Both officers transcended smartness as they marched towards the two Naval guards standing at the bottom of Belfast's aft gangway. And as expected one of the guards was standing slightly behind the other with his *SLR* semi-automatic rifle with bayonet attached. And he was pointed it directly at them as the second one asked them for their passes.

"Passes please, that'll be both of you, Sir's."

Salty handed the guard the passes, and the guard shone his torch studying their images for a couple of seconds then looked behind Salty exchanging a glance with Bucks, ` who was stood there nervously fiddling with his jacket pocket.

The Webley revolvers trigger guard felt cold strapped to the bottom of his right leg, and Bucks just hoped he'd taped it tight enough.

"Okay, that all looks fine welcome aboard Belfast Sir's, report to the officer of the watch at the top of the gangway. We have an Admiral aboard tonight, so security's at *Red level One*, so if either of you are in possession of any weapons of any kind, you need to hand them over now."

Both shook their heads in unison, giving the guard the impression, they were unarmed, as Salty quickly confirmed it by declaring; "Nothing to declare able seaman, we're only here to take a look at the Turbine's, apparently there's been a few problems recently."

"Okay Sir, you're free to come aboard, watch out for the slippery gangway, Chief Petty Officer Levied nearly broke his neck earlier."

Instantly Salty stopped mid stride as he recognised the name, sure in the knowledge there could only be one Chief Petty Officer Levied in the whole of the Royal Navy, and it had to be the same Levied he'd previously known as *PO Devil*, the rope climbing, sadistic bastard he'd loathed at TS Seaway.

And Levied would recognise Salty if he was wearing steamed up glasses on a dark night, so he'd be sure to warn Bucks`. But not just yet.

As they approached the top of the gangway the duty seaman piped them aboard, as the duty officer, a young midshipman asked them for their passes.

"Passes please Sir's, sorry about the extra security tonight, we've an Admiral aboard."

"Oh, don't apologise midshipman, we're all on the same team here." Bucks` said handing him the two passes at the same time as injecting a little camaraderie into his answer.

The midshipman looked down for a moment and studied the two passes, then carefully compared the photographs of the two

NIS agents with their faces, before he passed them back and asked.

"I see you're both from engineering Sir's, I presume you'll be needing directions to the ship's engine room then?"

"Yes, we will, but I must compliment you on your excellent security here tonight, you can never be too careful, so jolly well done midshipman."

Just as he'd been trained, Bucks` had complimented him, and that appealed to the midshipman's sense of importance. People respond easily to praise, it altered their perceptions, placed them temporarily off guard. Usually just long enough to either pick their pocket, pass by unhindered, or even kill them in cold blood. And because of that, the midshipman had failed the test. He'd forgotten to search them.

"Thank you, Sir, I appreciate that, the engine rooms along the gangway there eight decks down, have the steam turbines been playing up again, Sir?"

Salty was bored with the game by then and wanted to get out of sight before he was recognised, so he quickly answered for Bucks` this time.

"You presume right midshipman. Okay must be on our way, so the engine rooms along the gangway, and eight decks down. Thank you once again, and goodnight."

"Goodnight Sir." Midshipman Barret replied, feeling rather pleased with himself as he saluted the two senior officers thinking the pair were both; *Damn good sports* as they departed and made their way along the outer gangway, and down to the ship's engine room.

Eight decks down in the engine room, levied was busily conducting his rounds, checking steam pipes for leaks, wiping gaskets, taking down readings from all the various oil and water gauges, as the tannoy announced.

"CPO Levied, CPO Levied, report to the Captains wardroom, report to the Captains wardroom immediately."

Tossing his oily rags into an old metal oil drum. Levied removed his heavy blue overalls and steam boots and hung his overalls up in the stoker's locker, before he washed his hands and forearms with the heavy smelly soap, the Navy had so affectionately christened. 'Pusser's.'

The *soap* was really a mixture of turpentine and petrol, mixed with a small amount of bicarbonate of soda, but it did the trick.

As Levied washed the last remnants of the thick shale oil from his hands, he glanced up through the bright halogen lights overhead and noticed that the hatch above the engine rooms main gangway had been left slightly ajar, and immediately thought some *bloody stoker* must have left the hatch open.

So, he dried his hands, screwed up the paper, and angrily threw it into the bin. Then made his way up the steel mesh gangway stairs, before he disappeared through the door and noisily slammed it shut behind him.

Bucks` and Salty were watching hidden behind one of the massive red steam turbines, as Levied disappeared from sight.

"That's him all right, he'll be involved I'll put a month's wages on it, sneaky horrible little bastard that one, I always wondered what happened to him, thought he'd have been slung out of the Navy bloody years ago."

"Right, what's the plan then Salty?" Bucks` asked, "why are we down here when we should be seven deck's up in the Captains wardroom?"

"Because my dear Bucks somebody is here to help us, and that somebody is standing right behind you."

Buckley quickly turned around and saw the white bearded face of Captain Jack `Black` McPherson, standing just two feet in front of him.

"Good God Sir, how long have you been there?"

"Just about long enough to stick a bloody knife in your back, Lieutenant Buckley, you need to sharpen up my boy and remain vigilant! What did we teach you at Invergordon? Check all around you stay focused, that way you might just stay alive."

Bucks` was tired, but that was no excuse because he knew Jack was right and he should have checked, he wouldn't make that mistake twice, so he swallowed the second amphetamine tablet Salty had given him earlier, as Jack began his report.

"Anyway, here's the plan, we're alone for the moment, that treacherous Devil Levied won't be back for a while, the wardroom's seven decks up so we've got a bit of time, gentlemen."

"Sub-Lt Salt, you're going to take the aft gangway and you Lieutenant Buckley the forward, Cmdr. Prosser is already on station up there hidden beneath a tarpaulin in the aft lifeboat, right outside the Captains wardroom. So that you're both aware, your old friend Kapitan Leonid Medhev is also aboard, he's in there talking with Admiral whoever he is while the cargo's being loaded supervised by your other friend Franz, who is also up to his bloody neck in it. My Marines will deal with him and his Nazi cronies later."

Salty listened, and as always was apprehensive to interrupt Jack when he was in full flow, but he did anyway.

"Sir, are we being ordered to shoot to kill? And where will you be when all this is going on?"

Salty's second question was rightly interpreted by Jack as more of a concern for his safety, than hinting he might be purposely ducking out of harm's way, that wasn't Jack's way. But Salty didn't care. Losing Jack was never an option to him. Whatever the cost.

"Well Salt to answer your first question, you're obviously armed, I spotted the bulges on the inside of your leg's a mile away. But the short answer is no, we need to take Medhev, Levied, and the Admiral alive, the information they've got between them should fill the coffers of NIS for years to come."

"Don't use your NPD pens either, we don't want them stone deaf, but I must add that if either of your lives depend on it, or you are protecting one of our own, then you absolutely shoot to kill is that clear?"

Bucks` was the first to acknowledge Jack's order with a nod of the head, but Salty still waited for an answer to his second question. And Jack answered him.

"Salt, thank you for your concern for my safety, but my role in this will be to head up our boarding party entering the hold while you chaps wrap things up above."

"Here are six sets of handcuffs, if I hear shots being fired my Marines will be with you in seconds, make no mistake about that. Be bloody careful, these people will kill you given the chance, they're extremely dangerous, and I can't afford to lose you."

Jack quickly corrected himself by replacing the singular word *"you"* with *"either of you"* as he watched them both remove the heavy black insulation tape securing their Webley revolvers at the same time painfully detaching several leg hairs in the process.

Restored to his former rank, Kapitan Leonid Medhev felt proud to once again be wearing the uniform of his glorious Soviet Navy, he felt warm inside as he sat there holding court in the comfort of the Captains wardroom gently sipping on his thirty-year-old French Cognac.

Stanislav Koralev, Medhev's immediate KGB superior had allowed him to invite his former torturer *Mikhail Kuznetsov* along, and Medhev planned to employ his specialist services that very night. The British Admiral had become greedy and was constantly demanding more and more *Rubles* for his information. Unfortunately for him he knew too much, but much worse than that, he had a habit of talking too much. So, he'd be disposed of before Belfast's wet mooring ropes were winched aboard.

Captain Lewis Montagu-Smythe, Belfast's official master was sat at his desk speaking fluent Russian with the *Smithy* enjoying their little interaction as he listened to Boris reminisce about his glorious Motherland and the grand May day military parade's, and last but by no means least, *"his work"* as he referred to it. Smythe had even taken the time to write down Boris's home address in Gorky in the centre of Moscow and promised to pay him a visit one day.

Smythe a fanatical communist swallowed the whole communist ideology hook, line, and sinker, the fantasy where all citizen's irrespective of colour, creed, or nationhood, were treated as equals. He'd attended Cambridge in the late forties and early fifties and read all the communist articles they could throw at him. He'd watched the so-called *McCarthy* trials with scathing interest, he'd mixed with staunch hard-line red's, and that's what had made it so easy for *Lavrentry Beria's,* NKVD to recruit him.

Of course, the promise of his own *Dacha* on the Black sea, and a highly paid party job helped him along the way as well. Smythe was just looking forward to retirement, and his eventual defection to the east. What would his wife say? What would his twin daughters say? Well, he'd worry about that when the time came, because right now he felt he was among friends.

"Knock, knock."

Allowing the customary delay, Captain Smythe exhaled the smoke through his nose as he stubbed out his eighth cigarette in an hour, then looked towards the door and shouted.

"Enter." And in walked, Chief Petty Officer Levied.

Levied closed the door quietly behind him and stopped for a few seconds looking around and carefully made a mental note of who was in the room.

Captain Smythe, Medhev, Kuznetsov, and the Admiral coldly stared back at him, distrust apparent in their eyes. Because for the past five years Levied had been reporting directly to Stanislav Koralev and only him, he was acting as what Koralev termed; His eyes on the ground. And that exclusivity had made him Levied a very rich man, so, glancing around the room again and rightly sensing the hostility, Levied hoped and prayed that he'd live long enough to enjoy it.

"You sent for me Sir?"

"Yes, Levied I did, take a seat we need to discuss the unloading procedures when we dock in Portsmouth."

As the details were being explained, newly promoted Rear Admiral Lionel Humphrey Burton, KGB code name *Slim* sat sipping his brandy and quietly listening. Burton was the same ranting Commodore that had interviewed Salty and his mother at Portsmouth Fleet headquarters following his father's untimely death, four years prior. And he didn't match his code name in any form. His pompous nature and overbearing greed had made him the perfect target for the Soviets.

But lady luck had run her course, and Kuznetsov lustfully eyed Burton. His future prey. Kuznetsov although extremely cruel, and a full-blown psychopath to boot utterly despised perverts, and his pet hate was child molesters. He'd been shown photographs of Burton entertaining young boy's in his flat in Chatham and that was all the proof he needed. To him Burton was not only a pervert he was worse than that because he was a traitor to his country, and tonight Kuznetsov would enjoy removing him from the KGB's payroll for good.

Outside the room Bucks' whole body was shaking as adrenaline pumped through his body like a runaway steam train. In total contrast Salty felt the opposite he'd learnt how to control his feelings, his hands weren't shaking, he'd become the ultimate professional, a cold-hearted killer no less. His driving force constantly being fuelled by his loathing for Medhev, so, if he as much as twitched when he rushed into the wardroom; He'd end his days without as much as a sideways glance.

Cmdr. Prosser hated confined spaces, the cold damp insides of a lifeboat just didn't sit well with the well-groomed

Cambridge educated Commander, so when Salty unhooked the cover's he was absolutely delighted.

"Good God, I thought you'd forgotten all about me, not my cup of tea all this clandestine skulking around, glad to be out, ruddy glad. Right Buckley you take the left side of the door, Salt you take the right, there's no other way in. I've got the key so no need to smash the door in. We go straight in weapons ready, and make the arrests, got that."

Both the agents replied with a curt; "Yes" as the Commander pressed his ear to the door and listened to them talking inside, at the same time making a conscious note of roughly where each voice in the room was coming from. Then on the count of three he quietly inserted the large brass key in the lock turned it, and all three agents rushed through the opening.

Salty was the first to discharge his weapon as Kuznetsov reached inside his jacket for his gun and a millisecond second later Salty's bullet entered Kuznetsov's upper torso just above his *Costae Verae,* his seventh rib, before washing through his heart. Salty had been well trained, it was an excellent shot. Captain McPherson's earlier instructions to.

"Protect one of our own," mixed with the thunderous noise of the Webley discharging in such a confined space, caused bells to ring in Salty's ears. But it had the desired effect, it had caused shock and awe.

A second later Medhev's Tokarev automatic was pointing directly at Salty before a second shot rang out and Bucks` who'd jumped across to protect his friend dropped his gun to the floor and was gripping his stomach less than an inch below his bullet proof vest. Fresh warm blood was seeping through his tightly closed fingers, as he collapsed onto the floor, and Lieutenant David Buckley with a single mention in dispatches and two sortie's under his belt, aged just 23 years and four months old, took one final glance up at his friend, before his head fell back to the deck, and he was quite dead.

Medhev was smiling as he dropped his gun and raised both his hands, in an act of mock surrender.

"I surrender, you can't shoot an unarmed man?"

Cmdr. Prosser had never shot a man in cold blood, but there was always a first time, so as he aimed the barrel of his Webley between Medhev's eyes as his whole-body shook in pure unhindered rage, then pulled the trigger hammer back and cocked the weapon as Salty shouted out;

"Stop, stop! He isn't worth it sir, calm it, he isn't worth it Commander." The Commander was standing perfectly still his hands felt sweaty, the weapon was heavy as Salty's words echoed around in his head, and he just stood for a moment before he said. "Drop that fucking gun Medhev, drop it onto the deck or I'll blow a hole in your skull the size of an orange, you too Burton, and you Levied, don't you even twitch you little bastard."

"I'm assuming that includes me as well Commander?" Said a fifth voice from underneath Smythe's desk as the Commander swung his gun back and forth between the three remaining prisoners, and this new voice.

Seconds later, Captain Smythe who'd dived under the desk when the first shot had expired, emerged on his hands and knees and his capture raised the night's tally to five. Pulling himself upright the Captain placed his hands on his head and looked over towards the seething Commander. Who instantly ordered him to;

"Stand over there with the rest of your *commie* mates you traitorous bastard, and keep your hands on your head, or I'll finish you in a ruddy heartbeat."

Salty who still had his Webley pointing squarely at Medhev knelt down onto one knee and placed two fingers on Bucks` neck feeling for a pulse, but his pulse was absent. And his friend was quite dead. Seconds later alerted by the noise of the gunshots, Jack stormed through the open door closely followed by two hefty Royal Marines Salty immediately recognised as Sgt Steiner, and Corp Murphy from his Seaway days.

And just as Jack had promised earlier;

"He was there in seconds."

Albeit a few seconds too late. And Bucks` was gone…

Chapter 9. A Hero Returns.

Jack felt there wasn't any point in an autopsy, gunshot wounds inflict so much internal damage that the victims usually bleed out, and *Rigor Mortis* sets in within hours. To Salty, the loss of his friend was unbearable, he hadn't experienced pain like it since his mother had passed away and spent most of the trip back to Invergordon via Brize Norton slumped across the back seats of the Royal Air Force Britannia Aircraft, drifting in and out of sleep.

At Salty's insistence Lieutenant David Buckley's body wasn't placed in the hold, instead it was laying across row sixteen in an open coffin swathed in a Union Jack, with Medhev, Levied, Burton, and Smythe sat chained and cuffed four rows behind. And Salty detested the air he was being forced to breath.

Jack and Cmdr. Prosser dressed in full ceremonial uniform were sat quietly behind Buckley's body and hadn't exchanged a word in the whole of the three-and-a-half-hour flight. Commander Prosser's only comment to the RAF steward, was to tell him in no uncertain terms;

"That those four maggots behind us are not to receive any water, or food of any kind and the hoods are to stay on. So, don't even think about removing them." Salty had never seen the Commander so angry, he wasn't taking Bucks` untimely death at all well, at one stage during the flight he noticed Jack place an arm around the Commanders shoulders, and Salty could swear he'd heard him weeping. The Naval intelligence service hadn't lost one of their own in fifteen years and Jack was furious, he felt responsible and spent most of the flight staring out of the small portal window.

Half an hour later the aircrafts four Proteus turbo prop engines reversed their forward thrust, and the giant plane screeched down onto the tarmac runway, as it arrived at RAF Brize Norton.

Three NIS field agents raised their right hands in a smart salute as four Royal Marines in full ceremonial uniform hoisted the coffin onto their shoulders and exited the aircrafts large, rear opening doors.

The *Last Post* echoed across the wilderness of the deserted airfield, as three very tough and highly skilled NIS field agents openly sobbed without shame, as their trusted friends' young body was placed into the back of a jet-black hearse. The wind was up, and the large union flag covering the coffin was flapping wildly in the breeze, as they gently slid his body into the car's interior. And the hero that had once been Lieutenant David Timothy Buckley began its final trip to his home village of Rangeworthy in Gloucestershire.

Salty's nerves were at breaking point, and he was due some well-earned leave and watched as the three handcuffed traitors, and a Soviet killer were marched, more like dragged, unceremoniously to a waiting *Ferret* armoured car. Jack wasn't taking any chances this time; escape would be impossible.

Medhev would be questioned by the NIS, and then by MI6 respectively, and Jack hoped just that the threat of a return to his mother Russia, would result in a loosening of Medhev's tongue. The NIS would of course promise him asylum, that is, until the Soviets` offered a good prisoner exchange, and then Medhev would be returned to his very own *Smithy.*

Buckley was to be buried with full military honours in his home village, and his grieving parents would receive his posthumous Gallantry Medal, and his mention in dispatches. Burton, Smythe, and Levied were going to be tried by a full military court, and the details kept secret. Jack was eager to rush the trial through before the forthcoming vote in Parliament on the abolition of hanging.

Former Rear Admiral Burton was wailing like an overweight baby, shouting out and proclaiming his innocence from underneath his black hood, and had to be forcibly manhandled by two burly Royal Marines into the back of the camouflaged armoured car.

The screaming only ceased when Sgt Steiner's rifle butt made contact with his groin. But none of it seemed to make the slightest bit of difference to Jack, Cmdr. Prosser, or Salty. They had lost an agent in the field, and Bucks` could never be replaced.

As the black Rover Ninety followed the hearse through the driving rain, Jack, being Jack was becoming fidgety and blaming himself. He knew that this was just another thing he'd just have to try and live with, they'd told him right from the start that death was an unavoidable part of the job, but if he could only have been there a few seconds earlier. He knew full well that an agent being killed in the field was always on the peripheral, he'd experienced death first-hand throughout his whole career. But this time it felt different to him somehow. Bucks` death was going to be a bitter pill to swallow.

He'd been the youngest serving field agent lost in the line of duty since the modern Naval intelligence service was formed back in 1917, and Jack felt it to his core.

During the return flight back when deep in thought he'd promised himself he wasn't going to allow himself to wallow in it, to not drown in his own self-pity, he'd rebuild, he wouldn't give in, the grieving would pass, and the NIS would survive.

And above all, he, Captain Jack `Black` McPherson would lead from the front.

"Well Salt once the funeral is over, I'm ordering you to take a spot of leave, you see somehow and I don't know how yet, we must all try and put this dreadful business behind us. We need to move on, but before we can do that there is something, I need to share with you, something that for security reasons I wasn't able to divulge before, so this may come as a bit of a shock."

"You see, your old friend William Blake from your Seaway days has been working for us in Spain, and as a reward for his excellent handling of what we have now termed the *Sebastien affair* has been promoted to sub-Lieutenant. Blakes covert action had a great deal to do with the successful outcome of your mission *Lieutenant.*"

Salty recognised that Jack in his own Churchillian way was already trying to inject some morale back into the team. To install an *Esprit de Corps*, and to a certain extent it was working. Then suddenly he recalled that Jack had addressed him as *Lieutenant.* Without using the prefix *Sub.* And it dawned on him that he'd just been promoted, and in a way the news briefly lifted his mood. His mother and father would have been proud, but he just wished his friend, the swarthy dark chap they simply knew as Bucks', the man who'd saved his Naval career at Invergordon, and his life in Gibraltar, was there to see it.

But he wasn't….

The funeral was set for the following Sunday in a small Church in the idyllic village of Rangeworthy in Gloucestershire. It was packed with family, friends, and well-wishers. The neighbouring villages of Iron Acton, Bagstone, Charfield, and Wotton Under Edge had all turned out to pay their respects.

The official story recorded in the Sunday Times was that Bucks` had been washed overboard, and his body recovered by Wessex helicopter during a humanitarian mission, somewhere off the Borneo coast which explained, his medal and mention in dispatches.

"Ashes to ashes, dust to dust we commit this body to ………" The Very Reverend Andrew Gladstone hands shook in the biting cold, and the freezing wind was turning the water to ice at the bottom of the deep grave. Those gathered watched as the handmade mahogany coffin descended its muddy pit, and Lieutenant David Buckley NIS to the core, departed this world for the next. Unmarried, and without children, his parents Ada and David Senior listened and wept openly in the cold, as the *Last Post* echoed around the graveyard, and the Red Ensign was slowly lowered. All sortie members including the still badly wounded Captain Fox, who'd insisted on attending layed their wreath's and saluted the grave.

New to NIS operations, Lieutenant George Black safely back from his own sortie in the steaming hot Jungles of Belize was attending the funeral, he hadn't met Bucks` but the NIS had to be brought back up to strength. And Black was going to replace Bucks in the *(MTO),* the Mediterranean Theatre of Operations.

After the ceremony at the wake in Rangeworthy's only pub, the Rose and Crown, Salty thought it was about time he offered his own introduction to the tall tanned, debonair looking Lieutenant Black, who was standing on his own at the bar, sipping a large gin and tonic.

"Pleased to meet you Lieutenant Black and welcome aboard, I'm Lieutenant Salt. Most people call me Salty. Sorry we have to meet under these circumstances, but I'm sure if Bucks` were looking down on us, he wouldn't mind."

Pausing for a moment Black placed his glass down on the long bar before he answered, and to Salty's mind his slow but seemingly timed response felt a little guarded somehow.

"Oh yes, hello Lieutenant I've heard a lot about you, great to be aboard old chap understand we'll be working alongside each other after your spot of leave." Only then did Black offer up his own hand in return, and Salty's instincts were alerted, this new

NIS agent was no Bucks` his smile was awkward, his persona unfriendly, maybe even a little false, but in the interests of all concerned and considering the venue he chose to ignore them.... for now. After all, he'd been proven wrong before, hadn't he? His previous assessment of Cmdr. Prosser five years prior, paid testament to that...

Chapter 10. Hell. Now Walk.

Majdanek: SS Concentration Camp, outskirts of Lublin
Poland 1942

During the late spring of 1942, the SS were transferring thousands of Slovakian Jews from dozens of *Konzentration Lager's* and transit camps, with less infamous names such as Zilina, Novaky and Michalovce. The mass movement was in preparation for the Nazi's so called *'Final Solution,'* the transfers were the beginning of the massed annihilation of the Jewish race. The Shoah.

By the end of July, Majdanek Konzentration Lager was overflowing with its new influx, men, women, and children filled the dusty courtyards of the ten feet stone walls all looking skyward as the tall red brick chimney belched smoke, day and night dissolving the flesh of their loved ones.

Caught in the breeze by the funnel effect inside the camp's high walls, human ash was floating in the air and fell like confetti as thousands of filthy, emaciated, striped uniforms squinted skyward as they awaited their turn. They could see white smoke by day and red fire by night, as the never-ending selections took place. And all prayed to their own God, for deliverance.

The term head Jew or *Kapo* broadly translated as foreman in German, the Kapo was the boss. The camp bully. They were the survivalist's that implemented the SS laws and carried out their masters bidding, their commands were sacrosanct in the camp system. And you only crossed a Kapo at your peril.

That was why the Jew called Alex was so different, yes, he worshipped his God and the Catholic's there's, but Alex didn't really care which God was the true God. Why didn't the Jews just renounce their God? That could sometimes mean a bullet instead of a gassing, but it didn't really matter as in the end. nobody avoided the chimney. Not even the Kapo's.

SS Haupt Sturm Fuhrer Heinrich Zeigler wasn't a religious man by any means, he hated Jews and Catholic's alike, he'd been christened a Catholic in his hometown of Stuttgart, but to him it didn't make any difference which religion a prisoner was because they all went the same way in the end.

But Zeigler had formed a strange sort of attachment to Alex, who was by far the most efficient Kapo in the whole of Majdanek, and he would personally ensure that Alex got his bullet when the time came. He felt he owed him that. He'd worked hard for it.

Each morning Zeigler would stand and watch as Alex faithfully carried out the 'Forced Selection's' during what the prisoner's termed *rappel*. And he'd watch closely as Alex chose between life or death, condemning men, women, and children to depart this life for the next with a simple tick of his roster, followed by a gentle tap on the shoulder.

The sick, the very old, the infirm, even the young children were not excluded, nobody was, there were no exceptions. Everyone attended rappel. If they were unable to work, and couldn't provide, they would be deemed superfluous to Nazi requirements. And simply gassed.

The Pink triangle's, the Homosexuals, rapists, and sexual deviants wore on the front of their shabby striped uniforms would usually catch Alex's eye first. He had a rule that the *'Homo's* or *Perverts,'* as he referred to them would be picked first. It wasn't that Alex had anything personal against Homosexuals, no, but he had to pick somebody, and he might just strike lucky and pick a pervert, a rapist, or even better his pet hate, a child molester.

"Alex come over here, you've missed one, Alex. He's hiding at the back on the left, are you blind Alex? Bring him over here, bring him to me."

"Straight away Haupt Sturm Fuhrer."

Rabbi Yisrael Dorfman was silently praying with his eyes closed as Alex dragged him by his long white beard through the dust to the feet of his Haupt Sturm Fuhrer, he hadn't missed him at all, Yisrael's life had been purposely spared, bought and paid for in black stale bread and ersatz coffee by his fellow Jews. Alex had enjoyed the extra bread, and coffee, his payment for the Rabbi's life, and he wondered if the Haupt Sturm Fuhrer knew? And was he about to follow the gracious Rabbi up the chimney?

"You are either taking bribes Alex, or you are getting sentimental in your old age. Which is it Alex, which?"

The Haupt Sturm Fuhrer was continually tapping his shiny black riding crop against his boot as he awaited his answer and watched as the sweat ran cold down Alex's face as he looked up towards the wooden rostrum and started to hum a silent prayer.

"I am neither Sir I simply missed him, I simply missed him at the back of the line, forgive me Haupt Sturm Fuhrer it will never happen again."

It was at that stage that Alex dropped to his knees, and prayed not to his God, but to the Haupt Sturm Fuhrer, and Rabbi Yisrael felt only pity for his poor lost soul.

However, Haupt Sturm Fuhrer Heinrich Zeigler didn't. He thought pity was only for the weak, a disease and if it hadn't been for pity the Reich wouldn't have had to endure such a terrible defeat, and humiliation in the first war.

So, no, it wasn't pity, the only emotion Zeigler was experiencing at that moment was one of pure and utter excitement, after all he was a very big fish in a small pond, and Alex was a mere minnow swimming against the tide. A filthy, lying stinking Jew! And now he'd have to pay.

"Stand up you pig, stand! If you ever make the same mistake again, I will toss your rotten carcass into the oven's alive. Guards! Tie this filth to the wheel, give him twenty, so he never misses one again."

The *Wheel* to which Zeigler referred, was really a large iron rimmed gun carriage dating back to the first world war, and was where the lashing's, or the *fury* took place, among the prisoners it was the second most feared place in the camp. Only the hot fiery chimney held more notoriety, and more terror.

As the midday sun was beating down, SS Leutnant Hans Brauchitsh released the fury, and the twenty lashes were administered. And much to Zeigler's delight Leutnant Brauchitsh took his time, and he wondered to himself if Alex might survive. Perhaps? Brauchitsh as an SS Leutnant could easily have forgone the physical exertion and passed it over, but the pleasure was going to be all his. Rotten-Fuhrer Fritz Yuengling his corporal, or the *Bavarian beast* as they whispered his name in the darkness of the huts just wasn't good at it. He didn't have the right technique; he would administer the lashing's a little too hastily for Zeigler's taste.

Rumours had spread like wildfire through the camp that Brauchitsh's favourite method of dispatch was impalement, he would select a prisoner then take them into the dense *Krepiecki* forest nearby, and if they were lucky he'd simply shoot them in the back of the head and end their miserable existence there and then. But if he was feeling especially cruel that day, or maybe experiencing one of his painful migraines, he'd tie them to a tree and impale them while they were still alive; only finishing the job when the branch exited their mouth or anus, depending on which route he'd decided to take that day.

The Rabbi and twenty others were marched off, and an hour later the chimney once more spewed its fiery wrath, and Alex watched as the ash settled, and the large SS man untied his hands allowing his thin bloodstained body to drop to the dust. The blood droplets from his back and buttocks, mixed with the human ash formed a crimson trail to the hut where Brauchitsh kicked him to the wooden floor.

"You won't make that mistake again, will you Alex?"

Brauchitsh was Italian by birth, and had changed his name when war was declared, he had originally volunteered for the *Waffen SS,* the fighting arm that had stormed through Russia a year earlier. But, his talents and obvious leanings towards abject cruelty had been brought to the attention of one of his senior officers after he'd beaten a Jew half to death when drunk one night in the nearby town of Katowice. So, Brauchitsh had been chosen for the camps instead.

Brauchitsh hated Alex, he hated his country, he hated his beliefs, so he hoped he'd die in the filth of the block as he slammed the wooden door and left Alex alone with his pain. But Alex felt nothing, the scars would heal, the blood would congeal, but his hatred would always remain. So, he stood up and stared out of the huts filthy broken window and looked up to the sky, at the sun.

And as he looked out Alex promised himself something. He promised himself that the day would come when he would look towards the sun a free man again, and if Brauchitsh survived, he'd hunt him down and kill him, and his would be a slow lingering death. After that, it would be Ziegler's turn and his suffering would be much worse. But in the meantime, he'd carry out their bidding, that's what had kept him alive so far. So, Alex dragged his emaciated bloody torso onto the wooden bunk and ate the rest of the Rabbi's bread and carried on doing what he did. He kept surviving.

Majdanek descended into chaos during the late spring of 1943 as trainload after trainload of survivors from the Warsaw uprising began to arrive, and Alex carried out his forced selections at rappel, sometimes as many as three or four a day.

"You to the left, you to the right, leave your case's over there, they will be returned to you later. Stop crying mother! You will be looked after here the German's are kind to us."

It was all part of the act, and Alex had become an unpaid master at it. He was good at his job, but it wasn't made any easier by the half-starved German Shepherd dog's trying to jump aboard the carriages when the trains arrived, straining at their long silver chains and barking wildly with their yellow fangs exposed.

Consequently, those that had managed to survive the arduous journey would often refuse to exit the carriage. And that just made Alex's job so much harder. Alex felt he needed to speak with Brauchitsh, the dog's made the prisoners jumpy, and that made them harder to herd to the gas chambers. So, if he wanted the process to run like clockwork, the dogs would have to be held further back, and away from the carriages.

Alex's physical wounds were healing, but deep down inside his hatred remained, laying buried and dormant for now. He'd hidden it so deep, even Zeigler hadn't seen it. But it was there all the same.

The selections continued as bad news from the east started to filter through the camp, the German's were in full retreat on all fronts. So, as the brave Soviet army fought its way westwards in early 1944, secret evacuation plans were being put into place. The crematorium and the gas chambers would be blown up, under Heinrich Himmler's order number; 202/SS.

'We must leave no evidence.'

The Russians were less than 200 kilometres east of the camp and their guns could be heard by the prisoner's if the wind was in the right direction, what remained of the population was to be transferred further west, to places with more infamous names such as; Dachau, Bergen-Belsen and Mauthausen. The forced marches had begun. And Alex had been chosen to be among the first to leave.

"Alex, you will escort the weaker Jews with Brauchitsh here at the rear of the column, if they fall over, or are too weak to march Brauchitsh will shoot them, and you will help him. Remember Alex, I spared your miserable life once don't make me regret that."

"I will always remember you for that single act of kindness Haupt Sturm Fuhrer, I will do my duty, you can rest assured."

Zeigler wasn't at all sure of Alex's tone. Was he saying he'd been kind? If so, he'd gone completely mad. Or was he really that grateful for his life? Either way it didn't really matter, his camouflaged SS Kubelwagen was waiting to take him on the long drive west to Dachau, as its new commandant. And that was where he would await Alex and put a bullet in his miserable head as soon as he arrived. After all, Brauchitsh needed help now, not later.

After forty-five Kilometres, and three days of marching in the deep-freezing snow against the biting wind, seventeen souls had already been dispatched, and the hot barrel on Brauchitsh's Schmeisser, hissed as the snowflakes descended. The sickly-sweet stench of death lay all around, as thousands of barefoot prisoners from over twenty separate countries walked the lanes, the gravel roads, and footpaths as they travelled further west.

Townspeople lining the roads watched them pass, some offering a little bread, or the occasional gulp of water if the SS guards weren't looking, other's offering nothing more than a fixated hatred, and the most fanatical Nazi's among them simply turning their backs. The constant: *"Rat tat tat"* of machine gun fire up ahead, a reminder to all, not to slip or fall.

Alex, the survivalist walked at the tall SS man's side, and just as Zeigler had instructed was providing help where needed.

As the fourth days march came to an end, and the freezing night started to draw in, Alex and his column stumbled across a farmhouse with a small barn attached, a light was flickering from a lit candle in the front window of the stone porch. So, Brauchitsh immediately ordered the remaining prisoner's to bed-down inside the barn, while he accompanied Alex to knock on the farmhouse door.

After a short time, the door opened just enough to reveal the shape of a young girl probably no older than eighteen. And Alex straight away started to worry for her life.

"Fraulein, good-evening my name is SS Leutnant Hans Brauchitsh, this is my Kapo Alex, we are transporting Jew prisoner's west, and we must requisition your barn and farmhouse for the night, you must let us in it is the Fuhrer's directive, my men will guard the prisoners, but I will sleep in here."

"But I am not alone Leutnant, my mother is very ill in bed and my father and brothers are away, serving the Fatherland in the east."

That suited Brauchitsh's plan perfectly, he would eat the food, rape the Fraulein, then put a bullet in her mother's head, and if Alex got in his way, his name would be on the second one.

"Fraulein you have nothing to fear from us, nothing I can assure you."

The young girl reluctantly opened the wooden door, unaware that her fate was sealed the very second, she'd answered it.

"This way Alex, you can remove my boots while our friendly Fraulein here prepares me some food, isn`t that correct Fraulein?"

"Yes, yes come in I have some hot soup on the stove, please make yourself comfortable, sit over there by the fire and get yourself warm."

Brauchitsh sat down in the large rocking chair and raised his leg, and Alex started to pull on his mud encrusted leather boot, the SS *runes* on his black lapels were glinting in the flamey light. As Alex asked himself.

What can I possibly do on my own? He has the Schmeisser, the Luger, the knife. Should I warn her? Should I?

"Now get out of my sight and clean my boots Alex, I want them sparkling, we have a long way to go tomorrow, reports are already coming in that the Russian's are only eighty kilometres away, take them to the kitchen, there'll be water in there and see what's holding up my food, I'm starving."

"Yes of, course Herr Leutnant."

As Alex entered the small kitchen at the back of the farmhouse the young Fraulein was stirring the thin soup, and he could hear her sick mother coughing from the bedroom above. The girl was blonde with her hair tied neatly in a bun at the back, her hands were shaking, as she continued to stir the thin broth.

"Fraulein, what is your name? Mine is Alex, I am from a camp called Majdanek further east of here, you must have heard of it? Please excuse the Leutnant's manners, he's just a Nazi pig."

The last part of Alex's sentence was spoken as barely a whisper as he offered his hand, and Alicja gently placed hers in his, all the time keeping hold of the hot ladle.

"I am Alicja, in this part of Western Poland it is a common name, maybe you have heard of it?"

"No Alicja. I haven't but it's a beautiful name, and you are beautiful, you said your father and brothers were serving the Fatherland. Poles serving the Fatherland. Why?"

"They were conscripted, two months ago, I have heard nothing from them since three Wehrmacht officers turned up one day and took them away at gunpoint, they could be dead by now, for all I know."

"I'm sorry Alicja, things aren't going well for the German's in the east, they're in full retreat on all fronts. But you never

125

know, they may well have been captured alive and could be prisoner's like me, sorry Alicja I'm an idiot sometimes I didn't mean to upset you by asking."

"You haven't upset me Alex, it's okay, look I must take him his soup, or he will get angry, use the water pump over there to clean his boots."

Alicja wiped the tears from her face, she liked Alex, he had a heart, she could tell, but she wondered about the Leutnant?

"Here is your soup Sir, I have used all the meat and the few potatoes I had left, I have a little bread, shall I fetch it?"

"Yes Fraulein, but first tell me, what were you and Alex talking about in the kitchen? Was he mistreating you in some way? He's a filthy Jew, sometimes they behave worse than animals."

Brauchitsh sat for a moment with his cold Black eyes exploring her frame, as Alicja stood quite still wondering how to reply.

"No, Sir he was very polite to me, he is cleaning your boots, I will get the bread."

"Stop, stop, forget the bread for a moment and come and sit with me over here, the fire is warm, you look frozen, Mien Fraulein." Alicja swallowed hard hoping the fear would pass, and that he would be kind to her when he raped her, as she watched shivering as Brauchitsh placed the hot soup bowl down on the hearth and pulled his braces down to his waist.

"Alex go and see to the prisoner's and don't disturb me again tonight, you are to sleep in the barn with the others."

Alicja sighed, her mouth opened but not a sound came out, and in Brauchitsh's twisted mind her terrified stare just made her all the more attractive. And Alex the coward, the survivalist, obeyed his master's orders, and ran for the barn.

As the morning sun began its path across the eastern sky, Alex was listening to the birds warbling outside as he watched the SS guards button up their black tunics and shoulder their weapons. The prisoners were already lined up outside shivering in the cold, except for the five that lay dead, sprawled out amongst the hay. Their starved emaciated wretched bodies had been set free, and all Alex could feel was envy. Because for them it was finally over.

His thoughts then turned to Brauchitsh's boots he would be waiting. Then he pondered Alicja's fate, he'd heard her pitiful screams in the night, and hoped that Brauchitsh had spared her young life, and that one day she might settle down and have children of her own and try and forget this ever happened.

So, he prayed to his own God for her deliverance.

"Leutnant, I have your boots, I am waiting here at the door."
No reply.

"Leutnant are you there?"
Nothing.

Alex entered the small kitchen, Brauchitsh was busy boiling his shaving water on the stove, and looked shocked to see him, Alex thought he observed a hint of fear cross his face. But he couldn't be sure.

"Leutnant, I have your boots, I'm afraid I didn't have any polish, so I used a little gear oil and some petrol from the tractor outside. I hope they are up to your standard."

"Just drop them over their Alex and get out! I will be there shortly!"

"Yes, Leutnant, I will wait outside."

As Alex turned to make his way along the dark hall, he noticed the embers on the fire in the living room were still smouldering in the hearth, he also noticed Alicja's body sprawled out naked face down on the wooden floor with her buttocks splayed apart, dried congealed blood was spread around her womanly curves, a broken broom handle lay at her side, dried blood on its brittle shaft. And, Alex the survivalist, once more ran for the barn.

The prisoner's waited and the snow fell as Alex heard a single shot from the farmhouse echoing across the concrete yard and pretended not to notice. Some of the prisoners were so weak they could only stand if supported by a friend, as others simply collapsed where they stood and were quickly dispatched with a single bullet to the back of the neck. Those that were able, tried to straighten their broken bodies, to show the Leutnant that they were ready for the days march, that they wouldn't be a burden to him, and fit enough to walk another fifteen kilometres in the freezing cold wind without food, water, or footwear.

Brauchitsh arrived holstering his Luger and ordered Alex to remain with him at the rear and asked him how many of the prisoners were still alive.

Alex replied as he stared into the blackness of the Leutnant's eyes

"Thirty-five Leutnant, from the original sixty that is." Alex said curtly, as Brauchitsh smirked, and thought.

I might reach Dachau. I might not? But whatever happens I will rape and pillage along the way, maybe even steal some transport or hitch a ride, so the sooner the prisoners are dispatched the better.

Then Alex shouted;

"Right walk! Come on, move, move!"

Alex's shouted order impressed Brauchitsh, his booming voice reminded him of his hero Mussolini at one of his rallies He thought he could almost smell the fresh mountain air of his beloved Italy.

Later that afternoon Brauchitsh was relieving himself in a nearby hedge, and Alex overheard part of a conversation he was having with one of the SS guards, *SS-Oberschütze, Otto Ehrlichman.* Ehrlichman's favourite method of dispatch was to beat the prisoner to death using the metal butt of his Schmeisser. He'd always be sure to start at the feet, smashing the bones as he slowly worked his way up.

Their conversation was conducted in German, so Alex listened, he was from Slovakia near the Baltic states and had been taught German as a second language at school, that was another of the reasons he'd remained alive. That and his impressive ability to simply, *hide in plain sight.* They'd been discussing the march, and Ehrlichman said "the main column had broken off and was much further up ahead, so what was the point in keeping the remaining prisoner's alive? After all the Russians were close, so they needed to move quickly if they wanted to join the *Rat line* or the *Organization der Ehemaligen SS Angehörigen.* The *Odessa.*

Alex wondered what the Rat line was, he knew where the Ukrainian port of *Odessa* was, and he could tell by the smug look on Brauchitsh's face that something was very wrong.

So, that was the moment he knew he had to escape, and it had to be soon, so without Brauchitsh noticing he started to drop back slightly, slow his pace down, and fell in just behind him. He could sense Brauchitsh searching, looking for the perfect spot for the execution's they would need to be fast and efficient that was his style, behind him he could hear two SS men unloading the *MG42* machine gun from the cart, and he knew he had only minutes to live.

As they approached the stone bridge that separated the villages of *Leszno,* and *Nowa Sol*, a chance appeared, the bridges stone walls were low enough and the river below looked deep. The current was rapidly flowing down-hill, so it had to be now or never. So, Alex chose now.

As he threw the lit match at Brauchitsh's boots, he ignored the SS man's frantic screams as the flames engulfed his legs, and he jumped the stone wall, and the roaring river took him, the water was freezing but Alex didn't care, he would survive whatever. He was free now…

As he was being washed further downstream Alex shouted out their names over and over again; "Brauchitsh, Ehrlichman,

Yuengling, Zeigler" those names needed to be remembered. There were others too and he would pay them all a visit one day just to catch up on old times.

But he would be sure to leave the best until last.

"Brauchitsh, Ehrlichman, Yuengling, Zeigler......"

Chapter 11. God Forgive Him.

The Monastery of Saint Augustin. Vomero Hills.
Naples. Italy. 1964

Abbot translates as Abba's in Latin and Abbot Giovanni Francesco was a good Abba's, and a good father to his flock. Giovanni's regular bread deliveries to the local villages were a lifeline to his people, and he'd often be seen walking the tracks, and the dusty lanes of the Vomero hills with his faithful donkey *Benito* stacked high with fresh Pitta bread at his side.

Children would shout greetings from shuttered windows and fetch fresh water and dry hay for Benito, as the good father attended his rounds and fed his people. Little was known about Giovanni during WW2, those who could remember would tell you he'd run off the same day Great Britain had declared war on Germany, then simply returned a month after VE day. Then, he'd renounced his sins and taken his scared vows in front of the holy father's.

Giovanni's own father the last Abba's had bravely sheltered downed Allied airmen from the Nazi's when the bombing was at its height, and every year those same airmen and their siblings would visit his grave at *Saint Augustin* to leave flowers, gifts, pay their respects, and offer a special; "Thank you" to the devout Abba's for saving their lives.

Today didn't feel different to any other, the dusk was upon them as Giovanni returned from his visits, and Evening Prayers were beckoning. The cacophonous sounds of the monastery bells echoed throughout Vomeros in its beautiful green valley. Giovanni was suffering one of his excruciating migraine's and rubbed the water from his eyes, as he approached the stable to bed Benito down for the night.

As he was wrapping Benito's rope around the wooden manger post, a tall dark stranger suddenly appeared from behind the water trough and asked him in fluent Latin for some bread and water.

"Crustum, aqua, crustum aqua, gratificor, gratificor Abbas." So, the father replied in English.

"Please my son, you can speak English, German, or Italian here, I must admit to finding Latin a little tiring at times. Forgive me speak freely my son."
The tall dark stranger replied in English;

"I need water, food, and a bed for the night father, I was stranded on the mountain when my motor bike overheated and broke down in the hills this afternoon. I've been wandering around ever since, please help me father?"

"Yes, yes of course my son, I can see your face is a little sunburned, just let me attend to my old friend Benito here, then I will fetch you everything you need."

Giovanni smiled as he stroked Benito's wet nose and was about to offer him the water bucket when a heavy blow struck him from behind, and his bucket dropped to the stable floor.

He wasn't dead, that wasn't the killer's intention at that stage, so he stared up dazed and helpless as the tall dark-haired stranger pushed the hypodermic needle further into his vein as Giovanni asked; "God to forgive him."

A few hours passed, and Father Amadeo or *'God's Love'* came looking for his dear friend Giovanni. He remembered earlier hearing a hawk screaming during Evening Prayer's, but high up in the wild hills of Vomero, that was nothing to be alarmed at. The last Abba's, Giovanni's father had taken Amadeo in as an orphan after the war, and with bright blonde hair and blue eyes suspected was a German's child.

As he approached the barn Amadeo noticed that the door was slightly ajar, and he could hear Benito's hooves scraping the pennant floor.

Entering the half-darkness of the barn, Amadeo looked down towards the floor to see the faithful Benito with his legs curled up underneath him, writhing in agony with Giovanni's pitchfork impaled through his neck.

Amadeo screamed out for help as the monastery lights revealed Giovanni's naked body suspended upside down from the old timber beams with a jagged broom handle pushed up his anus, and the other end protruding through his mouth.

As the others ran in, Amadeo sank down to his knees deep in prayer, and looked up again to see Giovanni's eyes had been sewn together, and his forehead and eyelids tattooed with strange symbols, letters even. Amadeo thought it strange though that Giovanni had never mentioned the terrible burns and scarring on both of his legs? But that didn't matter, as his friend was no more.

So, he took a sacred vow of silence that night to shut himself away from the world vowing he would never utter a spoken word to a living soul again.

And he didn't. Not ever......

Chapter 12. Javea and a Rest?

The BOAC Britannia flight to the dusty patch of airfield the Spanish had recently re-named *Alicante Airport* had taken just under three and a half hours from London's rapidly expanding Heathrow. There'd been headwinds and turbulence all the way, so as the large four engined turbo propped monster touched down on the hard-tarmac runway, Salty felt relieved.

The sun was shining, the sky above was blue, and he was dressed in civvies and on leave for the first time in a year, so as he descended the plane's stairs and the intense heat greeted him. He felt good.

At the edge of the large runway was an old tin shed with the word *Aduanas* written in chalk on the corrugated sheeting. The man inside was sitting on a stool clearly trying to avoid venturing out into the midday sun and was instead happily nodding politely to anyone who chose to make eye contact with him. Once through what he rightly assumed was Airport Customs Salty started to look for a taxi on the long dusty road at the rear of the shabby airport terminal.

The sun was beating down and the heat was approaching the upper nineties, then as he was studying the map and out of the corner of his eye he noticed an old pickup truck parked near the entrance with the words *Pedro Pescadero* (Pedro Fishmonger) written on the door, and below that the letters *Xabia* he immediately recognised as the Catalan spelling for Javea. His destination.

"Amigo, hablas ingles?" Salty asked, repeating his request in English; "Do you speak English?"

"Si, Poco. A little senor," the small dark-haired man replied pinching his fore finger and thumb together in an attempt to emphasise his point.

"I need a ride to Javea, comprende, I will pay you senor, si."

"Si, senor, you are lucky, I was just leaving you pay me yes."

"Si senor I pay you." Salty confirmed as he threw his small case into the back and jumped in the front before the man had a chance to change his mind.

The two-and-a-half-hour journey in the old *Warszawa* Russian built pick-up truck to Javea felt like hell, the dirt roads and tracks were continually interspersed with Guardia Civil checkpoints and fallen trees. To Salty it felt as if he was visiting a third world country, but Spain, although lacking modern roads, industry, and commerce, was still a strikingly beautiful place.

Relations between Spain's fascist government led by Generalissimo Franco and Great Britain had pleasantly thawed over the last two years. Franco badly needed coal, tourists, and hard currency, and the British were desperate to keep hold of their strategic Naval base on Gibraltar. So, the Brit's were happy to supply them, hand over fist.

As the dusty pick-up's two stroke engine popped and smoked and stuttered to a halt outside Sandra's bar on Javea's sandy Arenal beach, Salty thanked his new friend Pedro for the lift, and handed him a five peseta note, and was not altogether sure if Pedro's radiant toothless smile was because he was happy with the tip, or whether he'd unintentionally overpaid him.

"Gracias Pedro por el ascensor de mi amigo." Salty said in fluent Spanish, repeating it again in English.

"Thank you for the lift, Pedro my friend." Salty's warm goodbye and perfectly pronounced Spanish impressed Pedro, Salty was the second Englishman he'd met who could speak Spanish, that was apart from the big soft lump everyone in the village called Blakey.

As Pedro and his fish van departed Salty waved and took a few moments admiring the scene, the warm crystal calm waters of the Mediterranean were glistening before him in the afternoon's hot sun, as *burro's* loaded high with fresh oranges and lemons trundled past, and laughter filled the air as amorous Spanish hombre's passed comment on Senorita's wearing tightly drawn blouses. Invergordon and its glum grey weather seemed a world away, and Sandra's bar was just as he'd imagined. The sun terrace or *Naya* was thronging with Spanish families enjoying jugs of fruit-filled Sangria. The bar's setting in Javea's beautiful bay was idyllic, the most beautiful he'd ever seen and the only emotion he could feel at that moment as he jogged up the steps, was that of pure raw excitement.

The first thing he saw was Fiona busily wiping down tables, clearing glasses, and doing what she did best, looking beautiful. Blakey was nowhere to be seen, so after clearing his throat he attempted his rehearsed quote from Shakespeare's *The Tempest,* directing his slightly altered rendition, towards his unsuspecting friend.

He'd been rehearsing the verse ever since he'd left the airport, and Pedro the fish man had heard it that many times he'd memorised it himself and promised to try it out on his wife *Adelita* when he arrived home later that day. Secretly hoping it impressed her enough for a mid-afternoon siesta.

Salty coughed loudly trying to attract her attention;

"Is that some beautiful Welsh girl I see yonder, for I would not wish any companion in the world, but her, and only her."

Fiona recognised his voice instantly, so she smiled and pondered and stood quite still with her back to him for a moment and instead of turning around, she calmly placed the dish cloth down on the marble table gently brushed her dark brown hair back, and turned towards the door, as the days sunshine delivered her friend, a true friend, and Blakey's best.

At the same time as Salty was arriving at Sandra's bar the newly promoted sub-Lieutenant Blake was busy packing the replacement Marconi high frequency radio receiver back into its steel cradle, making sure it was hidden and safely stowed away underneath the ropes, pulleys, and fish netting deep in Sébastien's hold, as Gonzalo and his newly acquired first mate Juan Carlos were securing Sébastien's heavy mooring ropes in Javea's busy harbour.

After three days at sea battling the elements, and intercepting hundreds of Soviet radio messages, Blakey was more than relieved to hear Gonzalo's voice shouting out the all clear, from above;

"Sebastien's secure, we are ready for off-loading." On hearing those words Blakey was topside in seconds, and with four days of well-earned leave to look forward to, his first port of call as always would be a couple of cold beers at Sandra's, followed by a warm soapy shower, a good meal, and after that whatever sprung to mind.

The trouble was that if past experience was anything to go by, he'd be fast asleep long before reaching the "sprung to mind stage."

Entering the bar, the first two things he noticed was that the place was empty, and the blinds had been pulled halfway down and an inert silence was filling the normally busy bar. Fresh cigarette smoke was dancing around in the air, so it was obvious somebody had recently been there.

As he adjusted his eyes to the half-light and he walked down the bar sand was crunching beneath his shoes on the marble floor, but that wasn't all he could hear. He could also hear a sound like a rustling, followed by a snort, like somebody was trying to stifle a laugh. So, he shouted out.

"Hello, Fi, Julia you there? Hello is anyone there?

Then, he waited. And at first, he heard a giggle, followed a loud shout, before all hell let loose and the two people Blakey loved more than anything in the world popped their heads up above the bar. And the box containing his newly purchased engagement ring fell down onto the marble floor, and then. The real celebrations began…...

"Four years, four years, my God has it really been that long mate? Salty asked, "we were what? Seventeen then I'll never forget the first time I met you when you were trying to stuff all that uniform in your locker, ha ha, wouldn't fit in would it."

Blakey's eyes were watering with laughter as they clinked their glasses together remembering that moment like it had happened yesterday.

"And just look at us now," Salty continued; "Who'd have thought, I mean us two officers in the Royal bloody Navy, we owe a hell of a lot to Jack don't we Blakey? So, here's to Jack."

Both friends lofted their glasses high in the air towards the setting sun as they gulped down the cold cerveza, and jointly recited;

"To Jack, God bless him. Firm but fair is Jack."

A few minutes later, still sat there reminiscing, Julia walked in and spread out a giant red and white check tablecloth on the table as Fiona arrived with selected cheeses, and `Jamon Serrano, before finally, a huge iron skillet filled to the brim with seafood paella was placed in the centre of the table and in her poshest but still broad Welsh accent Fiona named it. Her; *"Piece de resistance."*

As they sat down and ate the food, the subject of conversation, inevitably returned to work. To both of their covert roles within the NIS. Blakey was quietly playing with his half empty beer glass as he listened to Salty description of Medhev's arrest and a played down version of his own part in the sortie. Blakeys stomach turned as he heard about Agent Maria's demise in the Tangerine club.

"Ironic isn't it Blakey? If you hadn't intercepted that message from Kronštádt when you did, and Bucks` hadn't killed Andropov Captain Fox would be pushing up daises right now, that bullet nearly tore his bloody arm off."

"I'm really sorry about Bucks` mate." Blakey responded after a few moments spent deep in thought. "I never met him, he sounded like a really great chap."

"Yes, he was" Salty replied; "and if it's the last thing I bloody well do, I'll make sure that Russian bastard Medhev pays."

The venom and bitterness contained in those last few words weren't lost on Blakey, he knew Salty meant every word of it, so he joined him in a last toast, as once again they both raised their glasses towards the setting sun only this time to wish Bucks` a tearful "Bon Voyage."

As the sunrays gently disappeared behind Javea's giant wonder the *Montgo Mountain* and the stars twinkled in the darkening sky, they both sat outside and shivered as a breeze or a *Scirocco* cooled the evening air and wondered if it might be Bucks` thanking them.

The next morning during breakfast the atmosphere was a little tense, both had ignored Fiona's repeated requests to; "Go to bed!" And were paying for their heavy night's drinking, neither had slept more than a few hours, so Salty decided a reconciliation was needed, and quietly whispered into Blakey's ear.

"Come on, now's the time, get the bloody ring out, you clot!"

As if he was obeying a direct order from a superior, Blakey felt for the box in his pocket then noisily dragged the wooden chair back across the marble floor pulled out the ring then holding it between his thumb and forefinger he dropped down onto one knee. And Fiona wondered if he was still drunk.
But he wasn't.

"Fi, I know it's a bit overdue, but what with Salty here and all that, and with everything we've been through together I wondered if you would do me the honour of becoming my wife. You see. I really love you Fi, and…."

Fiona stopped him midsentence by calmly placing her finger to his lips as he knelt, and his whole body started to shake before she answered;

"Don't say another word you big soft sod, of course I'll marry you, took you bloody long enough though didn't it? I really love you Blakey, from the bottom of my heart."

"I love you too."

That was the second time Salty had seen Fiona cry, beautiful as she was whether laughing or crying, he'd always thought of her like a younger sister and she suited Blakey down to the ground, so, as he looked across the table as his two best friends embracing, he started to wonder what to write in his best man's speech.

Due to strict NIS security and with the exception of Julia and her twins, no friends, neighbours, not even any of the local inhabitants of Javea were invited to the wedding. Revealing either of their true roles and identities would be tantamount to a death sentence in the irrepressible country that was; Generalissimo Francisco Franco's, fascist Spain.

Instead, Blakey and Fiona had to travel twenty kilometres to the *Church of the Virgin* set in the centre of the quaint little village of *Xalo,* in the picturesque *Jalon Valley.*

Salty was obviously going to be best man, and without a father to give her away Jack had volunteered to walk her down the aisle and cajoled Cmdr. Prosser, Guns, and Asker into being witnesses. His unique way of persuasion not to dissimilar to an eighteenth-century press-ganging.

The Church bells echoed throughout the sunlit valley as Blakey and Fiona stepped out into the brightness of a beautiful day as a married couple, paper confetti littered the air above the arch the four sailors had created with their ceremonial swords. And a beaming Jack wiped away a tear.

Salty was overawed by the wonderful moment as his two best friends kissed and their laughter filled the air in the old Church garden.

The outside tables were set for ten, as they sat watching Julia's beautiful twin girls dance the Flamenco on the green lawn in their flowery Spanish dress's as Blakey attempted to strike a tune from his old Spanish guitar. The absent Captain Fox had sent flowers which adorned the long wooden table, his recovery in hospital was still an ongoing issue, following the wound to his shoulder.

As the warm day morphed transforming itself into a balmy summer evening, Salty was sat wondering to himself if this is how life was meant to be? Was this how normal folk lived?

With the speeches over and the empty *la Paella* tray's stacked high on the tables, Jack who was sitting opposite playing with his beard leant forward and looked across at his young sub-Lieutenant, and Salty could sense his life was about to change again. The next sortie clearly on Jack's mind.

"Walk with me for a minute, will you? There's something we need to discuss my boy."

Rising from the table, Salty followed behind as Jack walked down the sloped lawn towards the graveyard containing most of Xalo's former residents and propped himself up against the most ancient gravestone of them all, a sixteenth century Conquistador as he puffed eagerly on his pipe, and the smoke curled and danced in the evening air.

"Well, I do apologise if I'm about to spoil your day Salt, not the best of places to discuss your next sortie is it? So sorry about that but this really couldn't wait. Up until now you've had the benefit of either me, or Commander Prosser behind you as a backup, so you've been lucky. Well your next Sortie's going to be a little different, as this time you're going to be on your own."

"You will have sub-Lieutenant Blake in radio contact aboard our spy trawler Sebastien at a prearranged time for a few minutes a day. But I'm afraid, apart from that, that's about it. So, you need to concentrate Salt, correlate the facts and piece all the information together."

Jack paused taking a puff on his pipe as he savoured the taste, and the smoke from his mouth curled up through his nose.

Salty hated smoking, but he could see Jack was deep in thought, so he stood there patiently waiting for him to resume the conversation as Jack pointed the bowl end of the pipe towards Salty's chest and said;

"Now, this all started when a murder took place in the Italian village of Vomero, somewhere near the port of Naples, now I can see you're already asking yourself what the hell's that got to do with Naval intelligence? Well the murders didn't stop their Salt, no. Because following our aircraft carrier HMS Eagle's departure from Naples the slaughter continued right down along the whole of the Spanish coastline, in fact they occurred in every deep-water port HMS Eagle visited during her Mediterranean deployment."

"To date that's Alicante, Malaga, and Valencia. So clearly somebody aboard Eagle is venting their blood lust on these poor unsuspecting locals."

Salty already had a question and was dying to ask but knew better than to interrupt Jack when he was in full flow, so he simply nodded his understanding as Jack tapped the warm remnants of his pipe tobacco against the Conquistador's final resting place; Before returning to his brief.

"Now here's the thing Salt, as you're fully aware it's Naval policy to grant liberty to only one capital ship at a time, so as there aren't any disturbances or brawling between the crews when ashore. The common denominator in this is that the murders only take place when Eagle's crew are ashore. Nothing ever happens when any of the support crews of the destroyers or submarines are granted liberty."

"When the reports of these murders first started filtering through to us at NIS, I contacted Interpol here in Spain and according to them each time the killer strikes he leaves a calling card, the victim's bodies are tattooed with the letters *K* and *L,* and in each and every case there's a second tattoo, and here's the really odd thing the tattoos are in Jewish, and they spell out the Yiddish name for Evil."

Salty already knew the Yiddish name for evil, it translated simply as *Beyz* with the letter *E* rolled on the tongue and pronounced as an *A* but was still reluctant to interrupt.

"So, what the hell does KL mean Salt? You tell me? Is it initials for something or maybe a place? What is it? But I'll tell you this we need to find out bloody damn fast before Franco and his fascist wankers refuse entry to all our British warships, and worse than that the press gets hold of the story."

Salty didn't give a hoot about diplomatic relations between Franco's Spain and Harold Wilson's Great Britain, and he certainly didn't care much for the so-called *free press*, so his questions were going to be based on the facts, and to hell with Jack and his problem with interruptions. He'd ask anyway.

"Sir, I know how much you hate interruptions, but I need to ask you a couple of questions, so please bear with me."

"Go ahead Salt, ask away."

"Well the first question is this, on which part of the bodies do the tattoos appear? I mean the K the L and the word Beyz must be linked somehow, the word Beyz is only ever used in the Jewish community isn't it? It dates back hundreds of years, my other question is of course, how are the victims being murdered?"

Jack was impressed with his young Protégé. He'd finally reached the stage where his questions were relevant and meant something, so he deserved the respect of a decent answer, not a guess or a bad-tempered reply. To Jack's mind, he'd earnt that.

"Well Salt, the victims are always Franciscan or Benedictine Monks, and from what we can gather the killer seems to lay in wait for them in a quiet part of the monastery, then shortly after the call to Evening Prayer's he attacks them in either their hermitage or workplace by striking them on the head with a heavy object. Then once they're incapacitated, he simply carries on with the killing process."

"Killing process?" Salty asked; "What do you mean the killing process, Sir?"

Jack swallowed hard for a second before continuing as the photographs he'd seen on his desk at Invergordon flashed through his mind, and he wondered how best to explain to his young Lieutenant, the so-called *killing Process,* a term he personally detested. So, swallowing hard again and clearing his lungs with a gentle cough he attempted to explain.

"Well, once the victims are hit on the back of the head, they're tied up then stripped naked and injected with just enough *Propofol* to place them in a half coma so that they're completely paralysed, but still awake and unable to move or fight back."

"Then the killer proceeds to drive a broom or mop handle or whatever's handy up their back passage, and only when the end protrudes through the victim's mouth does, he deliver his killer blow by using the same heavy object he'd originally used to incapacitate the poor souls. These attacks are frenzied Salt, quite frenzied."

Salty couldn't quite take in or quite believe what he was hearing, the laughing and cheering from the ongoing party in the background seemed a universe away. So, he re-asked his original question.

"So, where do these tattoos appear, Sir?"

Jack stepped a little nearer to Salty and lowered his voice slightly, before providing his answer.

"They appear on the victim's eyelids Salt, that is of course only after the killer's taken the time and trouble to sew them up."

It was at that stage that Salty had heard enough and he bent down behind the Conquistador's gravestone releasing his day's food and sangria. Then wiping the sick and bile from his mouth he looked up and asked; "When do I go Sir? The sooner the better, we need to nail this bastard, and be double quick about it!"

"You leave by train for Valencia the day after tomorrow. Anstey and Ballard don't know it yet but they're being transferred from HMS Eagle to her support carrier Centaur in a couple of days, that is of course if they've sobered up enough by then."

Asker was now standing on the wedding table wearing a sombrero, clicking castanets and dancing his very own version of the flamenco, as Guns, Fiona, and Blakey clapped. Commander Prosser who uncharacteristically for him was in extremely high spirits was busily pouring the remnants of his Vino Tinto from a clay carafe, a full two feet away from his mouth. The Commander hated mess; his aim was extraordinary.

Re-joining the party Salty tried to hide his feelings, he'd already made his mind up that what he'd just been told could wait for another time. Today was meant to be for fun, and fun was what he'd have, so when he heard Guns and Asker wolf whistling towards the Church entrance, he looked away into the distance to see a figure only a woman could possess, and for the briefest of moments Louise's beautiful shape was silhouetted against the tall stone wall, in the half light of the evening sun.

Louise had arrived and her face was radiant and beautiful, and at last happiness and alongside it peace had returned for the young Lieutenant. Salty walked slowly towards her and took her in his arms, and the two lovers embraced and took their first kiss in four long years. Blakey was watching open mouthed and wondering if Julia should make up the spare room that night. Somehow, he just didn't feel up to it himself.

As the evening drew to its natural end and the last of the sun rays glinted as they departed the early evening sky the two lovers drank flirting the remaining hours away as they laughed and other times shrieked just happy to be in each other's arms.

Later that night as the taxi travelled through the valley and passed under the shadow of Javea's mystical Mountain, the Montgo`, Salty decided it was time to ask his question, the question he'd been itching to ask, since Louise had first arrived.

"Louise, I hope you don't mind me asking, but well who is Jack? You know the chap that took the photograph of you in Valetta harbour?"

Louise laughed, not in a mockingly cruel way but more at the way Salty had stuttered his way through the question.

"Jack, happens to be short for Jackie, you big overgrown dafty, she's my female roommate a nurse the same as me, now shut up and seduce me, or lose me forever."

Following Blakey's instructions Julia had dutifully prepared the room and sprinkled flowers lay across the thin cotton sheets, as a cool breeze entered the room from the open shutters.

To them everything was right in the world and this was only the beginning…...

Chapter 13. Eagle Day.

Salty was piped aboard HMS Eagle as Lt Charles Davies, or simply *Chas* to those who knew him, but of course Chas had no friends only the real Salty possessed friends.

"Welcome to HMS Eagle Lieutenant Davies, glad to have you aboard just what the doctor ordered, a new seaman branch officer. We've just lost two of our most experienced ratings to our support carrier Centaur, so your arrival here couldn't have come at a better time."

"Thank you, Captain Hargreaves, I'm very happy to be aboard Sir."

"I've bunked you in with Lieutenant Adam Bloom on deck five, he's a fine young officer and about your age, so you should have a lot in common, at forty-six thousand tons Eagle's an extremely large ship, so no doubt Lt. Bloom will show you around, you know show you the ropes and all that Davies."

Captain Clifford Hargreaves, Captain of HMS Eagle and her four Air Squadrons welcoming speech in the wardroom was music to Salty's ears, and just as Jack had advised earlier, he needed to fit in, to not stand out his life might just depend on it one day.

"Thank you, Sir, Eagle's certainly a lot bigger than I expected, so I'll certainly take Lieutenant Bloom up on that offer."

Salty liked his new Captain, at six feet two and at least sixteen stone in weight, Captain Hargreaves reminded him of Jack minus the beard of course, and with two thousand five hundred crew to search through he'd need all the help he could muster, and a lot more of the same.

Clambering down through the internal gangways and ladders, the words *"needle in a haystack"* crossed his mind a few times. Eagle was massive, the killer could be anyone and for all he knew he might have just passed him on the gangway. So, the only approach would have to be the logical one, and like Jack said;

"Piece all the information together my boy and just follow the facts." But Salty did wonder;

Why is he impaling his victims? What are the tattoos all about? They have to mean something. So, what the hell is it?

The next day during the morning Port watch, he was looking down from the outer gangway at the nights liberty crew noisily re-boarding the huge grey ship, many of them were returning much the worse for wear after their night out in Valencia's red-light district. And as the duty officer who greeted them referred;

"Some of em will be Brigged before their feet hit the bloody deck."

Watching the hundreds of tired faces staggering aboard, it was becoming blaringly obvious to him that he needed a list of the liberty boats and needed to cross reference them with the crew that were ashore on the night of the murders that would reduce the number of suspects. And his roommate Adam Bloom quite literally, held the key as he was head of personnel and crew welfare, so whatever it took, he needed to get hold of that key.

As he entered the twin cabin Adam was repairing the hem on his number two uniform trousers and seemed pleased to see him.

"Oh shit, Chas are you any good at this? I'm all thumbs, I've already pricked myself twice." Adam's mischievous tongue in cheek comment wasn't lost on Salty's sense of humour, so he laughed at his roommate's predicament and asked him to pass him the needle and thread.

"Give it here, come on let me do it, you'll bloody injure yourself in a minute. What's your day been like? Mine's been awful, I've carried out three kit inspections, organised a deck football tournament for the stoker's, and been duty officer of the Port watch since before six."

"Well if I'm entirely honest with you Chas, rather boring I'm afraid, same old nonsense filling out medical records, transfers, dental records and the like, so don't moan your day sounds much more fun."

Bloom, or Adam as he liked to be called, although a smashing fellow and in total contradiction to his six feet three stature muscular frame had a slight effeminate tone to his voice. And Salty wondered if his roommate might be gay.

"So, what time does personnel close Adam? I need to buy some stamps and writing paper."

"Oh, wrong department for that Chas I'm afraid, you should know that, you need the *NAAFI* up on deck seven port side aft, not personnel, they don't ever shut. We close at nineteen hundred even at weekends, thank the Lord, those dusty old files just aren't good for my poor little chest."

Adam feigned a cough to demonstrate his point and Salty smiled at his new friend, safe in the knowledge that tonight he'd remove the key from his locker and take a look for himself. He needed to work fast though, the previous night another monk had been slaughtered in a remote village monastery just outside of Valencia, so the clock was ticking.

Salty waited until Adam had completed his laboriously drawn out nightly routine of showering, shaving, and brushing his pearly white teeth, before pulling his bunk curtain across a little after eleven.

Adam was a prolific snorer the sounds were always patterned and rhythmic, a reasonable chance the victim, or in this case, his new friend Adam was sound asleep. Knowing he'd have to scrabble around in the dark Salty had previously counted the number of steps to Adam's jacket hanging on the chair by his bed. He'd also made a mental note of how many steps it was from there, to his locker.

The room was pitch black and hot, and the ship was deathly quiet as he tiptoed across the small cabin deck quietly opened the locker door then silently removed the key from its hook. Adam stirred in his cot for a moment, then just carried on snoring as he pulled the cabin door quietly closed behind him, then straightened his peaked cap and made his way aft, up to personnel and welfare.

Looking up and down the gangway checking to make sure there was nobody around, he inserted the large key and very quietly opened the door at the same time feeling for the switch on the inner bulkhead as the fluorescent tube immediately flickered to life. Inside the brightly lit office, metal shelves

160

screwed to bulkheads covered all four walls, dozens of grey lever arch files were stacked on metal racking and piles of untidy paperwork was strewn across the three central desks.

Looking to his right he noticed a wall mounted graph then after studying it for a few seconds he realised it was the filing coding legend, the coloured dots on the side of the files represented different departments. Red was for medical, blue training, and the all-important black one contained all of Eagle's liberty records. The file he was looking for was four shelves down on the left and within touching distance, so he quickly pulled it out and placed it down on the desk as he ran his finger down the index on the left-hand sleeve, before turning to the port liberty page.

Then he noticed that the night before when the most recent murder had taken place, all of Eagle's stokers, pilots, and admin staff had been granted liberty. Meaning that all aircrew, every single engineer, and over fifty from administration, were now prime suspects. Luckily for him, the clerk had typed the record out in triplicate using carbonated paper and the list contained over three hundred officers and men, even the Captains name appeared at the top. So, straight away over two thousand crew were reduced to just under three hundred, and one of those was potentially a serial killer.

It would be a few days before that same mixture of engineers, Fleet Air Arm pilot's, and admin were all granted liberty again. So, he'd be sure to accompany them in the clubs, bars and brothels of Valencia.

Before departing with the liberty boat on the Saturday, he was scheduled to make-contact with Blakey at 1800 hours. Sebastien was lying twelve miles off the coast just outside Spanish waters and Blakey was concerned because he hadn't heard anything from Salty in two weeks. But just as he'd been trained, he patiently waited, and listened.

Using 978.Megaherz in the ultra-high band, Salty tapped out his message using the NIS phonetic code on his portable radio transmitter in the forward laundry that seconded as his adopted office. The bare, unusable space although hot and humid, was otherwise perfect for the task.

So, he began his transmission:

.- .-.. .-.. / .. -. / ..... .- -. -.. / - .... / . -. -.. .-.-. / .... - --- .--. .-.-
.- / --- -. / -. . -..- - / .-.. .. -.... . .-. - -.-- / -... --- .- - / .. -. / ...- .- .-..
. -. -.-. .. .- / - --- -. .. --. ..... - .-.-. / .... - --- .--. --.... / .... ..- .... .--. .
-.-. - ... / -. .- .-. .-. --- .-- . -.. / - --- / .- .. .-. -.-. .-. . . .-- --.-- / . -. -
-. .. -. . . . .-. .. -. -. --. / .- -. -.. / .- -.. -- .. -. . .-.-. / .... - --- .--. --.... / -
.-. ....-. -.-. -.- / - ..... . / -.... .- -.-. -.- --. .-. --- ..- -. -.. / --- .-. / -.-.
.- .--. - .- .. -. -... .-. ... .-- -- --- -. -. . .-.. / .- -. -.. / .-. . . .-. --- .-. - / -....

The Message Read

All in hand this end. Stop.

On the next liberty boat to Valencia tonight. Stop.

Suspects now narrowed down to aircrew, engineering, and admin. Stop. Check the background of Captain Hargreaves and report back asap. Stop.

Next contact by radio same time tomorrow morning as arranged. Stop.

Over and out.

Message Terminated:17.20 HRS G.M.T.

As he descended the sloped gangway, he decided he'd follow the *wings* section first, their camaraderie and natural esprit de corps set them apart, and as Fleet Air Arm they always drank and partied as one.

But their first venue was not what he was expecting as he sat at a bar drinking coffee watching over fifty highly trained, intelligent, and very brave Buccaneer, Sea Vixen, and Wessex pilots racing donkeys up and down Valencia's beach, at the same time as downing copious amounts of Sangria. So, it didn't fill him with confidence that he was on the right track, so after leaving them to their antics he decided to take a look inside Valencia's notorious haunt. *Aunt Jemima's Nightclub* just off the Avenida Del Cid smack in the middle of the city's well-known light district, a regular haunt for ratings and officers alike.

At this stage, the term; *Needle in a haystack* crossed his mind again, as he began his search of the several bars in the club for a suspect, or any sort of clue, for anything, something that might point him in the right direction. But after a few hours and fed up with talking to drunken up matelots and saying; "No" to repetitive offers of; "You want some fun tonight sailor man?" He decided to change tack and get in a taxi and take a look at a nearby monastery for himself.

With fifteen of them within a twenty-mile radius of Valencia's town centre, even plan B would give him only a one in fifteen chance, but that was still better odds than plan A.

So, he chose the nearest monastery to the town centre. *The Monastery of San Miquel, in Del Reyes.*

"Señor por favor, donde puedo conseguir un taxi, necesito ir al monasterio de San Miguel de Los Reyes, por favour.

"Sir please where can I get a taxi, I need to go to the monastery of San Miguel de Los Reyes?"

"I speak a little English senor, so please talk slowly, you can find taxi from Valencia central market just down the bottom of this street, that is only place senor` all taxis are from there."

The street *Troubadour* deserved the tip Salty gave him and smiled at the smart Lieutenant, secretly wishing his daughter would meet such a man; Her boyfriend Miquel was a pig, and worse than that he was a terrible musician.

In the half light of the tree lined square four smiling taxi drivers all exited their cabs at the same time volunteering their services as he approached. "Senor, senor I take you, very cheap senor," but he ignored them and went to the first one in line asking him politely in English.

"Senor have you taken any fares to any of the monasteries surrounding Valencia this evening please?"

The driver although disappointed he wasn't one of his usual fares, a drunken Englishman, or an American sailor he could drive two miles and charge for ten, answered him honestly.

"Not tonight senor, very quiet for me, you want to go monastery I take you now, very quick, very cheap, yes?"

As politely as he was able, he declined the offer, then moved on to the next in line watching as two drunken American officers from the recently moored up *Essex* class carrier, the *USS Wasp,* noisily climbed into the back of the fourth taxi in the line, and he could feel his chances slipping away again.

Repeating his previous question to the next driver in line, he was pleasantly surprised to hear *Juan Jorge Carlos* confirm that less than an hour earlier he had indeed taken a sailor to that particular monastery. To the Monasterio de San Miguel de Los Reyes.

"Right, take me there, straight away driver! Pronto! Pronto! Por favor."

Juan although taken back the by the young officers desperate urgency, was more surprised by the way his whole persona had so quickly changed from that of a polite English gentleman sailor, to a rowdy bawling madman, even so he thought; *A fare's a fare,* so he threw his half-finished cigarette down onto the pavement and promptly started his rear-engined Renault Eight, and sped across the square, as his friend *Ramos* watched and wondered, if his friend Juan had gone completely mad.

The unlit road up the winding hill was covered in potholes and at each winding bend Juan used his handbrake to speed the turn, and the little Renault responded well as its small tyres gripped the gravel surface. Although utterly terrified, Juan had an inner feeling the trip was a matter of life and death as he prayed openly to the icon of the Madonna stuck on the front of his dashboard.

"Madonna, Madonna, por favor salve an este humilde chofer, incluso salve an este `loco` sentado aquí, y llegaremos a nuestro destino en una sola pieza."

"Madonna, Madonna, please save this humble driver even save this madman sitting here please, so we can reach our destination in one piece."

As the bright lights of the huge monastery started to light up the small track ahead, Salty removed his faithful Webley and Juan started to beg for his life, so Salty thought it was about time to explain to the terrified cabbie, that he was actually the good guy, and was on the track of a very bad guy. So, speaking as slowly as he could, he started to explain the predicament that Juan had unwittingly found himself in.

"Juan, listen amigo you must not fear me, I am tracking a murderer, possibly even now he is trying to kill one of the good father's, so please help me to stop this happening Juan. Si, comprende?"

"Comprende Si, comprende" were the only three words Juan could muster, but he believed the sailor and would help him. Nobody should harm the good fathers. Nobody.

The car skidded to a halt on the gravel drive just outside the monastery, and Salty quickly ran towards the light in the barn at the side shouting at Juan to go into the monastery and warn the fathers.

"Tell them Juan, tell them he's here."

Approaching in the darkness he pulled back the cocking hammer back on his Webley IV and pointed it towards the half open barn door then looked up at the single paraffin lamp that was hanging by a hook swaying from side to side in the night's breeze. Then as he glanced towards the large haystack at the back, he sensed a movement, and *Father Emanuel Rodriguez* leant the pitchfork against the manger and immediately noticed the gun Salty was holding.

"Can I help you young man? I can assure you there's no need for weapons, you're quite safe here my friend."

"Forgive me father but your life is in danger, a killer is on the loose, me and my driver tracked him here tonight."

"Yes, I have heard about these dreadful killings my son, but I can assure you nobody has visited us here toni…"

The good father's words were abruptly interrupted, as two feet from where he was standing, a tall, dark shape emerged scattering a pile of hay at the back then got up and darted straight out through the partially open door. Salty instinctively pointed his Webley towards the intruder's back and was just about to pull the trigger when Juan appearing from nowhere, blocked his field of fire, as he ran towards him.

"Get down Juan, drop to the ground!" Salty shouted as Juan dropped to the dust, and he fired two shots at the tall dark stranger, missing him by only an inch or two. But the stranger continued to sprint off down the gravel road and Salty made chase, then suddenly and without warning his shape suddenly disappeared as he jumped through the long rye grass and took a sharp right turn down a side path, before once more changing direction and increasing the distance between himself and his pursuer.

He was fast but Salty was faster, and was almost within touching distance with both arms outstretched, trying to grip hold of the back of his hooded jacket, when he stumbled and fell over an upturned rock, the forward momentum causing his body to literally somersault in mid-air, before he came to a sudden halt at the base of an old fig tree.

As he lay there winded and gasping for air, all he could hear were the stranger's footfall's dissipating in the darkness of the campo and the explosive clattering sounds of fireworks illuminating the black skyline in the distance. Trying very hard to ignore the pain from his bruised right thigh and cursing to himself that he'd allowed him to get away he limped back up towards the barn nursing a bruised thigh and a headache. As he entered the gates and holstered his weapon at least forty monks were gathered forming a ring of protection around their beloved Father Emanuel and Juan was kissing his hand as he blessed the *Archangel Saint Michael* for his deliverance. Although clearly shaken, the father was otherwise unharmed, but much more importantly than that. He was still alive.

"I thank you for my life tonight young man, but I'm afraid I cannot condone the use of firearms in this Holy place, but I thank you anyway."

To Salty's ears the father's words sounded more like a reprimand from one of his head teachers at his old Grammar school. So, after two hours spent asking the good fathers for a description and searching the grounds for any clues, he scratched his head, and decided it was time to head home, and climb back aboard Eagle.

Salty spent the whole journey staring out the window, as Juan continually thanked him for saving the father's life.

"Gracias senor, gracias, you are a hero, I love you, and God loves you, bless your heart senor."

Salty finally walked up the gangway a little after five in the morning as the sun was making its first appearance in the eastern sky. He was sober, tired, and fed up, and his thigh hurt like hell. As he entered the cabin his only reward for his night's toil were the sounds of Adam's incessant snoring and he wondered to himself if he should put in a request for a new roommate. Despite how close he'd come to apprehending the killer, Juan nor any of the monks had managed to take a good look at his face. So, in simple terms not one of them had a clue as to what the killer looked like.

"Tall, dark with a raspy cough" was the only description offered; So, clearly, he was back to square one. But Salty knew one thing for sure, the killer was a serviceman alright, there was no mistaking the distinctive sounds of those hob nail boots on the gravel surface, as he escaped down the road.

Tired beyond words, he pulled his privacy curtain across and opened his most recent letter from Louise, the envelope was readdressed to Lt Charles Davies, via the NIS sensor's.

My Dearest Salty,

I miss you so very much, our night together in Javea was wonderful, I re-live every moment of it daily and I can't wait until we're together again. In short Mr Samuel Salt (I know you hate Samuel!) This silly girl loves you, yes loves you, and I have since the first time we met at Seaway. I hope you feel the same way and I'm not making a fool of myself here, so if you do feel the same be sure to tell me in your next letter. I need to read it, but more than that I need to hear it.

We've been really busy here with all the casualties coming in from the insurgent attacks on our troops in Aden. Over thirty were medevac'd in yesterday alone, three were much worse than the others and died in the night, all three were husbands and fathers. Our Matron in Chief was up until midnight writing letters to their families. It's a really sad time here at Bighi, more casualties are arriving all the time, everyone's trying to do their bit, including our new Royal Naval Liaison officer, Lieutenant Black. Apparently, he said you'd met briefly some time ago, he seems quite a nice sort, a little bit guarded

172

somehow, but he's playing polo for the Navy against the Army on Saturday afternoon at the Fleet club, and has invited Jack and I along, don't worry though, I'm acting more as a chaperone for Jack, as I feel she may be developing a crush on him.

Anyway, must sign off now, there's been a terrorist bombing in Valetta, so we're expecting more casualties in tonight. I love you my dearest Salty, please write back as soon as you can.

Louise.

Petty Officer Wren: The Queen Alexandra's Royal Naval Nursing Service Royal Naval Hospital Bighi. Kalkara: Malta Garrison.

Just as he'd been trained and following strict NIS protocol, he burnt the letter the next morning and wondered to himself why his opposite number in the Mediterranean Theatre of Operations, the (MTO). Namely Lt. George Black was in Malta, not sure if it was plain old jealousy, or just old-fashioned inquisitiveness, he wanted to know. And he intended to find out soon, when he contacted Blakey later.

Chapter 14. Confessions.

St Mathias Nursing home, for Retired Naval Officers
Isle of Wight: (Present Day)

The dementia was becoming progressively worse, Salty the man Louise knew and loved came and went when the illness allowed. But Salty, being Salty he battled on. To him, finishing *Salt's War* was his first priority, and only after every sentence and every single comma had been checked then re-checked, would he start *Blood and Country,* it's sequel, or; *Volume two.* As he preferred to call it.

If anything, the writing helped him as memories of time's long passed were quickly scribbled down by Louise as and when he was able to recall them.

"Well I'm off to breakfast my little Angel, then I'll get on with some writing when I get back, I don't suppose you'd like to join me. Can I tempt you my dear?"

"No, you go and tip your trilby to our friends on your own this morning Salty, I'll be here waiting, might make myself a nice cup of tea and enjoy the sea view, it's beautiful out there this morning if you'd take a minute to look. Oh, and just the one rasher of bacon this morning Salty, remember what the doctor told you."

Leaving the sanctuary of their two comfortable rooms always made Salty feel a little uneasy, he'd walked the long corridor to the dining room hundreds of times over the past two years, but on the last occasion when he was quite alone, he'd become confused, and Louise had been summoned to escort him back. He'd simply forgotten where he was, but more importantly than that, he'd forgotten who he was, the illness had become a cancer, his lonely sanctum, a dark place that he couldn't share with a living soul.

Louise often wondered if the dementia had been caused by all the knocks on the head he'd had when he was in the NIS, she often wondered that, but who could tell? Maybe it was just Salty's time?

"Morning Sid, how's the leg old boy?" Tip of the trilby.

"Bloody playing up Salty, wheel me up to the dining room, will you? Since Jean passed away, I can't seem to grip the tyres like I used to, it makes me arm's ache."

Despite the dementia, Salty would always oblige, he enjoyed Sid's company, Sid was fifteen years older than Salty and in his eighty eighth year and was barely nineteen when he'd volunteered for the Royal Navy. The dangerous *Murmansk convoys* from Birkenhead up through the Baltic had been Sid's first posting, his leg problem was because four of his toes had been amputated, following a severe case of frostbite.

His ship the corvette *Monmouth* had been torpedoed by the legendary U boat *Kapitan Karl Schmidt* who'd allowed the crew of Sid's ship to safely evacuate her and board the lifeboat's, before carefully placing his killer shot.

Ten day's adrift in the freezing pack ice of the tempestuous Baltic Sea had put paid to Sid's leg. So, Salty felt a connection with him, he'd lost two fingers on his left hand himself, several years before, and no matter who asked him.

"How did that happen then Salty?" He'd simply reply. "Training accident." Before quickly changing the subject.
Salty liked Sid.

As the two pals entered the dining room, Louise was busily tidying up the two rooms they both called home, but as she looked out across the sea and sat down in her chair, her mind started to drift back to that awful day so many years before.
Her tiny hands began to shake as she held the letter, she'd received from Captain Jack `Black` McPherson.

The paper was tattered and torn where she had folded it, then re-folded it so many times, before hiding it when the Navy posted them somewhere. The wording was barely legible, but it didn't matter, she'd memorised its contents a long time ago.

She remembered the day it had dropped through the letter box like it was yesterday, it was a minute to one on the 5Th September 1990. the same day she was sat all by herself, crying and wondering what to do.

My Dearest Louise,

I understand from certain contacts I still have within Naval intelligence that Salty is away, I'm sorry to say I really don't know where he is, and I wouldn't be allowed to tell you if I did. You must forgive my impromptu contact, but time is what you might term. 'Of the essence.'

You see Louise I am dying; my doctor has given me a few weeks to live, please don't cry for me I have had the most wonderfully full life, and with just the one exception. I have no regrets.

That exception is for not having come forward before. I have put this day off far too long, so I'm sorry to impose my guilt on you especially at such a late stage, but you have always been such a rock to Salty, and only you, and you alone, can decide what you must do with what I am about to tell you.

You see the story begins in the late spring of 1944, just after I was posted aboard HMS Gould, the same ship I was torpedoed on, in the October of that year.

It was while I was attending a welcoming party being held for her new crew in Portsmouth that I first met Lieutenant Brian Salt. And that was also where I first met his wife, June. That night Brian had rather a few too many to drink and asked if I wouldn't mind giving him and June a lift back to their flat in Gosport.

So, of course, I humbly obliged. After all, Brian was an officer at the time, and I was a mere P.O. Anyway, that aside I'm ashamed to admit that it was also about the same time that June and I embarked on our affair, an affair that was to last that whole hot summer of 1944 when I betrayed my friend.

The affair ended just before we left for active service in the August, and both June and I agreed to never breathe a word to a living soul of our deceitful act, and although I was aboard HMS Gould with Brian at the time. He never knew.

It's no excuse Louise, but the war was on, and things happen in wartime that should never happen, everything just seemed so rushed somehow. It wasn't until years later when I was going through Salty's medical records at HMS Invergordon that I noticed his rare blood group, you see it's the very rarest of them all, it's 'Rh-null' and even now there are only a dozen or so donors in the UK and I should know, because I'm one of them.

So, you see Louise there's no doubt in my mind that he is my son and this stupid, dying old man, has left it far too late to confess.

My humble request is for you to love him and try to forgive his grumpy behaviour, his impulsiveness, and his failings, you see he can't help it: After all he is my son.

I will be gone within a few weeks, but my estate has been divided equally between my other two children and yourself, that way Salty will never know of its origin, what you decide to do with the money after that is completely up to you, but my suggestion would be to take him away, apply for an extended leave and just enjoy your time together, somewhere nice.

I must leave you now with these final words;
Take time out, be eternally faithful to each other, and please always love my son."

Yours Truly

Captain Jack McPherson RN (Retired)

Frenchay Hospital, Bristol.

Louise had decided twenty-seven years before to never tell him, and today was the last time she would ever read the letter. At the time Jack had only weeks to live, and Salty was away on a sortie so what could she have done? And what good could be achieved by telling him now? She'd asked herself that very same question nearly every day for the past twenty-seven years.

The letter burned in the ashtray, but the guilt still remained and hung like a great lead weight around her neck as she carried on polishing the sideboard allowing her tears to flow down her cheeks looking forward to Salty's return.

By this time, and although it wasn't his intention Salty had brought poor old Sid to tears, the poem he'd penned as he quickly ate his four rashers of back bacon had reduced his friend to a mumbling mess.

"What is a man without his partner?
When time is wasted so far apart.
What love transcends Oceans or time?
Only true love from the heart.
For ours is a shared love, a deep love, and given that time again.
oceans would seem only puddles, time only seconds, and we'd
never be apart."

"Well Sid old boy that's going in my next book, 'Blood and Country,' so stop getting all emotional, or I won't wheel you back."

.........Sid wiped his eyes with his hanky.

He loved Salty's company

Chapter 15. Good old Captain Hargreaves.

The humidity in the ex-laundry room was playing havoc with the sensitive radio equipment, and the awful high-pitched screeching sounds when the band width dial was adjusted put Salty's nerves on edge. Discovery of his true identity at that stage would be a total disaster, he was getting closer to the killer, he could feel it, and one more liberty boat and he might just get him. So, he started tapping:

.-.. .- ... - -. .. --. ..... - ... .-.. .. -... . .-. - .-- -... --- .- - --. -- .--
.- .... .- -.-. .-. --- .... . -....- .-. .. - -. - .... -. --. ... --- -.-. .-. .. -
-- .... . - --- .- .-. .-. .-. .. .. -. .... .. --- -. --- .... - --- .-- . ---...
....- ... .--. . -.-. - ... .. -... . .. .-. .. -. .. - . .-.. -.-- .- ... . .--. ..
-.-. . -- .- -. ---... ... - --- .-. --- ... -... .. .... -.-. .-. .. .-. . .. --- -. -
.- .-.. .-. -.-- -.. .- .-. .- -.-- .-- .. - .... .- .-. .- ... .-. -.-- -.-. ---
.. .- --. ..... .-. .- ... - --- .-. --- ...-- .. .- .-. .-. -.-. ....-. .-. - -- . -
.... .. -.-. .- .-. .. .-. . -.- --- .-. -... ... - --- -. .. -- ..... - ..- --- .- . .-
-. -.-- .-. .-. .-. .-. . -. .- ...- .. .. - .... - --- ... .. .-. .-. -.-. -... .- .- -
... -... --- ... . -. -- . ... -... -- -- .- . -- --- .... .-.- ... - --- .-. ---...
.-. .. .-. --- .-. .- - .. -. .. --- -. .-- .- .. --- -. . --- -. -.-. .- .-. .-. - .- ..
-. -... .-. .- .. -- -- --- -. .-.. --- ... .-. .. - ..- .-. .-. . ---... ... - --- .-. -- .
....- --- . - .-. .-. -- .. -. .- - . .-.. --- --- ...- .-.- .---- --...- ..... .-.
... .-.-.- -- .-.-.- -- .-.-.- - .-.-.-

The Message Read.

Last night's liberty boat was a close-run thing, very close to apprehension: Stop.

Suspect is definitely a serviceman: Stop.

Only description is tall, dark, and has a raspy cough. Stop.

Will try and check ships medical records tonight for any recent visits to sickbay by any servicemen experiencing coughing symptoms. Stop.

Report back with any information on Captain Hargreaves` background: Stop:

Final request: What is Lt. George Black doing in Malta: Stop.

Any information on his intentions, will be received in the strictest confidence. Stop.

Message Terminated 08.17 HRS. G.M.T.

The message sent, all he could do was sit and wait.

Blakey would come back in minutes, and although the murders were foremost in his mind, he couldn't help but wonder what the hell Black was doing in Malta?

A few minutes passed, and the Marconi 600 UHF receiver squealed to life and Salty started to write down all the coded dots and dashes, the message was definitely from Blakey. He recognised his style, slow and ponderous, but always deadly accurate.

The short message read:

NIS transmissions are compromised: Stop.

Suggest meet at pre-arranged place and time.

Code word: *Playtime.* Instigated. Stop.

All transmissions are to cease immediately. Stop.

Message Terminated at 08.23 G.M.T.

"Playtime" translated as "Abort-Abort" or in simpler terms, danger, so he quickly packed the green transmitter back into its cradle, and instinctively felt for his gun, knowing the pre-arranged meeting with Blakey would take place at the entrance to Valencia's main Railway station. The *Est del Nord`* at 20.00. hrs, that night.

Salty felt an emotion he hadn't really experienced up until that point; It was fear, and felt a cold shudder pass through his body, as he realised that the killer might at that very moment be adding his own name to the list. And maybe his time was running out.

Blakey approached the huge iron gates at the front of Valencia's Grand Central Station peering through the nights summer rain as he checked his watch, it was 19.55 hrs, and he knew his friend was there somewhere. He just wasn't ready to reveal himself yet.

Then just as the hands on the large station clock struck eight, a street vendor walked past, and the scruffy walnut seller, whispered "Playtime."

Quickly following him down a side alley, Blakey was fooled but not surprised by his friend's disguise, they were always on another level, but he did wonder where he'd acquired the white beard.

"Right, you watch the alley Blakey, while I get this gear off, this beards driving me mad, it's so bloody itchy it's part of the Father Christmas outfit on Eagle. How they wear the bloody thing is beyond me."

Blakey was laughing as he watched his friend removing the beard, and pull the raggy trousers to the pavement, then bundle them all together and throw the whole lot in the metal bin in the alley. Then Blakey stopped laughing as he turned serious and was the first to speak;

"The whole sortie's been compromised, don't ask me how or, by who, but somebody aboard Eagle has been listening in to our messages, they've broken the NIS code, whoever it is must be in signal's or have access to the radio room, but that's not the worst part. Listen to this."

"Captain Hargreaves's records said he was an orphan just like us. Apparently, he was brought up by Franciscan monks on Malta and that's why Black's there now, he's visited the monastery and spoken to the head Abba's, whose own words were, and I quote;" Blakey pulled out his pad.

"Young Hargreaves was a troubled lad and had to be regularly punished."

"Punished, what do you mean punished? What the hell did they do to him?" Salty quickly asked.

"Funny that," Blakey replied, "because when Black asked the same question, the Abba's became all defensive, and Black had to threaten him with exposure before he eventually admitted that good old Captain Hargreaves, was regularly beaten and most nights locked away in isolation, in his hermitage. Apparently, he'd scream and shout at anyone who came near him, he hated it there, he hated those monks. He fits the bill Salty."

"What a story. We thought we had it bad at Seaway, poor sod. Look tomorrow night it's liberty again, so we need to follow Hargreaves and find out what he's up to, so make yourself scarce while I climb back aboard Eagle. I'll meet you at the dockyard gates tomorrow night, dead on five. Okay."

"Yeah and be careful, I'll see you then."

Blakey left his friend in the alley and made his way across the deserted street towards his night's lodgings at the *Hotel Da Vinci*.

The next afternoon, liberty was piped aboard Eagle at exactly 16.30 hrs, and the gangways and exits all over the huge carrier were all jammed solid with officers, ratings, and civilian workers alike, as Salty walked through the dockyard gates and both friends dressed in civilian attire were lost in the mass exodus.

"Now look Blakey, Captain Hargreaves has already handed over command to Commander Bolton for the night, so he's off somewhere, so we'll follow him and see where he's headed, c'mon, we need to get over to the taxi rank and wait."

Half an hour quickly passed and as if on cue, dressed in his civilian clothes, the Captain appeared and quickly got into the back of the first taxi in line. From a discreet distance they watched as he got in the back and it pulled away, then they ran over to the next one shouting at driver to; "Follow that taxi will you mate, hang back a bit, but don't get too close he mustn't see us."

Juan couldn't believe his bad luck, the mad sailor had returned as he looked at Salty then across at Blakey with a terrified stare fully aware that for at least the next couple of hours, his life would once again be in mortal danger.

"Okay, but no fast driving this time senor, my nerves cannot take it, not at my age."

Juan dimmed the lights of the old Renault, as it snaked its way up the winding road, and as instructed kept a respectful distance behind his old friend Carlos as both agents checked their weapons, and Juan, once again prayed to his Madonna.

As the brightly lit monastery structure appeared, they drove under the Gothic arch and could see Carlos, Juan's friend standing by his car smoking a cigarette, totally indifferent to the unfolding drama.

"Juan, you old bull, are you following me?"

"No, my friend, but these gentlemen are." Juan replied.

In the time it had taken Juan to complete his sentence Blakey had drawn his revolver and was covering Salty's back, as they both ran towards the wide-open doors. Salty started to count as both took up position either side of the old stone archway.

"Right, on my mark, three, two, one!"

Then both launched themselves through the opening into the vaulted chapel and were astonished to see Captain Hargreaves with his hands on his hips standing by the altar, calmly talking with the Abba's.

They came to a halt a few yards from the altar their weapons pointing directly at the Captain, as he raised his hands instinctively, and the Abba's crossed himself.

Blakey was the first to speak this time.

"Okay, don't make any sudden movements Captain, we're from Naval intelligence so, place your hands on your head and walk very slowly towards me, you father, you walk the other way. Walk away from him. Now!"

The Captain was too terrified to argue and did exactly what he was told and placed his hands on his head, and started to walk towards the two agents, as the Abba's began to openly pray. "Oh, most heavenly father, please forgive these men, for they know not what they do."

Salty was not at all interested in what the father had to say and told the Captain to; "Stop, stop just there and keep your hands on your head, I'm going to walk a few paces towards you, if you try anything I will shoot you dead. Blakey search him, while I cover you."

As he'd been trained, Blakey started at the Captain's ankles and worked his way upwards patting him down, as he went.

"If you've any hidden firearms, or any type of weapons on you at all Sir, its best that you hand them over to me now."

"Now look here Blake, and you Davies you really have overstepped the mark here tonight, have you two been drinking or something? What on earth is this all about? I'm here to catch up with my old friend Father Francisco here, we go back donkeys' years. I think you may have just ended both your Naval career's. Father Francisco is a personal friend of mine, he's the most Senior Father in all the monasteries in the eastern and western Mediterranean. Now I'm ordering you both to stand down!!"

Salty started to slowly lower his weapon, as Blakey pulled his safety catch back and the Captains deep thundery words of warning had the desired effect as Salty suspiciously eyed his commanding officer up and down still not sure if he was telling the truth?

"Sir, as you can see, I have lowered my weapon, but I warn you, any sudden movement and I won't hesitate to shoot you, so go on explain to us what you're doing here tonight, we're all ears."

"May I lower my arms Davies? I am completely defenceless."

"You may Sir, but don't make any sudden movements. Okay." The Captain lowered his arms and nervously began his explanation. "Okay right, I came here tonight to talk with Father

Francisco in private, now I can see that in the circumstances that private conversation will now have to be shared.

You see Davies …...."

"It's Salt Sir, Lieutenant Salt NIS, and this is sub-Lieutenant Blake, he's also with the NIS."

"Good God man, NIS aboard Eagle well you can try and explain that to me in a minute. Anyway, you see Salt many years ago, I was orphaned after my parents were tragically killed in a plane crash in Malta, my father was stationed there in the war. Anyway, Father Francisco here was very good to me at the time."

"You see I was what you might describe as a 'little rotter' a stubborn wild child, and if it hadn't been for the kindness shown to me by the good father, I do wonder what might have become of me."

The father nodded his head at the two agents confirming the Captains story, adding; "Captain Hargreaves has been visiting me here for many years now, he is a very kind man his generous donations have contributed greatly to the children in our care, without his money we would have had to sell many of our precious items, please believe me, he's a decent kind man, can I also take my hands down?"

"Yes, yes of course father," Salty answered, "excuse my language father but shit! I think Captain Hargreaves is right, we may have just ended our Naval careers."

Salty followed by Blakey holstered their side arms both wishing the ground would open up and swallow them whole, as the father's explanation of events began to sink in. And both realised they had made a terrible mistake. But worse than that, they were once again back to square one.

It was at that stage that Captain Hargreaves said something that only a very kind man would say and showed them some empathy.

"Okay now look Salt, you too Blake I think we need to have a little talk about this privately, I think I understand why you might have thought me a *bad-un* shall we say, you NIS boys have access to all the crew records and mine probably doesn't make very good reading, so let's just see if we can sort this out quietly between us all, shall we?"

Neither of them could believe what they were hearing, the Captain was throwing them a lifeline, offering them a chance, so they grabbed hold of it with both hands and two very embarrassed, very uncomfortable and over-zealous young agents made their exit smiling at the Abba's as once more they apologised for their behaviour.

"Lo Siento Abad, lo siento" and the wise old Abba's smiled back and said. "No hay problema."

Back aboard Eagle both reported to the Captains wardroom wearing their smartest freshly ironed number one uniforms, still unsure if demotion to the ranks, or even the dreaded *Brig* awaited them. Captain Hargreaves was sat at his desk, writing out a report on the state of the Wessex helicopter that had crash landed in the sea yesterday, as he heard the knock on his door.

"Enter."

"Oh, it's you two is it come in, come in, sit down gentlemen, we need to talk, you were damn lucky tonight. Lucky that it was me you tried to arrest I dread to think what might have happened if you'd done this to one of my politically correct understudies. Anyway, that aside for the moment I do have the greatest respect for you boys at the NIS, you do a damn fine job but the next time you feel like boarding one of Her Majestys Flagships, do try and let me in on it."

"I mean I quite understand the need for secrecy, but surely some questions needed to be asked first? You see Father Francisco turned my life around. After my parents were killed in the crash I started to steal, drink, rob, fight, you name it. And it was him that put a stop to the beatings and took me under his wing and gave me an education. And I've never forgotten his kindness to me, those were very dark days indeed. Anyway, your turn now, please tell me everything, come on spill the beans Lt. Davies, Salt, or whatever your real name is, explain to me what the hell is going on aboard my ship?"

"You have a serial killer aboard Eagle Sir." Was Salty's terse reply.

"Good, God man, are you sure, I mean…."

"Quite sure Sir, in fact we're a hundred per-cent sure aren't we Blakey?"

"Yes, a hundred per-cent Sir."

"Well come on then give me a name, who the devil is it?"

"I can't not at this stage, the investigation is what you might call on-going, and even if I knew NIS would hang me from the nearest yard arm if I told you, you're just going to have to trust us on this one, we'll get him Sir."

"That's a tall order Salt, as Captain of this ship I need to be informed of all going's on, and my first priority will always be the safety of my crew. Are they at risk Salt? Is this killer likely to kill one of his own?"

"That's extremely unlikely Sir, you see there's a pattern forming, the victims are always either Franciscan, or Benedictine Monks."

"I've heard about these murders the good father and I were only discussing it tonight, when you two buggers decided to barge in. Only yesterday I received a dispatch from Portsmouth telling me about it, what a dreadful business Salt, dreadful business. Now look here I've no wish to end either of your careers, I am not a vindictive man so that's the good news, so the matter stays in this room, and from what you've just told me complete secrecy is the order of the day. And together Davies, sorry I mean Salt and you too Blake, we are going to smoke the bugger out."

Both young officers sat upright in their chairs and let out a joint sigh of relief listening intently as the Captain continued.

"My suggestion to you both is this, you simply carry on pretending to be Lt. Charles Davies for the moment, and as for you Blake you come aboard in the morning as our new radio officer, what do you say? We'll smoke him out together."

Captain Hargreaves felt a tinge of excitement ripple through his body in the task that lay ahead, He was a good man, but had a natural tendency to lead from the front. So, trying to ignore the Captains boyish enthusiasm Salty quickly decided that Blakey coming aboard and joining the investigation would be an asset, especially now that the whole thing needed to be started afresh.

So, without further debate the decision was made, and the next morning as six bells were piped, sub-Lieutenant Blake, newly appointed signals officer was welcomed aboard HMS Eagle.

Captain Hargreaves however, had conveniently forgotten to mention to them that as flagship of the Mediterranean Fleet, Eagle was pulling her moorings, and leaving with all haste for Malta the next morning in order to load stores and ammunition in preparation for their transit down the Suez-canal, to help in the fight with the insurrection in Aden.

So, without knowing anything about it, Blakey and Salty were off to fight a war. The Captains thoughts on that decision, were that if the NIS couldn't be bothered to inform him of their arrival, then why should he inform them of his departure.

It was small payback he thought, after all, they had nearly shot him....

Chapter 16. Off to War.

The trip down the Eastern Mediterranean was fairly uneventful, as escort frigates destroyers, and their support submarines zig zagged, cutting a twenty-knot dash to avoid the ever-present threat of Russian submarines, and searches by their long range *Tupolev TU 95,* maritime aircraft.

Blakey was busily intercepting coded messages aided by Adam in his secondary signal's role, while Salty was carrying out his seaman officer duties and organising live firing exercises off the back of the big carrier, for the three hundred Royal Marines aboard.

Four days later, the bleached white buildings of Valetta glistened in the morning sunshine, as the great Armada entered the harbour-gates line astern, and Eagle as flagship sounded her arrival with three loud blasts of her horn. The docks were thronging with Naval personnel, all lined up on the jetty as Eagle's four Buccaneer squadrons roared overhead in preparation for their landing at Luqa airfield.

The sight was something to behold as Blakey, Salty, and Adam looked on as the great ship tied up her giant mooring ropes and the Royal Marine band wearing their white colonial hats and smart blue suits, announced their arrival by playing. "Rule Britannia."

The only thoughts occupying Salty's mind at that moment were those of Louise, not the fanfare, the flypast or the serial killer, not even the fear of entering a war zone. It was simply Louise.

So, just a little under three hours after they'd docked, dressed in his best number one gold braided uniform, Salty entered the Royal Naval Hospital in Bighi with twelve red roses, a smile on his face. And Blakey as his wing man.

"Nurse, nurse, can you tell me where I might find Petty Officer Louise Taylor please? I'm not quite sure which ward she is on?"

"Well, that's an easy one Salty, you see I'm Jack or Jackie, you know the girl you thought was a man." Jackie held her finger to her mouth implying a shush, but her eye's betrayed the moment as she smiled and her lips curled upwards, and Salty felt the blood drain from his face, and Blakey broke into an uncontrolled belly laugh, trying to loosely disguise it, as a coughing fit.

So, Salty tried again; "Well you see, I'm terribly sorry about that misunderstanding Jackie, but we haven't known each other very long, I mean, well…."

"Oh, don't fret Salty love, me and you are going to be great friends I can tell, I've heard so much about you, in fact you're

197

all she ever talks about. My God if I have to read one more of your letters, I think I'll just pack up my things and "hop on the next tug as well."

Her last comment confirmed she'd read his letters, but Salty didn't mind, as by that time she'd linked arms with them both and they were heading along the corridor towards Winchester Ward. Bighi's intensive care unit.

Blakey was beginning to feel slightly uncomfortable as they walked down the stark white corridor passed all the smiling doctors, nurses, and porters, and couldn't help but wonder what Fiona would make of their newly found, flirtatious friend. The vivacious Jackie.

As they were about to enter the ward, Jackie disentangled herself from them both and asked if they'd rather wait outside.

"What you'll see in here is not for the faint-hearted boys, so if you're a bit queasy about blood then maybe you should both wait outside, and I'll bring her out."

Salty by that time was desperate to see her, and as usual replied for them both, without checking with Blakey first.

"No, we're fine it's quite all right, we've seen worse than that haven't we Blakey?"

"Oh, much worse, we're fine," Blakey confirmed; lying through his teeth.

Jackie didn't believe either of them, but she held the swing door open just long enough and just wide enough for them to either enter or change their minds.

But they didn't and the two ex-Seaway orphans, two NIS men to their core gasped as they encountered wounded men packed like sardines lying in white metal beds covering all four sides of the ward. The most critically injured were offered some privacy with a curtain drawn across, so they could pass away in peace.

They watched as nurse's cut blood-soaked bandages from head wounds or amputated limbs coiling them into kidney shaped silver trays, as the smell of iodine and disinfectant mixed with vomit filled the air.

"Shit, this really is hell on earth, I've never seen anything like this Blakey I never thought it would be this bad, you?"

Blakey couldn't answer the sight was too emotionally overwhelming for him, they'd both watched the television reports and read the newspapers, but to witness this type of suffering first-hand, was another thing altogether.

Jackie's radiant smile was now absent from her soft features, her eyes were misted, and she shared the same feeling of hopelessness, she'd experienced that feeling every day since first arriving in Bighi. So, she chose to whisper, rather than lecture.

"You never become immune to this type of suffering lads, somehow you just learn to get on with it all you can do is help in some way. Since Aden kicked off it's been like this nearly every day, some of them simply die on trolley's in the corridors before we can even get them into a bed."

Looking down the hot busy ward, Salty recognised the unmistakeable shape of Louise as she moved from bed to bed, straightening bed covers, emptying bedpans, and doing what she did best, caring for others. Amongst all that suffering the red rose's he held firmly in his hand seemed almost insignificant and inappropriate somehow. But after travelling this far he decided it was now or never, so he walked down the centre of the ward, tapped her on the shoulder from behind, and quietly whispered;

"Been a while Lou, so I hopped aboard a tug and came to pay you a visit."

Louise felt a sudden shiver run down the entire length of her spine and dropped the empty bed pan onto the marble floor, then turned around and flung herself into his arms, and the few men led out in beds that were able to raise a cheer, did so. As for just a moment their physical pain was temporarily cast aside.

Their short stay at the George Cross Hotel in Valetta was wonderful. He'd managed to wangle three days shore leave before their imminent departure to Aden, Blakey had remained aboard HMS Eagle rather than act as a gooseberry and for three mornings they'd enjoyed breakfast in bed, and so much more.

The small, hot bedroom was their temporary sanctuary, they'd only left its whitewashed walls once, in three days, and that was only so Salty could whip downstairs in his slippers to buy a newspaper. On their last morning together, the phone rang by the side of the bed, and he was called down to reception.

"Sorry to disturb you Sir, but I have a call for you, you need to come down to reception I cannot transfer it to your room, it is from someone called sub-Lieutenant Blake, he wants to speak with you urgently."

"That's okay, I'll be down in a few minutes."

Salty hung up the receiver, rose from the bed and apologised to the half-naked Louise by saying; "I won't be a minute so hold that pose, and don't move an inch, I'll be right back."

Louise didn't move apart from pushing the single white sheet further down the bed.

"Hello, it's Blakey somethings come up, now I know this might sound like I'm overreacting here, and it may be nothing at all. But I've been working with Adam in signals these past few days, well he's started to act a bit coy about his past, you know evading simple questions, like where were you born? How many brothers or sisters do you have? That sort of thing."

"So, I thought I'd take a peek at his records, well I'm up in personnel right now and it says here that he's Jewish and was born in Slovakia, now I know the Jewish thing probably applies to about ten per-cent of Eagle's crew, but here's the weird thing Salty."

"It also says he reported to sick bay a few days ago with a cough, now before you say anything look at the facts, he's tall, dark, experienced in signals and he's been aboard every liberty boat that went ashore when the murders were taking place, now am I going mad, or doesn't that make him a prime suspect?"

Salty held the phone tightly to his ear deep in thought as he looked across the reception at the hotel manager who was busily polishing the marble desk.

How could I have missed him, right there in plain sight? I've been sleeping less than two feet above him, how could I not have seen it?

"Right, make sure we're on the next liberty boat Blakey? We need to be on that one, if it's him we'll nail him then."

"Already done mate." Blakey replied. "It's tonight at eighteen hundred hours so meet me at the bottom of the gangway, that way we won't miss him getting off, we'll tell him we're taking Louise out for a bite to eat in the town."

"Okay, see you then, but make sure you bring everything, oh and Blakey, I really hope we're bloody wrong."

"So, do I."

Outside the main harbour gates, they were both standing watching as hundreds of matelots, some in uniform and others dressed in civvies ran towards the waiting taxis and cars, and a few minutes later looked up to see Adam strolling down the steep gangway in his typical nonchalant, untroubled manner. The afternoon sun was set high in the blue sky as huge seagulls screeched overhead, and Adam or whatever his real name was waved at his two friends and shouted out;

"Chas, old boy, Blakey hold on a moment, I'll grab a taxi with you guys if that's okay? We'll tie one on in the town what do you say. Heh lads?"

Adam's friendly invitation wasn't exactly what they were expecting, was this overfriendliness designed to throw them off guard? Was that what he intended? Was Adam that clever? Killer's usually were. Those thoughts passed through both their heads as they stood watching him jog towards them and mentally rehearsed their own story, as he approached.

Salty this time, took the lead. "Sorry Adam we didn't think mate, we've booked a table in the town with Louise, and it might be bit much to expect her to put up with three hairy arsed sailors all at once, so if you don't mind, can we take a rain check on that one?"

"Chas, not a problem, wouldn't want to intrude old boy, completely understand, anyway must dash off lots of Maltese *Anisette* to consume and after that I might try my luck with one of the local ladies, so, see you guys much, much later and don't wait up for me, bye."

Salty patted Adam's back feigning a laugh wondering about his heterosexual remark, all the time closely watching as he jumped into the back of the first taxi in the queue.

As Adam's taxi started to pull away they ran towards the second, with their officer ID cards in hand, and after a few polite requests backed up by rank, they jumped the queue just about managing to push three angry stokers out of the way and entered the back of the next taxi in the line.

A feeling of *déjà vu* suddenly overwhelmed Salty, and he started to feel he'd been here before, he'd seen enough of the inside of taxis to last a lifetime.

"Driver do you speak English please?" Salty asked as he adjusted his front seat to match his six two frames, at the same time as Blakey in the rear was checking his Webley holding the loaded weapon just behind the driver's seat.

"I certainly hope so Sir my father was born in Croydon, he was posted here during the last war, you know during the Battle of Malta, George Cross Island and all that. My earliest memories of Croydon were wet windy days spent listening to the radio while it pissed down outside, so, how can I help you gentlemen?"

The driver's English was so perfectly pronounced that it placed them at ease, his answer although mixed with derision, and a hint of mockery they felt amongst friends, a common language always has that affect, it breaks down barriers.

"Okay, see that taxi that's just pulled away in front. Well we need to follow it, you need to keep a safe distance behind if he sees us, well you don't really want to know the rest. Can you do that mate? Sorry what was your name?"

"It's Michael, or Mike if you like, call me anything as long as you pay the fair, I don't really give a shit."

And as instructed, Mike kept a discreet distance as the yellow Humber Sceptre made its way through Valetta's crowded streets and they approached the crossing between the town's Castille Hotel, and South street. Then a policeman stepped into the road and held up his stop paddle and they waited and watched as Adam's taxi just about made it through before a long line of schoolchildren walked across holding hands singing *"Frère*

Jacque" at the top of their voices as they enjoyed the afternoon sunshine.

Blakey in the back was hotter than hell, the Webley's grip felt greasy and wet, so he checked the safety catch was on and placed it under Salty's seat, before leaning forward and asking the driver. "So, what happens now then Mike? We're stuck here, don't you know of a short cut we can take? You know so we miss out this traffic and these kids."

"You two are Royal Navy, right? And there's obviously something going on here, now I don't really want to know any of the finer details, but if you can give me an idea as to where he's heading, I just might be able to help you. But without me knowing that we're up shit creek without a paddle, this roads got about twenty different junctions off it. He could turn down any one of them."

Salty sat forward and looked across at the driver, he thought he had an idea where Adam might be heading.

"Right Mike head for the Saint Ursula Monastery the quickest way you can. How far is it?"

"About eight miles, so just sit tight and I'll get you there before him, that driver's taking him the long way around, they're heading back towards the harbour, robbing sods these locals."

As the last of the schoolchildren reached the pavement, and the policeman lowered his paddle and waved them through, Mike pulled the column stick down, registered first gear and took the next right, and immediately the streets started to narrow as the Humber's large engine roared passed all the packed bars and shops, as the local's took to the pavement and looked on in disgust.

The bottom of the road narrowed again almost becoming an alley as he mounted the pavement and the tyres screeched, as he took a sweeping left turn. Salty noted the blue and white sign up ahead said; "St Ursula`s Monastery Five Miles."

This Mike might be an arrogant so and so, but he certainly knows how to drive."

As the car sped down Merchant Street, Salty looked behind nodding at Blakey and told him to prepare.

"Right you know the drill this could go either way so let's not get carried away this time, we'll park somewhere and wait for him to turn up, we can't afford another ball's up, so let's just wait and watch, okay."

"I still hope it's not him." Blakey replied.

"Me too mate, me too." Salty answered as the great ramparts of the monastery walls shadowed the scene. Centuries before it's thick stone walls had repelled thousands of Moorish hordes, when the *Maghreb* scaled its battlements and taken no prisoners, and Salty wondered if even now in more peaceful times, would it once again act as a venue for torture and murder.

"Park over their will you Mike, just behind those fig trees. What do we owe you?" Salty asked.

"Nothing, you owe me nothing call me old fashioned, but I miss the old country, you know my dad and all that and I've an instinct for guys like you. Anyway, apart from that I enjoyed the excitement it's not every day you get to speed around Malta with someone holding a gun at your back."

"How did you know about the gun?" Blakey quickly asked.

"What else would you be fiddling with in the back, and why else would you be following someone. You guys are some sort of Naval Police, I worked that out the minute you got in."

Salty sat for a moment and wondered how he knew, but decided not to ask, and instead simply thanked him as he got out of the car. "Thanks Mike, been an interesting trip see you around."

"Bye, boys certainly has. Enjoy the rest of your day."

Chapter 17. HMP Barlinnie.

"Slop out, come on slop out yeh wee little bastard, oh and you've a visitor, so after that get yourself down to landing two, Officer McDonald `ill escort yee."

Medhev's cruel eyes examined the officer as he bent down and gripped hold of his overflowing slop bowl gripping tight hold of the enamel rim as the urine and his own human waste fell to the cell floor.

"Be careful what you say to me McDougal don't overstep the mark, remember our little arrangement." Medhev said glaring up the Officer.

After nearly forty years in the Scottish Prison Service, Senior Prison Officer James McDougal, or *Jimmer* to his friends was coming up for retirement, and in all those years he'd never taken as much as a brass farthing in bribes, his unblemished service record was only interrupted when he was called to arms, to fight the Japanese in Burma for four gruelling years, in WW2.

As a consequence of those experiences, McDougal had adopted. "A no fear attitude" towards all prisoners, that was until he'd met Medhev during his induction to the *'Big-Bad-Barlee'* less than a year before. To him, Medhev personified the ultimate terror, pure unadulterated evil ran through the man's veins, and Officer McDougal was utterly terrified of him.

"Who is this visitor? Where is he from? M.O.D, NIS, MI6? Which is he? Quickly tell me who it is McDougal?"

"Not a clue Medhev, didn't catch his name all I know is he's Royal Navy, now slop out and make your way down to the twos."

Medhev knew the depressing caged landings like the back of his fat Mongolian hand. He'd walked them once a day for twelve long months after the Governor had sentenced him to solitary confinement, following his frenzied attack on a fellow inmate using a metal tray. So, as usual he waited and listened as the landing cell doors were all slammed shut, and only then, was he allowed to leave his own.

As he reached the giant sluice basin at the end of landing six, he was careful to balance the bowl on the side of the large ceramic sink, knowing full well that McDougal would enjoy watching him mop up his own spills, so using his index finger he started to break down his stinking excreta, allowing the watery brown mush to slush itself away down the sink's plughole.

Only thoughts of hatred occupied any part of his tortured mind, he couldn't stop thinking about how he was going to slowly kill that pompous prick McPherson, and how he'd cut deep into the meaty flesh of his side kick Salt.

Visiting rights had been removed the day he'd arrived in Barlinnie following the attack on the prisoner. He'd also been classified as a high-risk political prisoner. Prison number PO 5478. A class A. So, Medhev had eaten alone, masturbated alone, and shit alone. He'd even been beaten senseless alone. *So, who the hell was this visitor? Could it be McPherson, or Salt? Surely not. And if it was. Why the hell now...?*

Descending the metal treads to landing two, the infamous death penalty speech continually rang in his ears.

You will be taken from this place, to a lawful place of execution, and once there hanged by the neck until you are dead.

There'd been no trial, he hadn't even seen the inside of a court, but he'd heard those terrifying words whispered every night through his spyhole by Officer Bates just before lights out. Prison officers aren't very kind to murderers, especially when the killer's victims were two of their own, so they enjoyed taking it in turns to add to his torment. They all utterly despised Medhev.

Down on the two's Prison Officer Frank McKinley from Ayrshire was well known throughout Barlinnie for his easy-going nature and equable manner. He would often be seen offering a calming pat on the shoulder to a troubled inmate or writing letters for those who couldn't. And he detested Medhev, but unlike McDougal, McKinley wasn't afraid of him.

After all, Medhev hadn't kidnapped his family!

"This way Medhev keep four paces back and make sure you keep your hands behind your back, I won't hesitate to use my baton, remember that."

Medhev did exactly as he was told because he knew McKinley meant it, so standing four paces back he placed his hands behind his back, and waited, and watched, as the six feet two twenty stone prison officer unlocked the main landing door to Barlinnie's infamous inner courtyard. Where only five years ago, they'd hanged their last triple murderer.

As they walked across the yard, door after door was opened, then re- locked, and re-checked as Medhev walked the walk of the condemned through the long dark depressing corridor, towards the visitor's suite.

McKinley un-locked the door and presented the *V. O*, (Medhev's visiting order) to the half-asleep warden sat in his chair with his feet up on the desk. Medhev looked across at the row of screened glass booths all with their own black telephones attached and could see a young Naval Lieutenant sat on the other side. And although not a face he immediately recognised he had a feeling, an inner sense almost, that for him. Things were about to change.

Dressed in his best number one uniform, the Lieutenant motioned Medhev to pick up the bakelite receiver with a wave of his hand through the toughened glass. And still without taking his eyes off the Lieutenant, Medhev pressed the phone closer to his ear as he sat down on the wooden chair and began to listen.

"Comrade Kapitan, I am here to help you, so keep your mouth shut and listen to my instructions, you must follow them to the letter, I don't have very long. I am here to interview Paddy 'O Hare but our handler, and we both know who that is, has diverted my attention to you. So, just listen."

Medhev nodded still holding the receiver tightly to his ear, the sweat running down his neck made it feel uncomfortable, but he listened anyway.

"My name is Lieutenant Black, and I am from the Naval intelligence service, now tomorrow night at about this time Officer Bate's will pay you a visit and just as he always does every night, he'll recite the *Hangman's verse* through your cell door."

Medhev wondered how a complete stranger could know that. But the outcome interested him more than the intelligence.

"Now after he does that, he'll throw a little white tablet into your cell, you have to swallow that tablet immediately, because that tablet spells freedom for you comrade."

"But you could be....".

"I told you to listen Medhev, so, shut up! I've only got few minutes left, be silent! Let me finish."

"The tablet contains a stomach irritant that will raise your temperature to just above 101 degrees, that is exactly the temperature where the prison authorities have to legally take you to an outside hospital. So, when McDougal carries out his rounds and finds you on your cell floor vomiting and writhing around, they'll have no choice, he'll have to raise the alarm just as he's been told, and you can leave the rest to me."

"One very important point to remember, is that when you wake up in the hospital bed you must remove the saline tube from your hand, that part is vital, so don't forget."

"But, how can I be sure Koralev doesn't want to dispose of me," pleaded Medhev, "I mean the tablet could contain cyanide, I w...."

"Shut your mouth! You half-wit! Never mention his name, the answer is you don't, but it's your choice Medhev and if it were me, I'd take the chance, because what is your alternative?

If you stay here, they will either hang you, or prisoner exchange you for some worthless British agent."

Medhev sat with his mouth open considering his fate for a moment, his gold teeth Koralev's dentist had fitted felt cold as he ran his wet tongue the length of his mouth and swallowed hard. But gradually he reached the same conclusion as the Lieutenant, he was right, he didn't have a choice.

"Okay times up you two love birds, come on let's be having you, come on back to your cell you ruskie bastard."
Then before he got up, Lieutenant Black whispered;

"Bye Medhev see you on the outside," then smiled at him as he carefully replaced the receiver.

But Medhev hadn't heard him, because by then he was deep in thought, as he looked first to the floor, then up to the ceiling for an answer. "I don't have a choice." He mumbled to himself as McKinley took his arm.

As the inner courtyard clock struck its tenth hour, the prison lights extinguished with a loud *"clunk"* as the electrical contactor disengaged from its circuit, and only silence, dread, and misery remained.

A few minutes later with his eyes starting to adjust to the darkness, Medhev heard a familiar voice coming from the open spyhole. *"You will be taken from this place, to a lawful place of execution, and once there hanged by the neck until you are dead.*" This time though the spyhole wasn't immediately slammed shut, this time there was a tapping sound as the tablet dropped and rolled along the stone floor as it rattled and rolled its way to the side of his bed.

As the spyhole closed, Medhev listened to the officer's footsteps clanging on the metal grating as he walked further down the landing. Then he looked down from the bed at the pearl white tablet that lay glistening on the filthy stone floor.

His hand reached out, but then he stopped, as he whispered to himself.

"Is this it then? Is this the end? Should I?"

A few minutes passed as he pondered his fate then he sat up in the bed picked the tablet up from the floor and held it tightly in his shaking hand, and once more he asked himself.

"What do I do?"

It was then that he did something he'd never done before. He began to pray whispering all alone in the darkness to the only person he hoped would be listening. "If you are there and listening, please I want to live I don't want to die, I don't want to die. Okay."

Medhev put the white glossy tablet to his thick Mongolian lips placed it on his tongue and swallowed hard, then lifted the grey woollen blanket off his body as he sat up and waited. Was it freedom he was awaiting? Or was it hell?

Medhev was under no illusions the Kingdom of Heaven wouldn't be beckoning him. But, there again, it wasn't to him he'd been praying…...

Chapter 18. Saint Ursula's, Malta.

The early evening sun was beating down, the temperature was well in eighty's the only respite from the heat was from the shade provided behind the graveyard's stone wall as they both waited and took it in turns to watch the monastery car park. They'd been there for three hours, and no one had appeared.

They'd seen the odd relative here and there placing flowers on a loved one's grave, or now and then an American or Japanese tourist turn up asking the Maltese nut seller to take photographs of his family, who'd happily oblige in exchange for a Maltese pound. But, apart from that it was just them, them, that and an inert troubling silence.

So, they waited as Salty cupped his hand and looked down at the ticking phosphorus hands on his Pulsar watch, it was 19.40 hrs, and he couldn't help but think the balmy evening would be better spent sitting outside a quaint little bar with Louise. Rather than hunting killers in a deserted graveyard.

Blakey wiped the sweat from his eyes for the fifth time in as many minutes, they'd already checked the other entrance at the back, and patrolled the grounds three times, checking every bush, and every possible hiding place. They'd watched monks come and go, but not one walked, acted, or even remotely looked anything like Adam Bloom.

At exactly 22.00 hundred hours, the monastery bells rang out, announcing their call to Evening Prayers, and the hollow sounds reverberated across the graveyard as Salty realised that the killer's preferred slaughter time had arrived.

Keeping both their heads held low, they looked over the top and watched as the devout father's started to file in, in two lines through the large wooden doors, and they all but the last in line, crossed himself. Instead he stopped and looked around and pondered for a moment looking towards the monastery courtyard like he was searching for something.

Then a few seconds later he stepped over the threshold and through the big oak doors still without crossing himself.
And Blakey asked Salty;

"Did you see that, did you? What was he looking for?"

"Us, I reckon, and he didn't cross himself either, it's got to be him he's the right height same build, come on you take the front, I'll take a look around the back, we'll nail the bastard this time."

Blakey watched as Salty crept along the grass verge as he made his way along the monasteries' tall stone walls towards the back. And as agreed, he'd hide behind the trees just outside the front entrance and wait for the signal the three loud whistles. And only then would he rush in.

219

Darting between the stone pillar's that supported the covered atrium at the rear, Salty stopped for a moment to cock the hammer on his Webley and check his pocket for his NPD pen. And although he'd never used it, he'd like to, he wanted to take Bloom alive, so placing the gun down on the stone floor he put his ear defenders in, and almost instantly a remote silence ensued.

They'd both rehearsed the move a dozen times since their awful debacle when trying to arrest Captain Hargreaves, and both had agreed that this time they weren't about to go in with all guns blazing.

As the last of the evening sunrays were breaking through the pine trees at the bottom of the garden, Salty sensed a movement up ahead, so he removed one of his ear plugs and could hear the shuffling of hooves and the *clip clopping* of the mules as they moved around in their stalls. But more important than that, he could hear two people talking. He couldn't quite make out what they were saying from where he was standing but he knew they were talking in German because the harshness of their pronunciation so easily betrayed the language. As the light started to dim, and the sun was lowering its flaming orange ball behind the mountain of St Peter it began to form a halo casting orange and black shadows across the courtyard as Salty darted across and began inching his way along the barn's stone façade, towards the two open doors.

Just as he was about to re-insert the ear plugs, and pull out his NPD pen, he thought he heard another noise, but this time it was from behind him, and whatever it was, was moving quick. Then, just as he was about to turn around.

It was upon him….

Blakey looked down at his friend fearing the worst, thick red blood was oozing from an open gash on the side of his head and his chest was heaving up and down like a stricken animal, so he was still alive.

"What the? Shit Salty! Sit up, sit up, come on, breathe, take deep breaths, come on," Blakey shouted pulling his body upright into his arms. He watched as Salty's eyes gradually flickered to life and he mumbled his first words.

"Did we get him Blakey? Did we?"

"No."

"Let me up, we've got to get him, before…."

"It's too late."

"What! It can't be, it's only been a few min…."

"He's gone, the father's dead the bastard got away.

Blakey hadn't been privy to the awful scene that had greeted Father Amadeo's that night in the Vomero Hills, neither had Salty. And although Salty had hung on every word of Jack's description of Father Giovanni Francesco's demise in the graveyard in Javea, words can never visually express what your own eyes reveal in a live situation.

Blakey wiped the blood from the back of his friend's head and holding him upright to support his weight the two NIS Agents stumbled into the barn. And straight away Salty understood what Jack had tried so hard to explain to him. It also explained why he'd broken down that day.

Father Christiano De-Angelo the head Abba's body was hanging upside down from two central wooden rafters with his legs splayed, a metal pole had been inserted through his mouth. But the rust covered end hadn't quite reached his anus this time. Instead, it was protruding out through his lower bowel, and had pushed his dripping entrails outwards and down, leaving the swaying bloody ends dangling an inch or two above his eyelids. The same eyelids that had been sewn together, the same eyelids that bore the tattooed letters.

BEYZ., and K L......

Chapter 19. Bighi Hospital, Malta.

Salty hated hospitals, the knock on the head was his third in his short career, and quite by chance he'd been struck in exactly the same place each time. The X rays hadn't revealed a fracture to the skull, so the doctor's recommendation was complete rest, and most of all keeping his head still, until the swelling subsided.

Louise would spend most of her lunch times sat on his bed, sharing his grapes and reading him the papers, she couldn't quite understand why Salty of all people had been mugged in the back streets of Valetta, and she didn't understand at all why he'd been out without Blakey that late at night.

She didn't even care that his medical chart listed him, as a Lieutenant Davies. She just didn't care. Just so long as he recovered. Louise had always known he was different, and that something odd was going on, she also knew Blakey was involved somehow. But she didn't care about that either as long as she could spend time with him. He was safe with her, and she felt safe with him.

"Lieutenant Davies, you have a visitor, there's a Lieutenant. Adam Bloom to see you shall I show him in?"

The nurse was hovering at the end, as Salty instantly pushed his arms down into the bed and tried to sit himself up.

Louise wrongly interpreted that as a sign for her to leave and stood up and gently patted his pillows kissing his hand before saying; "Bye see you a bit later then, I'll pop back around teatime okay."

Salty didn't want her to leave, but he did want her out of harm's way. So, looking into her beautiful brown eyes, he quickly replied; "Yeah, bye, love, I'll see you later." Then he looked back at the nurse who was still stood there hovering and asked her to; "show Lieutenant Bloom in, please."

"Of course, Sir, I'll fetch him in now."

"Oh, and nurse, can you pass me that glass of orange juice over there please?"

"Shall I refill it for you Lieutenant?"

"No, nurse, that bit at the bottom will be just fine."

The nurse then passed him the half empty glass, quickly swallowing its warm contents, he hid the empty glass underneath his sheet, and wouldn't hesitate to smash the bastard in the face if he as much as twitched.

"Chas old boy, what the hell have they done to you?"

Was Bloom's cheerful greeting as he arrived and gripped the end of his metal bed stead.

"You look like an Egyptian mummy with all that rigmarole wrapped round your bonce, must have been quite a blow, back of the head wasn't it?"

"Yes, back of the head Adam, how did you know?"

"Oh, the nurse must have told me, anyway, look I've brought these in for you, I know you love detective novels, so I scrounged a few out of Eagle's library, they're written by somebody called *Mickey Spillane*, thought it might help to take your mind off things, old boy."

Salty sat for a moment wondering how he knew? How could he possibly know he read, Mickey Spillane novels? Then he remembered. Bloom had access to all crew records, and he'd obviously read his.

"I've brought you some grapes in as well, but judging by your locker you've already had a few visitors today, so I'll just pop them on top of the pile over here, now Chas, tell me what on earth were you thinking going out all alone at that time of night? I mean that part of Valetta is renowned for muggings. I put the poster's up on Eagle myself warning about the dangers of lurking around at night in the dark, especially, if you are alone. I mean whoever attacked you, could just as easily have killed you Chas, couldn't he?"

Is the bastard warning me? Threatening me? But it doesn't really matter, the game needs to be played out, he's certainly a clever one all right. Killers usually are.

"Well I don't want it to be public knowledge Adam." Salty said tapping his nose and sitting forward looking him straight in the eye. "But I was shall we say, visiting a lady of the night, but keep that between us Adam, I wouldn't want Louise finding out, now would I?"

"Oh, I bet you wouldn't so mum's the word, must say though didn't have you down as a philanderer, you've certainly gone up in my estimation, Chas old boy."

Bloom patted Salty's leg, as Salty's tightened his grip on the glass, and Bloom's patronising smile washed over his face as if he was warning him to stay away, and just let it go. But Salty couldn't. And he wouldn't.

"Well got to dash Chas old boy, I'm on starboard watch at eighteen hundred, replacing some invalid who ended up in hospital apparently. I'll leave the books over here shall I?"

"Thanks Adam, yeah leave them on there, I'll have a look at them later, my heads banging at the moment."

"Ta for now Chas, see you soon I hope." He said turning around and walking slowly down the ward. Salty looked over to the bed side cabinet at the books, and the titles.

At the bottom was; "You are not my Jury," above that was, "Kill you Deadly," and the top one was entitled, "Vengeance will be Mine." It was a message and it was clear Bloom was warning him.

"Nurse, nurse can you telephone Lieutenant Blake aboard Eagle, it's really urgent, can you ask him to get over here straight away."

"Certainly Lieutenant, I'll call the ship."

"Thank you, nurse, it really is urgent."

Nurse Flanagan didn't move as quickly as she used to, aged sixty-two and a veteran of the *Quarns* she was a tad overweight, even so she'd picked up the desperation in Salty's request, so she ran down the ward like she was running from a fire to make the call.

Twenty minutes later out of breath, and panting like a wet racehorse, Blakey appeared at the end of his bed.

"What's so urgent? You're meant to be resting, keeping your head still, what is it? The nurse said you were acting like a man possessed."

"Bloom paid me a visit less than half an hour ago, see those books over there, take a good look at the titles."

Blakey looked over at the pile of three books as Salty started to explain.

"They're a cryptic message, he's telling us to not; "Judge him," warning us, "he'll kill us," that; "vengeance will be his. He's telling us to stay away Blakey, to let him finish what he's started!"

But Salty wasn't the only one with news that day, so Blakey sat down at the end of the bed and started to tell him what he'd found out as Salty listened with his arms folded staring up at the whitewashed ceiling.

"Well let's just say things may have started to unravel, when Bloom was visiting you here earlier, I used your key to get into his cabin and I found this under his bed, it all ties in, take a look at the title."

Blakey placed the black and red book on Salty's bed, it was first written in the 1950s and was authored by a certain *Wolfgang Schuster*. But it wasn't the German author's name that interested him. It was more the title. Shuster's book was entitled, *Konzentration Lager,* and the K and the L were highlighted in a deep bloody red. The same deep red they'd both seen at the cinema on the thousands of flags at the Nazi party rallies on *Pathe* news. Finally, things were starting to make sense. So, Salty started to work the puzzle.

"Beyz, means evil in Yiddish right, we know that, so this must mean that the K, and the L, stand for Konzentration Lager."

228

"We also know Bloom's a Jew, now let's just suppose for a minute that his mother, father, or even an aunt or an uncle were interned in one of these camp during the War, why would that make him attack defenceless monks? How are the monk's linked in to all this?"

Then, still staring up towards the whitewashed panels on the ceiling he suddenly remembered something he'd once read at school about the last months of the Second World War where hundreds of Nazis, especially members of the SS, disappeared down what the famous Nazi hunter *Simon Wiesenthal* had termed, the *Rat line*. Apparently, the Catholic church were complicit in their escape, or at least some of the more hardened Jew haters were. Not only that, they still hid them within the monastery walls for years after the war.

After a few moments bringing Blakey up to speed, with the historical facts, Salty continued with his appraisal.

"Now let's just suppose that's what's happened here, let's suppose for a minute that these monks he's bumping off are all ex Nazi's, where would he strike next?"

Salty sat bolt upright again and placed his glass on the table and asked Blakey to pass his clothes. "I've got an idea, get me out of here we need to contact Father Francisco in Valencia. Can you patch us through to the monastery on Eagle's radio? I've got a lot of questions I need to ask the good father."

"Yeah, piece of cake, but what about....?"

"What about nothing Blakey, get me out of here."

As they approached Eagle and before reaching the gangway, Blakey carefully re-dressed the bandage on Salty's head, his peaked cap was only just covering the sodden red and white creped material. Bloom was on starboard watch facing the sea, so he wouldn't see them climb board.

Salty was still weak from the injury, he felt tired and dizzy as Blakey gripped his arm, and they walked up the angled gangway, towards the port watch officer.

"Lieutenant Davies and sub-Lieutenant Blake requesting permission to come aboard Sir." Blakey asked, as both men offered a crisp salute towards the smart Lieutenant Commander.

"Permission granted step aboard…. Seaman Dyer pipe the two officer's aboard lad."

"Yes Sir."

As they reached the radio room door four decks below, Salty made a mental note of the time, Valencia in mainland Spain was an hour ahead of GMT so mirrored their time in Malta. So, he hoped to catch Father Francisco before he was called to Afternoon Prayers.

Dozens of sailors with white flash-hoods were sat around busily staring down at green cathode screens dotted along a central desk that provided Eagle's air cover. But not one looked up as they entered, they hadn't even noticed them.

"Right Salty, if we dial up using the ultra-high band, somebody in here's going to listen in, but if I use NIS at Invergordon on the tri-band to patch us through the signal will be scrambled both ends, that way nobody knows where we're transmitting to, or from."

"Crack on, just get him on the line and make it quick, we don't have long."

Blakey picked up the microphone then pushed the transmit button down at the same time as he adjusted the two green dials on the front of the Marconi set. Then as quietly as he was able, he started to talk;

"Invergordon, Invergordon, this is a flash message, stand by."
A few seconds late a woman's voice, replied.

"Invergordon receiving you loud and clear, ready for flash message, over."

"Invergordon, we are agent's Salt and Blake aboard HMS Eagle, coded numbers for tonight are.... Sorry, Invergordon stand by."

Blakey pulled out a small grey notebook from his pocket, and quickly scanned the numbered codes, irritated with himself that he hadn't been better prepared.

"Coded numbers are; Three, Niner, Six, Four, Niner, acknowledge, over."

The radio set hissed and squealed for a moment as Blakey twirled his black biro in his sweaty palm, and looked down at the notebook, whispering the numbers to himself again.

"Three, Niner, Six, Four, Niner."

A few seconds passed, and the Marconi set screamed to life again.

"This is Invergordon, acknowledge code is correct go ahead, over."

"Thank you Invergordon we need to be patched through to the main telephone line at a monastery called 'Sant Jeroni de Cotalba St Paul.' I repeat a monastery by the name of Sant Jeroni de Cotalba St Paul, it's in Valencia, on mainland Spain, we need to speak with the head Abba's there, his name is Father Francisco, this is an urgent message, a code one, repeat a code one."

"Stand by Three, Niner, Six Four Niner, I'll have you patched through in less than a minute, over."

Salty could feel the blood seeping through the bandage, staining the top of his white cap, so he wiped his brow, the heat from the masses of electronic equipment inside the room had raised the temperature to way above a hundred degrees, and it was stifling.

A minute came by and went, and the set intermittently buzzed as Blakey tapped his fingers noisily on the desk, and Salty started to feel the room spinning. So, Blakey grabbed his arm.

"I'll fetch you some water mate, it's just over there okay."

"Yeah, yeah that would help, it's just so bloody hot in here, how the hell do you work in this heat?"

Blakey didn't answer him and instead walked towards the stainless-steel water container in the corner of the room, and placed the white ceramic mug below it, as Salty waited listening to the sound of the liquid life being poured, and the set buzzed again.

"Here drink this, I'll get you some more in a minute, take these too I knicked em out of the cabinet in the ward when the nurse wasn't looking." Blakey handed his friend two aspirins and watched him place the tablets in his mouth and gulp down the water. He'd never seen him look so bad.

"Stand by again Three. Niner, Six. Four. Niner your contact is on the line, patching you through now…...Invergordon over and out."

"Hello this is Father Christiano to whom am I speaking with please?"

Immediately recognising the father's distinctive tone, Salty picked the second microphone up before Blakey had a chance to reply;

"This is Lieutenant Sam Salt, and sub-Lieutenant William Blake aboard HMS Eagle in Malta, I'm sure you remember us, we're the two that…"

"Yes, yes Lieutenant, how could I ever forget."

"Father, I am sorry to trouble you again, but our investigation has reached what you might call a *critical* stage, and we need your help."

Salty paused for a second allowing the *"help"* word to firmly imprint itself in the father's head.

"Carry on Lieutenant."

"Well father we have managed to identify the killer, we don't have much time to stop him before he strikes again, so…..".

"What's all this got to do me Lieutenant? I'm a simple Abba's how can I possibly help you, I mean….?"

Salty was the one to interrupt this time and said just one word, "Odessa." And the line went silent.

He could sense the father's angst mixed in the silence, the line was scratchy, but the father's heavy breathing was so easily betraying his guilt. Salty knew he was complicit but at that stage how deep his involvement had been, he just didn't know? So, he tried something else, this time by way of a threat.

"I'll ask you one more time father, or my next call will be to my good friend, *Inspector Générale Salvador Montoya*, you probably know him better as the head of Franco's secret police. And when he questions you, he won't be anywhere near as polite as me, I mean think about it father, if it gets out Franco has been harbouring war criminals in his monasteries all these years, can you imagine what that would do to Spain's economy? Britain would dissolve its interest in the country overnight, and the rest of Europe would follow suit."

"So, which is it father? Do you help us save a life no matter how worthless that life may seem to you, or do I make my call?"

Seconds passed and the line was silent again, before a trembly voice did reply, fear was etched in every spoken word.

"Those were very difficult times we lived in back then, you are young so you wouldn't understand Lieutenant, I was against

235

it, I even asked for an audience with his Holiness the Pope himself, but I was refused of course."

Salty was becoming even hotter, and more impatient by the second. "We don't have time for this right now, come on we need names, no more stalling come on!" Salty replied banging his fist down hard on the metal desk. "Come on father give me a name."

"Okay, forgive me it's just so difficult all this happened a very long time ago, but I will tell you what I know. Now one of these murders took place in Vomero that was Abba's Giovanni Francesco, otherwise known as SS Leutnant Hans Brauchitsh. Brauchitsh, was quite possibly the cruellest of them all. Of, course a few of the other murders that took place were father's who'd played only minor roles in the camps, a few actually repented their sins, not that that made them any less guilty."

"The next murder was of Father Emanuel Rodriguez at the monastery of San Miguel De Los Reyes. If I recall his body was discovered the same night that HMS Eagle departed for Malta. Rodriguez's real name was Otto Ehrlichman and his favourite torture was to beat the prisoner's to death using the steel butt of his machine gun."

The line was silent again, as the father tried to gather some composure, his words were faltering as he struggled to recall each ugly detail, to comprehend and relay in words somehow what he himself had kept secret for far too long.

"About a year after the war ended a man calling himself Alex came to visit me at the monastery here, Alex was a Jew from Slovakia and hunting Ehrlichman and the others here in Valencia. He told me everything that happened on that terrible march west from Majdanek, he described every detail, I think the poor man's mind must have gone by then. He said he'd met a young woman on his travels, and she'd borne him a son, the youngster's name escapes me at the moment, but Alex was already quite insane by then his eyes were glazed over, the Devil's hatred had devoured him."

"I'm ashamed to admit that at the same time as I was having a conversation with Alex, I was also hiding Ehrlichman in the cellar. And for what good it might mean now, Ehrlichman did try and repent his sins. But a man like that can never really change and a few weeks later I had to physically restrain him from beating one of the young boys with a bull whip in his hermitage."

"He'd do it every chance he got I despised the man he was so terribly cruel. That is probably why *your* killer attempted to murder me, my name must also be on his list."

"Correction father he's not *"our"* killer, he's yours. So just tell me how many are left, we need to know where he's going to strike next."

The father sighed; his reply was interspersed with static.

"Well I was only told about Christiano De Angelo's murder this morning, his real name is Fritz Yuengling so that only leaves the one, I'm so very sorry Lieutenant I should have told you about this before, I feel so ashamed. So, that just leaves the guiltiest of them all, the commandant of Majdanek…..."

"Look who is it father! A name, a place come on we don't have much time……"

Blakey offered him some water, and Salty used his sleeve to wipe the sweat from his face, as the tannoy announced; *"Lieutenant Bloom, Lieutenant Bloom report to the radio room on deck six. report to the radio room on deck six."*

"Quickly father we're all out of time here, quickly the name, the place."

"The man you're looking for is Father Benedetto, previously known as SS Haupt Sturm Fuhrer Heinrich Zeigler, he's the head Abba's at the St. Frances of Assisi monastery right there in Malta. But I warn you now he still has his SS contacts, he's surrounded by them, so be careful Lieutenant, he's a very

238

dangerous man, I shouldn't say this, but I must admit there are times when I almost wanted the killer to complete his list."

"List, that's twice you've said that, what do you mean by list father?"

"Don't you see Lieutenant. The first initial of each man's surname make up the Yiddish name for Evil, BEYZ, and Zeigler is his last........."

"Lieutenant Bloom to report to the radio room on deck six immediately, Lieutenant Bloom to report to the radio room on deck six immediately."

"Shit, shit, sorry father look we've got to go, thankyou father."

The line then crackled for the last time and went dead.

"Blakey, there's no liberty tonight because Centaur's in port, so write out a brief report and get it up to the Captain, tell him we'll fill him in with all the other details when we see him in the morning. Tell him all about the SS guards, the rat line and all that, but don't tell him Bloom's the killer. Not just yet."

"We'll save that little gem until we meet him face to face. I'll go off now and get cleaned up, let's get out of here before Bloom arrives ...."

Chapter 20. McDougal You Old Fool.

"Take that thing away from me, and get that stupid woman out of here, who are you? Where am I?"

"You're in Glasgow General Hospital, and you're still under arrest so close your stinking mouth you Russian bastard and shut the fuck up."

McKinley was sick of Medhev, his constant demands grated on him. He had his suspicions that he was either blackmailing or threatening his friend McDougal, he'd noticed a change in his behaviour recently. And it bothered him. He'd find out what was going on, and if he was proved right, Medhev would pay. He'd take personal care of that.

McDougal was standing at attention outside the door with his arms behind his back, his shoulders back, and his chest puffed out, every now and again he'd look down at his brightly polished shoes, and bend his knees to relieve the cramp, just as he been trained during his time spent fighting the Japanese in the steamy jungles of Burma.

McDougal wasn't a weak man by any means, no, he'd been a very brave man, the row of medal ribbons including the Burma Star on his chest paid testament to that.

As he stood guard his thoughts returned to Burma, to all the brave men and the good friends he'd had to leave behind, and kept repeating to himself under his breath, the famous *Kohima epitaph.*

"When you go home, tell them of us, and say for your tomorrow, we gave our today."

And today McDougall was about to do just that. Give up his today for his families' tomorrow.

Lieutenant Black was waiting in the hospital car park outside with the Austin A35's engine gently ticking over, watching the entrance for Medhev to appear. It was five to twelve, five more minutes and he'd drive him to the safe house and call the *smithy* at exactly one PM en route and tell him to release McDougal's family. He hoped for McDougal's sake the smithy hadn't been too impatient this time and would await his call.

McKinley looked towards Medhev disturbed by a movement as Medhev sat bolt upright in bed and noticed that the saline tube in his left hand was detached. So, as he walked towards the bed and picked up the tube and was distracted just long enough for McDougal to enter the room and creep up behind him. McDougal clubbed him around the back of the head with his baton, then caught his friend's twenty stone frame just an inch from the floor, the weight even for a fit man like McDougal was enough to take the wind out of his sails.

The blow had connected perfectly just below the hairline on the back of the neck and had been dispensed just hard enough to put him to sleep. The technique perfected in the Jungles of Burma when capturing Japanese behind enemy lines for questioning. And it worked.

Even so, McDougal felt for a pulse and was relieved to find his friend Frank was still alive, so he dragged his heavy body to the side of Medhev's bed then placed his head gently down on the tiled floor as he looked towards Medhev, scathing.

"I'm telling you Medhev if you've as much as touched one hair on my family's……"

"Oh, shut your fucking Scottish mouth McDougal, shut it, what do you think we Russian's are animals? Your family will be released as soon as my comrade outside makes his call, now hand me that bag over there, the one behind the curtain it contains my civilian clothes, quickly now! We don't have much time."

McDougal's instructions were to raise the alarm exactly one and a half hours after Medhev had escaped, he'd try and explain how nature had called, and while he was away from his post with a bad stomach cramp, Medhev had escaped.

After all he was sixty. What McDougal didn't know at the time was that at one thirty-five that afternoon, at exactly the same time as he was making his call to his wife Madge to make sure she'd been released. His neighbour Ernie would pick up the phone, and tell him that Madge, and their only son Donald had both been found dead.

Ernie would refuse to describe the scene to McDougal over the telephone, because he hadn't seen anything like it since his time spent fighting Rommel's Afrika Corps in the Western dessert. And even then, the German's had at least taken the time and had the decency to bury their dead…. Whole…...

As Medhev was being driven up the long gravel drive towards the big house he wondered why the smithy hadn't answered his call. He thought he had an idea, but he didn't really care, all he cared about now was saving his own skin and how he'd try and explain to Koralev why; he'd allowed himself to be captured by the British for a second time.

So Medhev swallowed hard, as Lieutenant Black pulled up outside the large Victorian mansion and ominously stated; "It's time to face the music."

"Is Koralev here?"

"Yes, he's here."

"Who else is here?"

"The smithy."

Black didn't say another word and once more took hold of Medhev's shaking arm as he marched him up the stone steps towards the big oak panelled doors at the top. Medhev stopped at the top and looked over at the gloating Lieutenant and asked.

"Please, allow me a moment will you Lieutenant?"

Medhev was in a sort of dreamlike state up and was staring up at what he imagined would be his last sight of the sun as its golden glow leaked through the branches of the willow trees in the well-tended grounds. Then he sighed a sigh of the condemned, and it slowly started to sink in that his life would soon be over. He could feel a warm form of acceptance washing over him, that was until he looked up at the door and was staring straight into the cold blues eyes of his handler. General Koralev.

"My dear Medhev we meet again so soon where have you been? I've missed you, come in, come in."

"Sir, comrade Koralev I can explain everything."

"First come in Medhev, we've a lot to talk about you and I."

Medhev stepped in through the doorway as Koralev blew his Turkish cigarette smoke upwards, and it spiralled above his head as he straightened his red party tie. Stepping into the dark hallway with its grand staircase the scene reminded Medhev of the inside of the *Kremlin*, where only a few years before he'd received his *Hero of the Soviet Union* medal. Placed on his chest by none other than Premier *Nikita Khrushchev* himself. But those days were long gone now. And he expected no mercy.

"Come on, this way Medhev through here."

Black kept hold of his left arm as Koralev pulled open the two tall white doors to the main reception room.

Inside was what could only be described as opulence, that was bordering on vulgarity; Paintings of long dead Czar's adorned each of the four walls. Peter the Great, on his great white charger by far and away the most prominent. Medhev thought that if these were discovered outside the confines of the Kremlin, then a Gulag or worse would await their keeper.

But Koralev head of the KGB and prior to that the NKVD was way beyond rapprochement, his well-documented friendship with the newly elected Soviet Premier *Leonid Ilyich Brezhnev* had been long in the making, their sons were best friends at the Naval academy, their wives, inseparable.

So Koralev, was what Medhev termed; *A member of the inner circle.* Koralev had made sure of that.

"Sit Medhev, sit, comrade Black fetch three brandies from the cabinet over there. Medhev and I have a lot to get through."

Koralev's tone wasn't conciliatory by any means but it wasn't threatening either, so Medhev started to wonder what sort of game he might be playing as he sat down in the gold braided winged back chair and awaited the smithy's appearance.

"Okay, good, just sip it Medhev, sip it." said Koralev handing Medhev the small glass tumbler. "Take only small mouthfuls you never know where your next drink will come from, do you comrade Black. Heh?"

"No comrade Koralev, you don't." Black coolly replied sitting just behind Medhev. The last comment from Koralev had unnerved Medhev, *is he threatening me? What is going on here?*

"Now you're probably sitting there wondering why you're not already dead, am I correct Medhev?"

"You are comrade Koralev." Medhev nervously replied.

"Good, because the last time we met, I distinctly remember telling you to never get caught again. Now didn't I Medhev?"

Koralev's tone had altered again, his words were sharper somehow, so Medhev uncrossed his legs and sat nervously upright, before offering his reply.

"Comrade there simply wasn't enough time for me to escape, I managed to kill one of the capitalist pigs before they took me. But there just wasn't enough time, I have told them nothing comrade, nothing, I swear this to you."

"Well I must say I was very disappointed in you Medhev, you see in all my time heading up our secret service, I have never, not once given somebody a third chance, and if I was to allow that to happen they'd laugh at me, they'd say I had gone soft, my reputation would be in ruins. But.... my dear Medhev, providence has shone it's light on you today, as I am going to do just that, and offer you a third chance."

Medhev dropped his empty brandy tumbler to the carpet as he sat there open mouthed and rubbed the back of his thick Mongolian neck, the room was hot, and the curtains were wide open. A clue to Koralev's intentions he wondered? As they only ever tortured their victims in the dark, and Medhev should know.

"What have I done to deserve this comrade. How can I repay you a third time? I will do anything; anything just name it comra...."

"Stop your whinging you coward, Black pass me that file on the table over there, before I am sick."

Black passed the file over and leant across the back of Medhev's chair, his silent ghostly presence behind causing Medhev to wince and cower.

"Do you recognise this man Medhev? I'm sure you do."

Medhev looked at the grainy black and white picture of Lieutenant Sam Salt taken by a KGB Agent during his passing out parade in Invergordon, and straight away felt the fear drain from his body fully understanding that Koralev needed him, and his life would be spared after all.

"I do comrade that's that pig Salt, the one that took me prisoner aboard Belfast, let me kill him for you comrade I will do it with my bare hands, just give me the chance."

"Your chance is coming Medhev, but I don't want him dead oh no, I want him very much alive you see what we really want is the real Paddy O'Hare back and we know if Salt is offered in the deal, the British will trade. Our little operation in the Mediterranean has all but ground to a halt, Paddy's influence as head of the IRA was priceless Medhev, priceless. So, you see you are going to act as bait, the bait that will lure him out."

"And you are going to do exactly what I tell you to do this time Medhev, do you hear me! You will do exactly as I say!"

"I hear you comrade; I will get Salt for you."

"You certainly will Medhev, and Lieutenant Black here will be there to assist you."

Koralev offered Medhev one of his Turkish cigarettes and Medhev pulled it out from the packet and quickly lit it. It was his first smoke in over a year and it felt good, and it was only then that his heartbeat began to slow. And his hands stopped shaking. Providence really had shone its light on him that day his prayers had been answered.

But none of that mattered as Salt was now his for the taking…...

Chapter 21. To Catch a Killer.

Captain Hargreaves was sat at his desk in Eagle's stifling wardroom reading the report from his two agents. The squeaky ceiling fan was cooling the room to a far more acceptable eighty degrees, the breeze providing a welcome respite from the hot, humid day.

Chief Petty Officer Mike Wheeler had been working on Eagle's air conditioning all day, so as he heard the door being knocked Hargreaves hoped it was him with the good news, that it was fixed.

"Enter."

Salty and Blakey entered the wardroom, saluted the Captain removed their caps and stood at attention in front of the large desk as the Captain looked up and said.

"Well Salt, Blake, I was just reading your report on yesterday's little sortie he could have bloody killed you, is your head okay my boy, are you fit enough for duty lad?"

"Well not officially Sir, I've been down to sick bay and they've re-dressed the wound and given me something for the pain, but I'm still up for it."

"Up for what Salt? Sit down and explain yourself."

On the Captains order, both, simultaneously pulled out a chair and sat down.

"Well Sir, what sub-Lieutenant Blake's report doesn't reveal is the name of the killer, we thought it better to give you that news, face to face, as it were."

Captain Hargreaves's interest was captured.

"So, go on tell me then, who the hell is it?"

"The killer is our very own Lieutenant Adam Bloom from personnel and welfare, my cabin mate, its Bloom no doubt about it Sir."

"Good God man! How, how can you be so sure? I mean, Bloom of all people."

The fan was squeaking a rhythm above their heads, thrusting its cooling air downwards as the Captain sat for a moment scratching his head, then Blakey placed the book down on his desk and started to explain his version of events.

"Sir, take a look at the title of this book it's called Konzentration Lager, now look at the way the *K* and the *L* are highlighted in red, the books are about a Nazi death camp in eastern Poland called Majdanek, now our theory is that one of Bloom's relatives or maybe even a friend was interned in this camp in the last war."

251

"Yes, yes, I read that part in the report, but how does this book implicate Bloom in all of this Blake. Tell me how?"

"Well, at the same time as Bloom was visiting Lieutenant Salt yesterday, I took the liberty of searching his cabin, at first I found nothing, you know just the usual things, porn magazines that sort of stuff."

"Yes, yes, but get to the point Blake, I've no interest in what he does in his spare time."

"Sorry Sir, well, that's when I came across this book hidden underneath his locker, you see the locker looked like it was leaning slightly to one side, and…..."

Captain Hargreaves was becoming impatient, the heat coupled with the noisy ceiling fan and Blakey's meandering report was beginning to grate on him, so despite his normally good nature and patient manner, he slammed his fist down hard onto the desk demanding.

"Get to the point lad the bloody point!"
Salty thought that might be the right time to take over.

"Sir, if I can interrupt please."

"Please do Salt. The book how does it implicate Lieutenant Bloom in all of this?"

"Well, as Blakey was explaining, you see the red highlighted K and the L."

"Yes, yes."

Well, that's exactly what the killer is tattooing on his victims' eyelids. That's after he's killed them Sir."

"Good God man, carry on."

"He's also tattooing the letters *BEYZ* the Jewish word for Evil, and they also happen to be the first initials of his victims. *Brauchitsh, Ehrlichman, Yuengling and Zeigler.* Zeigler is the last one on the list, you see each one of these Nazis escaped down what the Allies then termed the rat line, or the Odessa to escape Allied justice in the last days of World War Two."

"These four, in particular were offered sanctuary by the Catholic monks following the collapse of the Third Reich in 1945. And there's only one left Sir, and that is Father Benedetto who is really Heinrich Zeigler of the SS, the main man. And the ex-commandant of Majdanek, he's now the head Abba's at the monastery of St Francis of Assisi of the Franciscan brothers. Right here in Malta."

Captain Hargreaves mood had deteriorated again, he was clearly annoyed; "It's incredible," he said "we fought and so say won the bloody war, and these Nazi thugs, these murderers are still at large and right under our sodding noses. Anyway, that aside if memory serves me right Bloom is on starboard watch this morning so his next liberty is tonight, the question is Salt, will he take the chance to kill this Zeigler chap if he knows we're onto him?"

"Yes, I think he will Sir, you see he's quite insane and driven by pure rage and hatred, these attacks are so cruel and so frenzied, only a madman would contemplate killing Zeigler tonight. But Bloom will I guarantee it, especially as it's his last chance as we're shipping out for Aden in two days."

"How on earth did you know that Salt? That information is classified."

"Because why else would we be topping off our fuel supplies last thing on a Friday night? And why else would we be receiving weather reports on the sea state off Suez? I placed the orders for the oil myself, while Blakey here took the weather reports, you don't have to be *Albert Einstein* to work that one out, sorry Sir, I didn't mean to sound impertinent."

"That's quite all right Salt, I suppose it is your job to know these things but be sure you keep it under your hat, it's still highly classified Lieutenant."

Captain Hargreaves, although slightly annoyed by the young officer's bold presumptuous statement, could see why Jack `Black` McPherson had recruited him so early in his career, he could do with an officer like him aboard Eagle, he liked the cocky, arrogant sway Salt portrayed. He'd go a long way in the

Navy. Captain Clifford Hargreaves RN would bet a year's pay on that. So, as he sat there trying hard to ignore the heat, and maintain a semblance of composure then rather than issuing an order, he simply asked a question;

"So, what is going to happen next? I mean how do we play this one out Salt. I mean do you have a plan?"

"I do, I mean we do, don't we sub-Lieutenant Blake?"

"We do?... I mean yes, we do Sir. But I think Lieutenant Salt here would be much better at explaining it to you, than I Sir."

Salty had set Blakey up for the answer, he did have a plan, it was just that Blakey hadn't been party to it, but he'd guessed right. And Blakey played along.

"Well without actually catching him in the act, we've got no evidence, all we've got on him is that he just happens to be Jewish, is interested in WW2 books about concentration camps, and just happened to be aboard Eagle when the murders were taking place. Bloom's a sharp one-alright, but it's just not enough to stack up in court, we need to actually catch him in the act. So, here's the plan......... We go tonight, but this time we take the marines along with us and post four each side of the monastery walls and allow Bloom to walk right through them. Then we follow him inside and grab him while he's attacking Zeigler. The marines will take care of the SS."

The Captain sat and thought for a minute, it was the second time he'd heard Salty mention marines?

So, he posed another question.

"Well that's all very well and good Salt, but the report says the place is riddled with bloody SS, you can't take them all on surely not, not with just sixteen Royal Marines and you two?"

"Well I also took the liberty of asking some of my old friends along Sir they're specialists in this sort of thing, their names are Sergeant Steiner and his spotter Corp Murphy, they're *SBS*, you know, from the Special Boat Squadron."

"I'm fully aware of what *SBS* stands for young man, I am Captain of this ship you know!"

Salty chose to ignore the Captains re-buff apologised, and simply carried on;

"Sorry Sir, but what's needed in this case is a small specialised team, if we plant too many bodies in the rough outside the walls, Bloom's bound to stumble across one of them. This way, we've a better chance of taking him alive, the men I've picked are the best Sir, the very best."

The Captain twisted awkwardly in his chair, then asked him. "Okay, so where do I fit into all of this? I mean I can't just sit here and twiddle my bloody thumbs and watch you lot take all the glory, now can I?"

"Well with the greatest respect Sir you are the Captain, so the choice is yours, but my personal advice would be to do just that and stay here and sit it out. But I've a feeling you aren't going to do that, so each four-man team will be designated a team leader, and if you want you can head up the south wall team. Sub-Lieutenant Blake here and I will head up the east and west teams respectively, Sgt. Steiner will take the north."

"You really do have this all worked out don't you Salt, my God, how do you sleep at night?"

"I don't Sir."

Salty had purposely given Captain Hargreaves the south wall, the front entrance to the monastery. He had a hunch Bloom would come in from the sea, or the west wall. His own wall.

"Okay Salt, Blake, what time does this all kick off, where do we meet, and tool up, if that's you boys call it, "tooling up," that is."

"We don't Sir, but we meet in the Wessex hangar at twenty-three hundred sharp, you'll need to be cammed up, you'll meet your team then. You've got Corp Murphy acting as your second in command. Murphy's a damn good man."

"Okay, it seem's like a good plan, but that doesn't mean something can't go wrong, so I'll call down to sick bay and have them stand by to take casualties just in case. I'll tell them our old friends the IRA are planning something. So, on that note I think that wraps everything up for now, and I'll meet you in the Wessex hangar.

Any questions Lieutenant's?"

"No Sir."

"No Sir."

"Good, then you're dismissed."

Chapter 22. Monastery of St Francis of Assisi.

Malta.

Father Benedetto ran the monastery like his own personal camp. He'd been there since forty-six, the good fathers had taken him in after finding him on the monastery steps, starving, emaciated, and driven half mad. He'd hidden for a year in farmhouse lofts, barns, and public toilets, following his escape from an Allied prisoner of war camp in Munich. He'd purposely cut out a section of his left underarm, that bore his SS blood group tattoo with a blunt knife informing the `naïve Americans it was from a bullet wound sustained when he was trying to reach Allied lines.

It had worked, but the American's were looking much deeper than an old blood group tattoo, so humble Corporal Fritz Meyer as he was known then, a mere Wehrmacht cook stabbed and killed Private First-Class Joe Graziano while they were playing cards one night, then donned his uniform and escaped right under their noses. And now he was here, safe he thought, that was, until the murders had begun…

Uncle Heinrich as he was affectionately known to the rest of the SS murderers looked out across the sea towards the distant horizon from the top of the monastery walls, he could feel the cold stock of his Luger tucked inside his habit, he'd walked the perimeter a dozen times that night, checking for movement, then checking again, the whole place was on lock down. The wind was up and the breeze from the sea was causing his muscular frame to shiver.

For years he'd felt safe, then the murders had started, should he run? Hide? Where could he run? Where could he go? After all the monastery was his camp, and he enjoyed the weekly visits by the young girl's shipped over from the *Gozo archipelago*, a few of his men even enjoyed the boys.

So, either way he'd decided a long time ago, that he was going nowhere, let them come and face his ten brave SS men they'd have to get through them before they got to him. After all these were not your everyday men, these were brave fearless men who'd fought at *Stalingrad*, *Monte Casino*, and *Kursk*, they were tough men like him. No, this killer Jew would not find it easy, oh no.

Former SS Unterscharfuhrer Kurt Stangl, or Father Benedict pulled his hood back and lit his third cigarette of the night as he cast his eyes surveying the dark scene from the monastery tower. The glossy black barrel of his MG42 machine gun glinted in the moonlight, casting its shadow over the walls below. Kurt was old school, *Waffen SS*, a fighting SS man, a former,

260

Einsatzgruppen Schutzstaffel (SS), and he'd murdered more than his fair share of Jews across Russia and Latvia. And he'd kill even more if they tried to take away his beloved Uncle Heinrich. Let them come, let them try, bring it on.

His spotter, or Kurt's ammunition loader was much younger than Kurt, he'd only just turned seventeen and was too young to remember the war, but *Hans* as they'd christened him was by far and away the most fanatical of them all. He'd been left at the monastery steps as a baby, aged just three months old and the SS men had made sure that he was truly indoctrinated into the fold. Hans with his blonde hair and pale blue eyes was pure SS, a perfect aryan, and Kurt loved him like a son.

"Quiet tonight isn't it Kurt?" Hans whispered;

"Yes, but keep your eyes peeled they're younger than mine, if you hear as much as a mouse fart out there, you tell me, okay?"

"Okay, I will Kurt."

"Take over for a minute will you Hans this old SS man needs to take a pee, I'll bring us some schnapps from the kitchen, remember what I said, keep your eyes peeled."

"I will Kurt, you can rely on me."

Kurt was the only father Hans had ever known, so he smiled as he looked down the shiny machine Guns` perforated steel barrel and he'd be sure to release the red warning flare, if he did hear as much as a mouse fart.

Kurt made his way down the towers stone steps and at the bottom pulled open the vestry door as Uncle Heinrich walked towards him.

"Quiet tonight isn't it Kurt? Uncle asked. "Too quiet almost, is Hans manning the *MG* in the tower?"

"He is uncle, he's very alert I needed a pee, I'll only be a few minutes."

"Take your pee off the top of the tower Kurt! Hans is too young to be left alone, now hurry up and return to your post; Schnell, Schnell!!"

"Sorry uncle, I'm sorry."

Kurt decided to forget the schnapps, Hans would be disappointed, but Uncle Heinrich was someone you only crossed at your peril, so he turned around and ran back up the way he came, and he'd wait until he reached the top, and then take his pee.

As Kurt opened the wooden door to the tower battlements, he could see Hans still holding the wooden stock of the machine gun with his legs splayed, just as he'd left him.

Good boy Hans. Kurt thought.

"Anything to report Hans, see anything?"

But Hans didn't answer him, so Kurt knelt down beside to take a closer look. Han's pale blue eyes were wide open, but it was his head turned at such a strange angle that worried Kurt, so he placed a hand on the back of his head as he supported his body with the other. But then as he looked, Kurt could see and feel the warmth of Han's blood on the inside of his palm. And it was at that exact moment as he reached for the flare gun, that Kurt Stangl, a true Nazi and an SS man to his core that a sharp serrated blade slowly tracked across his throat.

And Kurt Stangl was no more.

Outside, below the monastery walls the four teams had taken up position, and as Salty had instructed two men were facing the walls, while two others faced the rear, and if Bloom approached, they'd have him covered from every angle. Heavily camouflaged marines with night scopes scanned the whole area for movement, and from the shoreline on the western approaches, in his sand revetment Salty waited, and watched.

The South Wall:

On the south wall, Corp Murphy suspected that a frontal approach would be too obvious, and he also suspected that was why Salty had placed Captain Hargreaves under his protection.

The Captain hadn't been out on night manoeuvres since his time spent as a young cadet at Dartmouth, but he was keen, and he was keeping a good eye out, and had the radio glued to his ear. So, Corp Murphy was happy.

The North Wall:

With his finger resting on the trigger and the barrel pointing skyward Sgt Steiner was holding his *SLR* tightly to his chest with a condom hanging down covering the end. Steiner hated blockages, a dud round had nearly cost him his life but his faithful old bayonet had saved him, and it might again. Steiner hated being parted from Murphy. But he looked and he watched like the professional soldier he was, and he'd kill the first SS bastard that popped his head up above the parapet wall.

The East Wall:

Blakey looked up to the top of the east wall, his hearing was exceptional one of the reasons he had specialised in signals, a few minutes earlier he thought he'd heard a scream, or a shout, but didn't feel it worth reporting. After all, *Salty's got enough on his plate.* He thought.

The West Wall:

With the sea constantly rolling its thunderous waves onto the beach to his rear, Salty listened and watched as Marine Jeff Lansdale from Yorkshire passed him a hot coffee.

They'd been hidden for two arduous hours and seen nothing. The marines incessant talking seeming to blend in with the screeching of the seagulls, or the occasional falling rock. Marine Jeff Lansdale had attended a Catholic School, so too Salty his knowledge of all things Catholic felt as though he was listening to a stuck audio tape, at his old Grammar School.

"Don't you think it weird Sir? You know these monks and all that, I mean the isolation, no birds, no booze, I mean I couldn't handle that could you Sir?"

"No Lansdale, I couldn't."

But Lansdale wasn't finished.

"Religious beliefs were all that mattered back then, weren't they Sir? I mean you know, years ago when places like this were attacked half of this lot would have been murdered in their beds, if it wasn't for the tunnels."

Salty was only half listening to Lansdale, his voice had a dull monotonous tone to it, that was right up until Lansdale had mentioned the word. *"Tunnel."*

"What do you mean tunnels? Explain Lansdale."

"Well Sir, it didn't matter if it was the Brits attacking the Moors, or even the bloody French come to that, but when they did attack, the Monks holed up in the monastery would escape down the tunnels, they'd bring in local labour from the surrounding village's to build them, you know strong young lads. They'd offer them safety in return for free labour, and it worked, because once the Brits, the frogs, or the Moors had buggered off after ransacking their village's and raping their women, they'd all come out of the tunnels and have a right good piss up."

According to the plans Salty had seen there were only four ways in or out of the Monastery of St Francis of Assisi. So, was there a fifth?

Acting on instinct, Salty ordered Lansdale to pass him the radio. Then fingered the mic button.

"Calling all commands this is the west wall, this is the west wall, all commands to carry out a thorough search of the perimeter base on each wall, there could be a hidden tunnel somewhere, expedite immediately. Bloom may already be inside, report back when search is complete. Over and out."

A few seconds later the radio crackled to life, as three return messages acknowledged his order;

"Message received and understood."

266

Then it went quiet again as Salty started to pull himself out of his sand revetment and ordered the young marine to follow him;

"Come on Lansdale pick up that rifle, we're going tunnelling."

Lansdale grabbed the green webbing strap on his SLR, checked the magazine was secured as Salty held his hand out and pulled him out. The sand was bone dry after the day's heat and crunched beneath their boots as they made their way up to the rock foundation, at the bottom of the perimeter wall. As they walked tiny sand crabs were darting around busily burying themselves deep, in the whiteness of the sandy shale.

Then from the monastery ramparts high above they heard a noise, but it wasn't an ordinary noise, it was more of a *"whooshing"* sound followed by a loud *"clump"* as a lifeless body fell and hit the ground, only feet from where they were standing.

Marine Landale quickly pointed his SLR towards the lifeless shape, but it didn't move, so slowly he walked towards it and looked down and could see blood running from the body's smashed head onto the silver SS runes just beneath the good father's habit.

Salty was the first to react.

"Shit, shit, he has to be inside, the bastard's used the tunnel like you said, quick Lansdale get your ass over here."

He didn't need to be ordered into the protection offered by the small inlet at the base of the rock, he was already halfway there as Salty barked out his next command.

"All command's, calling all command's this is the west wall repeat this is the west wall, a body's been thrown over the ramparts, all commands to split, repeat split, send two Marines each to the west wall, repeat two marines to the west wall. Remaining Marines to stay in position, and remain alert, over."

Salty didn't hear the three acknowledgement messages from the other command's this time, all he could hear was the steady *"Rat-tat-tat-rat-tat-tat"* of machine gun fire from above, and men screaming and shouting out in German.

Just as he'd been trained, Lansdale immediately pointed his weapon upwards and towards the threat and watched as Salty entered the small inlet and cursed as he caught his right foot on something jagged sticking out from a rock in the sand. So, he felt for his torch from the inside of his camouflaged smock and switched it on.

Two feet either side of where he was standing were six jagged rusty metal bars that at some stage had been forced upwards and out. Behind the bars was an opening and what looked to him like a tunnel. So, he knelt down on the wet sandy floor for a moment and shouted back at Lansdale, who was guarding the entrance.

"I think we've found it Lansdale; it was right under our bloody noses the whole time; you wait there for the Marines to arrive. I'm going in alone, so you follow me the minute they get here, and Lansdale make sure you leave a sentry posted at this end, got it."

"Yes Sir, got it Sir" Lansdale shouted back, as he mumbled something under his breath;

"He's bloody mad this one."

Salty hadn't heard Lansdale's last comment, as he had already switched his torch off and was crawling in through the small opening and pulling himself through into the darkness of what he could only assume must be the tunnel's lower ante chamber.

He tried to stand up and was feeling for the ceiling with his hands pitched above his head. The room was dark and cold, and he couldn't see his legs, but he could hear the sound of water as his feet splashed in the puddles on the stone floor. So, bending slightly forward he reached into his pocket for his torch. And switched it on. The scene was enough to take his breath away, the stone walls and vaulted ceiling of the ante chamber had been flawlessly constructed centuries before, each single stone looked like it had been hand-carved and placed together like a giant jigsaw puzzle, they all fitted perfectly. The ceiling could only be described as a work of art, the arch had been constructed to allow the water to drip off at exactly the right angle, allowing the surplus water to empty into the small flint gutter's, built into the sides of the pennant stone floor.

As the beam of light from his torch walked its way further along into the darkness, he could see the floor start to gently rise. The monks who'd built it back in the tenth century had thought ahead. No need for stairs when you can simply dig down from above at exactly the right angle. Much better for a quicker escape, no clogging on the stairs. *Clever those bloody monks,* he thought as he started to walk up the incline with his torch in one hand, and his trusted Webley cocked and ready in the other.

The incline gradually increased, as each laboured step was taken, and after what felt like an hour of steady walking his calf muscles were beginning to tighten, as each cold breath was inhaled. He stopped every few minutes to place his hands on his knees panting and bending his body forward, as his lung's attempted to take in more oxygen.

The dampness was making him cough and wheeze, the steepness of the incline had increased to a murderous one-in-twelve angle, but still he laboured on, repeating to himself; "One step, two steps…three."

Then as he rounded what he hoped might be the last bend, he saw a big oak door just up ahead with some light escaping around its edges. The floor had thankfully levelled. He'd reached the top, so, ignoring his natural instinct to run straight through, he placed his ear against the door and listened for any sounds from the other side.

But there was nothing, the *"rat tat tat"* of the machine gun fire had stopped a good half an hour ago, so switching his torch off he took hold of the doors rusty handle and opened it.

First an inch, then another, it slowly opened and creaked a sound not unlike a broken cartwheel. In the distance he could hear the dull rumble of heavy footfalls far below him echoing a steady beat within the stone walls. The marines had clearly started their ascent. The Cavalry were coming albeit a good hour away, with all that heavy equipment and seventy-pound *Bergen's* to carry it could even be longer. So, he decided he'd carry on alone.

With the big oak door now fully open, he entered the huge circular courtyard and straight away noticed two draping bodies sprawled out across the upper stone balcony. Their arms outstretched their red clotty blood was dripping to the floor below. Holding his Webley firmly in both hands, he looked quickly left, then right, but still there was nothing, only more doors.

Unsure of which route to take and with the circular courtyard in front of him he decided he'd turn east, towards the front wall, and started to quietly make his way around the circular walkway as he darted from one column to another. After every third column he'd turn around and check his six o'clock. Across the courtyard and up above he could see the bell tower and the sloped barrel of the MG42 machine gun protruding out above the battlement. Its owner long dead by now. Then before he was able to take another next step, he heard somebody laughing from above, so he slowly walked backwards into the centre of the courtyard with his gun pointing upwards. And up above he could see Lieutenant Adam Bloom holding Zeigler, with a gun to his head.

Zeigler's legs were buckled, a wet patch from his crotch spreading across his midriff as Bloom's large hands yanked his head back from behind. Bloom's eyes were betraying an animal like rage, he looked crazed, his hands were shaking and a wound to his left arm was spouting blood.

"Hello Chas, old boy" Bloom shouted down as he yanked Zeigler's head back even further, to Salty the strangest part was

Bloom was pronouncing each word perfectly, like he was almost un-hurried and not bothered. Salty was still pointing his Webley but couldn't be sure he'd get a clean shot.

"Well, well Chas you made it at last, come here for the finale` have you ah? Well, it's going to be a good one, I'm going to give old Zeigler here a really good send off, aren't I Zeigler?"

"Nein, bitte, nein, ich bin ein. Freund, bitte, Freund, hilf mir!!

"No, please, no, im friend, please friend help me!!"

"There's no helping him now is there Chas? So just drop that weapon of yours and come up the stairs, and I'll let you live, tell you what I'll even pretend you took me prisoner, that is of course once I've disposed of our friend here. I've nothing against you Chas old boy, a long life's a happy life that's my motto, what do you say?"

Like all NIS agent's in the field, Salty always kept a snub nosed *38 Saturday night special* tucked away in a holster strapped to his right leg, the chances of Bloom knowing that were remote, so he nodded his head, and placed his Webley down on the stone floor, and looked up again.

"That's better, much more civilised wouldn't you say Chas?" Bloom shouted spitting blood from his mouth.

"Like you'd know anything about being civilised Bloom."

273

"Oh, Chas, don't spoil it now. We've had such a wonderful friendship you and I, come up and watch me prepare old Zeigler here, you can have the exclusive. I'll tell you the whole sordid story I promise."

Salty turned on his heels and jogged towards the stairs, not wanting to present his back to him as a target for too long, he didn't trust the bullet proof vest he was wearing under his smock. His arms and the back of his head were still exposed, and Bloom was holding a .44 Magnum, that made his .38, look like a pea shooter.

As he reached the top, Bloom and Zeigler had dissapeared through the only open door on the circular landing, so he quickly dropped down to one knee and loosened the buckle a notch on the .38 strapped to his ankle. The fastest recorded time he'd ever reached down, drawn his weapon and fired it was in just under four seconds and he'd hit the moving target. He'd have to be the one on the move this time. That's if he didn't want to end up as the target.

"Come on in Chas, and make sure you lock the door behind you, the keys are in the lock pull the bolt across as well, you can see old Zeigler here's pissed his pants, so we don't want to be disturbed."

In the time it had taken him to come up the stairs and enter the room, Bloom had suspended Zeigler's body from the central roof spar by his legs.

His face was glowing a flamey red and his hands were bound behind his back with thick white rope, and Salty immediately recognised the knot Bloom used as the same knot he'd used on all his previous victims.

Bloom took a second to look down at his watch but was still gripping hold of the menacing silver Magnum and pointing it directly at Salty. By this time Zeigler was crying like a baby. And Bloom was clearly enjoying himself.

Salty couldn't picture this person, this ugly fat thing at the Nuremberg rallies saluting his Fuhrer shouting out *"Zeig Heil"* at the top of his voice. He just looked so helpless, how did this thing before him dangling helplessly at Bloom's pleasure ever command respect? Salty's thought moment ended, when Bloom started to speak.

"Now by my reckoning it should take your marines another twenty-five minutes or so, to reach the top. I know that because I timed it on my way up. So, before I stuff this pole up this bastard's throat, there are a few things I wanted you to know." "Go ahead Adam, I'm all ears." Salty replied as he watched

Ziegler's eyes bulge, his body swinging back and forth as the industrial duct tape bit into the sides of his fat mouth.

Salty was playing for time, he'd used Bloom's first name he was trying to appease him, but it hadn't worked.

"Oh, I see it's Adam now is it? Taught you well at Naval intelligence didn't they Chas, bet that's not even your real name though is it? What is your real name by the way? Seeing as I'm about to tell you everything about me."

"It's Salt, Lieutenant Sam Salt NIS, my friends call me Salty. You can if you like."

"Still trying it, well no matter I'll call you Salty anyway you see I really do like you, none of this is personal."

"I know."

"Well Salty we've only got twenty minutes left, so let's get started, shall we. Take a seat, this shouldn't take very long."

Salty cleared his throat and sat down on the hard leather upright chair scratching his right leg, lifting the bottom of his trousers only an inch, the same inch that would translate as time in the next few minutes.

"Well, here we go you might already know this, I don't know, but you see my father was a Jew, a Slovakian Jew, so originally I was born a Slovakian, my dear papa's name was Alex, and by all accounts before the war began he was a quiet gentle type of man, he herded sheep or something. That was until the Nazi's sent him to Majdanek, and shall we say, *altered* him forever."

"I wasn't born until forty-six, so it wasn't until I was aged about nine, maybe even ten that he started to tell me all about the things he'd seen, he explained everything in great detail, names, places, the death march across Poland, the awful cruelty. As he was telling me, he'd make me write everything down. I knew by that time that he was quite insane, he'd constantly break down in tears, he was drinking all the time and he'd beat mama` for the slightest of things. She'd only have to drop a loaf of bread on the floor and he'd beat her, then once finished with her. He'd start on me."

Salty's eyes glazed over, he knew his half of the story but was blown away by Adam's, so as Adam paused for a moment, Salty wiped his eyes. And without Adam noticing raised his trousers another inch.

"Anyway, where was I?"

"Your father beating you Adam."

"Oh yes, yes, forgive me, well when I was about eleven, I came home from school one day to find my father in one of his drunken rage's. He was ranting on about Majdanek, how he was going to kill Zeigler and the rest of his SS bastards."

"I'd never seen him as bad, and it was then that he took the bread knife out of the drawer and he slit my mother's throat from ear to ear, and she fell onto the kitchen floor."

"I can still remember her holding her throat, trying to stop the bleeding, I even remember holding her head in my hands as her eyes stared into mine, and her last words were gurgled as the blood started to fill her mouth. But she said it anyway;"

"Milujem t'a beh beh."

"Do you know what that means Salty, do you?"

"No."

"Well it means "I love you son now run, run", so I did Salty I ran as fast as I could, and that same night my father threw himself under a tram in *Bratislava*. After that old boy without brothers or sisters to turn to, I was left quite alone. A few weeks passed and I was picked up by the local authorities, half-starved wandering the streets of my hometown of *Samorin*, the court decided the best they could for me was to place me in an orphanage for delinquent's, located on the border with Austria. It was run by the so-called Christian Brotherhood, a charity, and it was there that I was abused nearly every night, so what a cliché Heh Salty? What is it they say? The abused so often become the abuser. I think the experience must have changed me forever, you know, altered my sexuality and all that, what do you think Salty?"

"Adam, I don't...."

"Oh, don't answer that, oh where was I?"

"You were describing the abuse Adam."

"Oh yes, that's right, so anyway a few months after my twelfth birthday I met my new parents, apparently, they weren't able to have any children of their own and they'd read some magazine article about orphan's in former war-torn countries from the eastern bloc needing homes. So, they travelled all the way over from Britain especially to see me, they were two wonderful human being's, they didn't care that I was a Jew, they fed me, pampered me, they even sent me to a private school, but it changed nothing."

"What do you mean, it changed nothing Adam, surely their kind...."

"No nothing changed!! Don't you see I still had the list, and I'd sworn an oath to my father that one day I'd hunt these bastards down and make them pay, the same way they made my family pay, don't you get it? Nazis pretending to be monks after what they did to me. It was irresistible Salty, irresistible."

"What a story, you're very ill Adam, you do know that don't you."

"Yes."

"Look, let me help you any Judge in the world would understand, after what's happened to you, they'd prob…."

"Stop it, it's no good I've got to finish this, let me finish it then it's done and it's over for good, then we can both walk out of here together."

"I can't let you do that Adam; I can't allow you to kill him."

Adam picked up the end of the broom and his attention was temporarily distracted, as Salty reached down for his .38, but Adam noticed the sudden movement and pointed the large Magnum to the exact spot that Salty had occupied a split second before.

The high calibre bullet blew the back of the wooden armchair apart reducing it to splinters and horsehair in a split second, as Salty fell to the floor and fired his .38 twice. Just as he'd been trained.

Adam staggered around for a second, then looked down at Salty with the blood from his stomach wound steadily dripping onto the timber floor below, then briefly smiled and with his dying breath said. "Thank you Salty, you're my friend." Then his body slumped forward and his eyes closed, and Lieutenant Bloom, the abused, the abuser, the tormented Jew, was finally at peace. Salty kept the smoking .38 pointing towards his dead body but there wasn't a sound to be heard in the room, only silence and the pungent smell of cordite remained, as he looked up towards Zeigler and his swinging torso he noticed the shit running downwards as it dripped to the floor below. Then once more he looked towards his smoking .38.

Getting up off the floor as Zeigler's body swung in circles, he looked at him searching his terrified eyes then once more he looked back down at Bloom. And wondered and for a moment he considered. And Zeigler thought he knew what he was considering as the smell of the faeces and urine entered Salty's senses and he raised the .38 and pointed it directly at him as Zeigler twisted and bucked wildly and his body spun on the rope.

The whites of Zeigler's pale blue eyes were now only blood spots, his whole body was moving around and around, the fear had gripped him. But still Salty considered.

Somebody was banging on the door, then he heard a crash and he watched as the door splintered before his eyes, then fell inwards and towards him. But he couldn't hear Blakey's words, his mouth was moving but not a sound left his lips. Then in one giant stride Blakey threw himself towards him and pushed him to the floor seizing the gun.

"Stop, stop, stay down, you're safe, your safe mate, it's all right." And as Zeigler looked on, he wondered if his next hanging might be by his neck.

And not his feet....

Chapter 23. Leave Time.

HMS Invergordon: NIS Headquarters.

Commander Terry Walker fingered the intercom button as Lieutenant Black sat patiently waiting outside of Captain Jack `Black` McPhersons office.

Eager for news, McPherson had called him in to discuss his interview with the infamous and very real Paddy O`Hare, in Barlinnie Prison.

"You can go in now Lieutenant," Walker said, "he'll see you now, but I warn you the old man's not in the best of moods today, so get to the point and cut a dash, you know how much he hates long drawn out reports."

"Thank you, Sir, I'll do that."

Walker wasn't keen on Black, he wasn't his cup of tea at all and felt there was something very odd about him, but he couldn't put his finger on it. Black was by no means an open book, but it wasn't just that, it was instinct more than anything else. Walker had checked his records several times. Black was from Aristocracy and had been reared by a good old English family. He'd attended Cambridge and held a master's degree in political science. So, what the hell was it then? He'd be sure to look again the next time he paid a visit to records.

"Sit down Lieutenant draw up a chair, now the report what have you managed to learn from your visit to Barlinnie, and that IRA thug Paddy O`Hare?"

"Well he's a tough one all right Sir, he's off hunger strike now and at first he refused to see me, so I had to interview him in his cell, he wouldn't say a word, not one Sir. He just kept smiling at me and spent the whole-time gluing matches onto the lid of an old tobacco tin. Very odd behaviour. So, in my view a total waste of time Sir. He wouldn't say a damn thing."

"Well something's definitely afoot Lieutenant, Soviet and IRA signals traffic are at an all-time high and have doubled, even trebled since Medhev escaped, trouble is they've changed the code at least a dozen times in the last two weeks. So, our chaps are blind Lieutenant. We're completely in the dark."

Black was pleased with that and was trying to stop the corners of his mouth from raising, so he looked down at the floor and away from the Captain. He'd be sure to warn Koralev later, the traffic had to stop, or it would just be a matter of time before some clever dick at NIS cracked the code, and that wouldn't do at all.

"Well, after the successful outcome of their sortie in Malta Lieutenant's Salt and Blake are taking some well-earned leave in somewhere called Javea, so I suggest you do the same and take some leave Lieutenant Black. I've prepared a travel warrant to Cambridge for you, it's all signed, a week off will do you good, so you're dismissed."

"Thank you, Sir, I could do with a break, I appreciate that."

Lieutenant Black stood up saluted the Captain and wondered what the weather would be like in Javea at that time of year. He might pay his old friends a visit. Why not?

He'd contact Koralev and Medhev later, they'd take Salt in Javea. What could be simpler....?

Chapter 24. Back to Black.

The Flight from Valetta to Madrid had taken just under three hours, and the internal flight from Madrid to Alicante another one hour and a half, so as Pedro the fish man pulled up outside Sandra's bar, Salty and Blakey, quite literally fell out of the van. The long trip had been hard, they were tired, but they'd also managed to consume more than enough beer to put a baby elephant to sleep. So, Pedro watched as the two friends swayed from side to side clinking beer bottles as he wished them well. He also wondered what Fiona would have to say.

Blakey shouted out towards the kitchen.

"Fi, Fi, it's us we're home Fi, it's me Blakey, I've got someone here to see yooooooou."

Fiona instantly recognised Blakey's slurred pronunciation, so, without immediately replying she placed the dish cloth down on the enamel drainer, slipped off her apron, flicked her hair back, and walked into the bar.

"Well look what the cat's dragged in, two dirty old sea dogs, sorry, my mistake, I mean two very drunken dirty old sea dogs."

Salty felt it was all his fault, it was him who'd hidden the beers in his case, so his bottom lip dropped in resignation.

But Blakey's didn't, so Salty tried to explain.

"Fi, it's all my fault, it's like this, we......"

"Oh, shut up Salty, come here and give us a big kiss, and bring that overgrown idiot of a husband of mine with you."

And the celebrations began and continued.... Long into the night.

The next morning despite an awful hangover, Salty was up at the crack of dawn, he'd promised himself he'd watch the sunrise over the *Montgo Mountain*. So, he sat down on the cold curved tiles of the `naya` roof marvelling at the colours of the mountain changing from a darkish grey to a bright pinkish hue, as the sun accelerated its path towards the glistening Mediterranean.

Blakey was right, Javea was truly an undiscovered pearl, *years from now people will be flocking here* he thought, and it was about then that he thought he'd write to his very own pearl. His Louise.

My Dearest Louise.

Well our sortie is complete, and I'm afraid as usual I'm unable to describe it to you in any detail, so I'll just say it was an interesting one, and leave it at that. I've been granted a week's leave, but I'm sorry to say they wouldn't allow me to take it in Malta.

It's Naval protocol after a sortie, security reasons and all that. So anyway, I decided to come back here to Javea and spend it with Blakey and Fiona. I must admit that Blakey and I held our own private celebration on the flight's between Malta and here so we're both a bit worse for wear this morning.

As I write it's about six thirty in the morning and I'm perched on top of the roof above Sandra's bar, the sun is coming up, the air is fresh, and for once I feel totally at peace. My only regret is that you aren't here to share it with me and see this beautiful sunrise.

I miss you so terribly. I have another week's leave coming up in about a months' time according to Jack, so it won't be long before: "I can hop on a tug," and come and visit you.

On that note, I must leave you as I can hear Fiona shouting up at me for breakfast, so I'll sign off now.

I love you.

Signing off with a kiss and a hug.

Salty

As he clambered back across the tiled roof and re-entered the small window to the bedroom, Salty could hear Fiona's voice calling him from below;

"Salty breakfast, we're sitting here waiting for you."

"Coming Fi, just putting a shirt on we don't want you getting yourself all worked up at the sight of a proper man, now do we?"

The laughter, mainly Blakey's got louder as he descended the dark wooden staircase and stepped through the fly curtain into the kitchen. The round wooden table was covered in warm croissant's, jams, butter, ham, and cold eggs, but despite all that he still felt quite queasy.

"How are you feeling then mate?" Blakey asked looking across the table, heavily buttering his second croissant knowing full well Salty had the weakest of stomachs. Fiona kicked him hard under the table and told him to. "Stop it and leave him alone. Come on love, you sit down and get something down you, it'll make you feel better."

But it didn't because he'd left the table by then, and only just made the tiny white sink in the toilet, before busily discharging copious amounts of spent alcohol down its shiny plug hole as Blakey carried on laughing.

In the late afternoon and leaving Julia to tend the bar the three friends decided to visit the local market that was held every Friday in a dusty old field just behind the sea front and shops in Moraira. A local village some five kilometres due west of Javea.

The market was amazing, the local produce and goods ranged in variety from food stuff's such as pepper's, fruit's, and olive's, to clothing like sombrero's and ladies' hand-stitched cotton blouses.

The blazing sun was hanging high in the vastness of the clear blue sky as the temperature started to nudge the mid-eighties and life felt really good as the three laughed together searching the alley's and stall's drinking the local Vino Tinto and enjoying their day. But that was when he saw him....

"Did you see him? Did you see him? It was him, he's here." Salty said pointing at the long line of people standing in the midday sun all holding wooden plates, waiting for the seafood Paella to be served from the stall.

Blakey and Fiona looked towards the spot where Salty was pointing and both answered in in near unison as they looked back at him and considered their friend's terrified stare.

"Who Salty? Whose here? Who?"

"It's him, I saw him he's here, Medhev's here."

Blakey recognised his name straight away. But, of course Fiona didn't.

"Who the hell's bloody Medhev," she asked, "are you feeling all right Salty? Has he had too much sun Blakey?"

Salty was stood like a frozen automaton, whose battery had run flat and didn't answer for a moment, instead he felt for his Webley, but it wasn't there? So, he turned to check his six-O`clock at about the same time as Blakey grabbed hold of

Fiona's arm, and the three of them started to walk, then ran towards the exit.

"Will somebody tell me what the hell's going on? I'm not a bloody child." Fiona shouted out, wrenching her arm from Blakey's slowing up. But Blakey grabbed hold of her again.

"Fi, I've never said this to you before, but please just shut up! Just keep going, don't make a fuss and everything will be fine."

Salty was attempting to explain as they ran.

"Look Fi, this Medhev is somebody you don't want to mess about with. He's a cold-blooded killer, someone I've been chasing nearly the whole of my short career, and believe me right now, we really do need to get the hell out of here."

Fiona's blood ran cold as they sped up, and she looked towards Blakey and the protection he offered and decided to.

"Shut the hell up," for the moment.

But she would wait until they were alone and in private before she'd warn him to never talk to her like that again.

Blakey hailed the first taxi passing outside the market entrance, and the short trip back to Javea alternated between moments of complete silence and rapidly expanding truths. And as the more truths were revealed, the more terrified Fiona became.

As they drew up outside Sandra's bar, Fiona was the first to notice that the exterior blinds had been pulled down, and the doors were closed. Sandra's was shut.

"So, where's Julia then?" Fiona asked.

"Blakey you wait here with Fiona, I'll go and take a look." Salty said as he exited the front of the taxi and Julia suddenly appeared from nowhere, waving her hands wildly in the air towards the taxi from the entrance of *Taqueria* the little fish restaurant opposite. Salty was the first to run towards her, with Blakey and Fiona following just a few steps behind.

"What's happened Julia? Why is Sandra's shut?" Salty demanded. But Julia's face was ashen, her usually bright cheery persona was hidden beneath a veil of fear, and her hands were shaking as she attempted to draw breath and looked up and down the dusty road, before finally turning towards Fiona and broke down crying.

"Just after you leave a man came, oh God, he was a terrible man, he had gold teeth, comprende?"

"Go on." Salty said.

"He tells me, to tell you Mr. Salty he wants to meet you he says he has information you want. I no understand him, he grips my wrists, pull me over counter, then he tells me again you must meet him at six tonight at the harbour entrance, and he tell you to make sure you come alone."

"What else did he say Julia? Did he say anything else?" Salty asked coupling her shaking hands in his;

"Yes, he says if you not come alone, he come back here, he kills my girls, then me, and after that he kills Fiona and Blakey. Oh, my God what sort of man is this?"

"You're not going alone I'm coming with you." Was Blakey's first remark.

"No, you heard what he said I have to be alone, you've got to stay here and take care of Fi, Julia, and the kid's this moment's been coming for a long time, he only wants me Blakey he's not interested in you, if I go alone you lot will be safe."

Blakey fully understood that even he couldn't be in two places at once, they were in Spain, there was no back-up from anyone at NIS, so no quick way of handling this. Salty would have to go alone. But Blakey did have an idea.

"Can I use Taqueria's telephone a moment Julia? There's somebody I need to talk to, urgently."

"Yes, yes please come in we are all friend's, it's just over there."

Blakey made his call and a little under two hours later Pedro the fish man pulled up outside Sandra's in his pickup. As he got out, Fiona noticed the hessian covered bundle he was carrying under his right arm and pretended not to notice as she carried on serving the Sangria, bread rolls, and Vino Tinto to the locals as Pedro disappeared through the fly curtains at the back.

Pedro, and his father before him had fought for the Republican side during the Spanish Civil War, his father was killed in the terrible bombing of *Guernica* by the German's in thirty-seven. But before he died, he revealed to Pedro where all his weapons were stashed. The very same weapon's, Pedro was now so proudly displaying to Salty and Blakey across the dining room table.

"These two are Astra model 900's my friends, they were handmade right here in Espana," he proudly announced, "they take a 7.63mm bullet, you see this long magazine at the bottom it contains ten rounds, and they are full. I have no other ammunition; I am afraid the rest were used killing Franco's fascist pigs back in thirty-eight."

The weapons although ancient were very similar in design to an earlier version of the world-famous German *Luger* and had been hand polished and kept in an excellent condition, but none of that mattered really. After all it was all Salty had.

"Can't thank you enough Pedro," Blakey said as he patted Pedro's back and stared down the barrel testing its balance trying the grip. Salty was doing the same thing but making sure his was pointed towards the other end of the kitchen.

"Are you killing fascist's or communist's my friend?" Pedro asked smiling at the two agents', who were still fully engrossed in the style of their new weapons.

"Neither" replied Salty without looking around, "just a cold-blooded killer Pedro."

"Good enough." Pedro announced folding up the hessian cloth and placing it in his pocket. "Good enough."

Five O'clock approached and Salty looked toward the Montgo mountain mumbling a silent prayer to himself knowing full well that without backup his chances of survival were extremely slim. But he also knew if he didn't go, Blakey's, Fiona's, and Julia's would be non-existent.

So, he checked the gun's magazine a final time, clicked the safety to on and pushed it firmly down the back of his belt, and started his forty-minute walk to the harbour.

He took the most direct route the footpath with the rocky beach and the turquoise sea to his right, he was savouring the coolness of the Mediterranean sea air in his lungs and stopped for a second watching as the local Spanish carved out huge chunks of *Tosca* stone from the rocky beach, using double-grip handsaws, chisels, hammers, and all sorts of hand tools to excavate the precious rock.

Burros ferried the yellow chalky stone packed neatly inside pouches and were delivering it to handcart's lining the dusty beach road. The local Guardia Civil looked on, either too afraid to intervene, or had simply been paid off to look the other way. He really didn't know. And right at that moment he really didn't care.

He began to wonder if this might be his last walk. Had he viewed Louise's beautiful face for the last time? Had that been his last drink with Blakey and Fiona? He wondered.

As he crossed the small stone bridge just before the entrance to the harbour gates, and the fish market, he noted the time, it was 5.45 PM. And he was early. High above him the sun was still beating down relentlessly, it's light casting shadows on the harbour wall as he wiped the perspiration from his brow, and he looked towards the two open gates and realised that Medhev was already there. He could feel him, sense him, he could almost smell him, he wouldn't be far away. So, he drew his weapon took another five steps forwards and took cover behind the upturned hull of a disused sailing boat. The harbour was quiet, and deserted, the inert silence only disturbed by the noise of the seagulls as they passed overhead, and the sea as it gently lapped against the quayside walls.

All of a sudden, he sensed a movement from behind him, and heard a noise like somebody tapping, then it happened again, "tap, tap, tap…." Then he heard a whispered voice. So, he looked behind him.

"Salt, it's me Lieutenant Black, I'm over here, just behind you covering your six, Blakey sent me so stay where you are, and I'll come to you."

Black was crouched down behind a stack of empty wicker fish baskets with his gun pointing inwards, towards the fish shed. And Salty thanked God he finally had backup.

Black stood up and looked around quickly darting from boat to boat, keeping his large frame low to the ground, only stopping for a second or two to catch his breath before he reached Salty's upturned hull. His act was faultless.

"Blakey said I might find you here, seen anything yet?"

"No, but what the hell are you doing in Javea?"

"It's a long story, I'll tell you later. Let's smoke this bastard out, you take the left flank towards the fish shed and I'll take the right; he's got to be in there somewhere."

Salty nodded in acceptance, all that mattered was taking Medhev and at that moment he didn't care if he took him dead, alive, or somewhere in between. Whatever it took. He'd get him.

Wrongly assuming that Black had taken the right flank, he got up and sprinted as fast as he could towards the huge fish shed doors and crouched down to check his weapon and wondered if two of the Astra's 7.63mm calibre bullets would suffice. One to the upper torso to maim and stun, then finally a head shot, and it would be all over.

He assumed that by this time Black must have reached the shed's back doors, and if Medhev was inside… they'd trap him in the crossfire. It was also about then that he decided he didn't want to take him prisoner. He needed to end Medhev's existence there and then, and bollocks to the fall out after.

The smell of dead fish mixed with disinfectant from inside had started to irritate his eyes, the deserted space was cold and damp, the concrete floor was littered with puddles. What to do? He wondered. He knew that if he ran in with all guns blazing, he'd be picked off in seconds but if he stayed where he was, his chances weren't much better. So, what to do?

So, he decided to shout.

"Medhev, if you're in their come out! There's no way out, the place is covered front to back, so drop your weapon and come out with your hands up."

The line although a little cliché and sounding more like something one might hear in a forty's western was all he could think of, but at least Black knew he was ready, and in position. Then he heard Medhev's high pitched shout from inside.

"Salt come in; come in I've been waiting for you."
Salty immediately fired two shots between the small gap in the metal lathe of the doors towards where he thought the voice was coming from, then quickly darted back into a crouched position.

"Ha ha nowhere near Salt, not even close, just take a look to your left Lieutenant."

He thought Medhev was mocking him, playing with him, but where was Black? Why hadn't he fired? Then he looked to his left and saw him.

Black was standing prone with his legs spread two feet apart with both his hands tightly gripping his Naval issue Webley MK IV and he was pointing directly at Salty. It took a few seconds for Salty to comprehend what was happening, and take it all in. *Is Black covering my back? If so, why is he pointing the gun at me?* And then the penny finally dropped as Black motioned him with a nod of his head telling him at the point of a gun to; "Drop your weapon Salt, drop it to the floor. One wrong move and I'll shoot you where you stand, drop the weapon and kick it over towards me… Now!!"

Salty thought for a moment and time seemed to stand still. *Should I try a shot?* Black's gun was pointing directly at his chest and he would probably get one off before he could even raise his arm, and without a bullet proof jacket on he wouldn't stand a chance of surviving a chest shot. On the other hand, if they wanted him dead, he would already be lying in a pool of his own blood by now, so he did just that, he bent down and placed his weapon on the concrete floor and without taking his eyes from Black's kicked the gun over towards him.

The gun slid across the wet concrete floor and came to a halt by his right foot, but it wasn't Black that picked it up. It was Kapitan Leonid Medhev.

"So, here we are again then Salt. You know what? You have been a Royal pain in my fucking ass! I should have killed you when I first saw you, but it wasn't to be, you have no idea how much joy this brings me, you have made my day my whole century in fact. You are going to pay Salt, oh, are you going to pay."

Medhev snarled his words and bit down hard on his gold teeth as his fist clenched and he threw his first punch Salty completely unaware as it connected squarely with the lower part of his abdomen.

As he doubled up in pain and his knees crunched down hard onto the concrete floor Medhev, like a deranged madman just kept kicking, screaming, and raining blows down onto his curled-up torso. And Salty started to wonder.

Is this was it? Is this how it was all meant to end

Only darkness followed…...

Chapter 25. Dead and Buried.

The smell of freshly dug earth was all around him, he could see a flicker of light as his eyes opened and he tried blinking. He tried to move his hands, but couldn't, his legs wouldn't bend either, so he tried to turn over, but he couldn't. ......Every instinct he possessed pleaded with him to, scream out, to kick and shout. He scratched the sides of the coffin then tried to stretch his legs and could feel and hear the sounds of his toenails scraping the wooden bottom. So, instinctively he tried to sit up and wiggle sideways, but he couldn't. Anyway, there was no point, because he was buried alive.

Then he saw the tube, as a small flicker of light danced across his eyes, and the tube was dangling just above his forehead. And then he heard the voice, Medhev's voice and it was coming from the end of the tube.

"You just keep thrashing around down there, you're two metres down it'll make you nice and hot and your air will run out sooner, tell you what Salt fuck you! Enjoy this!"

Medhev capped the end of the tube and total darkness and intense heat was all that remained as the panic tried again as he writhed around, shouting and screaming, but nobody was listening, and he clawed at the sides like a deranged animal. Until finally he passed out.

As he woke up the flicker of light caught his eyes and the tube had returned and as he lay there his thoughts travelled back to Invergordon. To the time two years ago, when Jack had told him this was his last test, and whatever happened he had to pass it. All the others could be retaken. But not this one.

He'd been buried underground and entombed in a wooden coffin for three days and three long nights buried deep below the heather just above Invergordon on the moor. At the time Jack hadn't told him how long he'd be underground. Saying that was the whole point of the test, but that was different, because he knew someone would eventually turn up and rescue him. But not this time.

He remembered that on his third day or night whichever it was he was led there in the cold blackness and doubts had started to creep in, and he started to wonder. Dark thoughts passed through his head bizarre terrifying thoughts that made no sense at all.

"What if they've forgotten about me? What if Jack's been killed, and no one knows I'm here? They might have forgotten where they've buried me?"

Then on the third night he thought he heard spades digging nearby, so he shouted and screamed, scratched and clawed, then the noise suddenly stopped. And the light returned, and Jack was standing over him, he'd been camped the whole time less than two feet away. He hadn't forgotten him. Not Jack.

Seven of the recruits on the course had failed the test, one was brought out punching, kicking and screaming after only two hours underground and it had taken three burly marines to hold him down, but not Salty. No, Salty had passed.

So, he needed to remain calm, to focus his thoughts and cast his mind back to what Commander Terry Walker had told him during the lengthy debriefing afterwards.

"Always remember one thing Salt, if there's an air hole, there's a good chance they want to keep you alive, why else would they put one in? The simple answer is they wouldn't."

The commander's wise words were all that were keeping him from the edge of madness and from going completely insane.

"Training Salty, always remember your training, keep calm, take shallow breaths, flex your muscles, exercise, stretch Salty, stretch." The Commander had told him.

So, for three days as the air tube was randomly opened and closed, he counted the hours and minutes that the tube remained open. Then he calculated the number of cubic feet inside his box by stretching out his toes and touching his nose on the lid, finally he splayed his palms out to the sides then divided the sum by the oxygen needed for the average sized man to remain alive, and he realised that Medhev wanted him alive.

The thirst came on the second day as an unquenchable gnawing wrenched at his stomach and he swallowed his own spittle as he licked the sweat from his lips, his fingernails were bleeding from his incessant uncontrollable urges to scratch and claw his way out, and he was crying. He wanted to give up, he wanted it to end. But it didn't.

So, as he entered his fourth day underground and heard the sounds of shovelling from above his heartbeat spiralled out of control as he shouted and screamed, and the coffin went black again.

They're topping me off. That's it I'm dead.

But then he heard this scraping noise on the lid and could hear the screeching noise of a crowbar as it pulled and wrenched on the nails and he listened as they moaned their way free.

It was such a blinding light that he had to scrunch his eyes up he could hear Medhev shouting at someone, telling them to, "Pull him out, pull him out."

As they dragged his limp body up out of the coffin, every single limb was aching, and he could hear wet mud falling from his clothes to the wooden floor below, he could feel the rough coldness of the wooden floorboards beneath his bare feet. Then his legs buckled, and he fell to the floor. And Medhev laughed.

"Quickly drag him over here, tie him up to that chair."

He could feel the tightness of the rope as it bit into his wrists, and his back arched as somebody wrenched his shoulder's back. And it was only then that he dared to open his eyes. The room seemed odd somehow. It wasn't like anything he'd ever seen before, something was wrong, the furnishing's looked old, foreign somehow. For sure he was on the ground floor, the uplifted floorboards and the piles of earth surrounding the grave proof of that, but the room was odd, it even smelled odd.

"You're probably wondering where you are Salt? Well I'm not going to tell you exactly where, but I will tell this, you are in the east Salt, yes you are in the Motherland, the U.S.S.R. no less. So even if you try and escape you won't get far, our troops will hunt you down and their dog's will tear you to pieces in seconds. Isn't that correct commissar Black?"

Black was standing in the far corner of the room with his arms folded looking out through a small crittal window, his presence in the shadow's until then was undetected by Salty. He was wearing the uniform of a full KGB Major complete with yellow starred shoulder boards of a *Commissariat*, a fully-fledged Soviet Political Officer. So, Salty looked over towards him and

306

spat the mud from his mouth, the disdain in his question matched only by the loathing contained in his words.

"Why you Black? You of all people. Why? You had it all, the family, Cambridge, the posh education, the money. The houses." Salty spat the last remnants of the mud on the floor just missing one of Black's shiny brown leather boots.

"Oh, you disgusting pig." Black replied as he walked around the spittle and leant in towards the chair a few inches from Salty's face.

"Do stop that incessant whimpering Salt, this has nothing to do with money you idiot, and it has even less to do with my social standing, not that you'd know anything about that mind you judging by your manners. Yes, I did attend Cambridge where I mingled with certain individuals who let's say, took a different slant on life, and like me, hated its inequalities."

"You mean Burgess, McClean, and Philby don't you." Salty quickly replied struggling to expand the ropes by using his thumbs behind the chair.

"I must admit I met them a couple of times, although I wasn't that impressed really, don't tend to see much of them these days. Anyway, that aside, you're right my family are well to do but you see Salt they represent the *bourgeoise* and the elite in our society. They're enemies of the state, enemies of their own people and when…"

"You always were a prick Black, the first time I met you I worked you out, you're nothing but a spoilt overgrown little pri…"

Before the last words had even left his mouth, someone or something kicked him hard in the back from behind that sent him and the chair flying across the room, the chair came to rest against the far wall and for a second, he was led there twisted and upside down, with his face on the floor.

And it was then that he heard a new voice in the room, a Russian voice; "Shut your fucking mouth, you fascist pig, or I will shut it for good." The voice demanded.

The next voice he heard was Medhev's as the new voice pulled the overturned chair upright, with Salty still strapped in it, and two large hands pushed him further down onto the seat.

"Now this is somebody I was desperate for you to meet Salt you've already had the pleasure of meeting his brother. In fact, if memory serves me right it was you that shot and killed him. I was right there so I can bear witness to that, let me introduce you to Boris. That's Boris Kuznetsov. Boris here, is going to be your very own smithy……"

Chapter 26. Glienicke Bridge.

Stasi Secret Police Headquarters
Potsdam. East Berlin. Eastern Germany. October 1968.

A little less than five years earlier, the most famous prisoner exchange in history had taken place on Glienicke Bridge. When *Francis Gary Powers* an American CIA U2 Spy-plane pilot was swapped for Soviet agent, KGB Colonel Vilyam Fisher.

Glienicke Bridge separated West Berlin from its Soviet held counterpart, the Berlin suburb of Potsdam in the G.D.R. The Soviet army had crossed in droves, paddling wooden assault boats back in April 1945 and had paid in human blood for every single yard they'd gained, and Stanislav Koralev hero of the Soviet Union now head of the KGB had been there. Koralev was reminiscing as he lit his third Turkish cigarette in an hour as he looked down at the city from high above in his office at Starsi's Polizei headquarters.

Potsdam, or the city of *Prussian Palaces* as it was famously known, stretched far and wide to the horizon below, some of its lavish opulent buildings had fallen into disrepair, but good Soviet money wouldn't be wasted on their reconstruction. No, Koralev thought as he drew on his cigarette, what the people need are flats, homes, jobs, and state school's that's what the people craved. That and the biggest land army in Europe.

"So, let them collapse, let them all fall down."

Koralev had served with distinction as a Captain in the third *Belorussian* shock army led by the famous Soviet Marshall, *Georgi Zhukov*. They'd fought the Nazi Fascists for every street, every basement, and ceded no quarter. And in fairness they expected none in return. Koralev had personally ordered the shooting of every SS man or woman they'd encountered, irrespective of age, and if it had been up to him, *Rudolf Hess*, and that Nazi lying pig *Albert Speer* would have been hanging from their necks in *Spandau*, years ago. But it wasn't. And that infuriated him.

Six floors below, the basement had been converted from the kitchen of the once gay and lively *Prinze Albert Strasse Hotel* and was now the holding cells for all the political prisoners, murderers, rapists, and general troublemakers the city regularly spewed from its depressing streets, flats and sewers. And Lieutenant Sam Salt was one of its newest residents and occupied a cell all of his own because his heavily bandaged left hand had become so badly infected that, if he was confronted by other prisoners, or even guards the fever induced delirium would cause him to act hysterically.

His weight had dropped from a healthy twelve and a half stone to just a little under eight, the loss of two finger's slowly sawn from his hand by the smithy Boris Kuznetsov had seriously affected his physical health, and his mental state fared only slightly better. But after eleven and a half months of continuous questioning with the same question's repeated over, and over again, cracks in his psyche had started to appear.

In short, he was slowly but surely losing his mind.

"Guards, guards, I want to see Louise, where's Blakey? You there Blakey? Dad, I can see you, please get me out of here dad, I'm afraid dad, get me out."

The shouting was always followed by an awful sobbing that would sometimes go on for hours and Oberleutnant Hans Cramm, the hardened East German Stasi border guard found the ranting, intolerable. So, he'd simply beat him some more, drink his schnapps and enjoy the temporary silence as he watched football on the East German channel; *Deutscher-Fernsehfunk.*

One night he'd found his prisoner unconscious; bleeding out on his cell floor hallucinating with a raging fever after he'd pulled his stitches out. By the time Cramm had found him Salty had lost over three pints of his very rare blood, and Cramm thought he was dying. Koralev contacted the British embassy within the hour and arranged for six pints of the rarest blood on the planet, *RH-Null* to be handed over, the delivery took place two hours later made by a Red Cross Jeep crossing the border, via *Checkpoint Charlie*. Another hour and Salty would have been dead, and his exchange for the infamous IRA leader Paddy O'Hare. Postponed Indefinitely.

On the other side of the border, Jack stared upwards towards the tall grey watch tower waiting at the entrance road to the bridge on the western side as he listened to the incessant barking of the German Shepherd dogs contained behind six rows of barbed wire on the eastern bank. He watched as they fought to find a way out, or an escaping East German citizen to kill or maul.

Machine guns with blinding floodlights imitating giant suns manned by trigger happy East German border guards were pointing westward and constantly scouring the thirty metres of river, the opposing powers had so unimaginatively renamed; "No man`s land." The Americans, Russians, and the British, the *Big Three* all paid up members of the exclusive nuclear club, faced each other like squabbling tribe's, in a tense nuclear stand-off. Each waiting for the other to make the first move. Or, maybe the first mistake. And Jack wondered. To him this wasn't just a normal prisoner exchange his son was over there somewhere beyond the search lights and the barbed wire, but only he was party to that, the guilt hung around his neck like a giant lead weight. And if they'd as much as hurt one hair on his head, he'd hunt them down like dog's, and kill every one of them.

"Pass me the binoculars will you Commander?" Jack asked, unable to remove his eyes from the bridge.

"No sign yet Sir, it's only twenty-one fifty, I make it another ten minutes by my watch."

"I don't bloody well care what time you make it Commander Prosser, pass me those bloody goggles!"

Cmdr. Prosser was used to Jack's sudden flare ups especially when dealing with difficult or stressful situations, but this time it felt different somehow. He'd never seen him so het up, so nervous and angry. And he'd never seen him allow himself to get so personally involved. So, he wondered.

Jack brought the binoculars up to his eyes as he apologised to the Commander for his last remark.

"I'm sorry Commander Prosser, I'm just...."

"I completely understand Sir, my nerves are in shreds as well you've no need to apologise to me Sir."

"Thank you, Commander, what time is it now?"

"Just short of five minutes to go Sir."

"Is everybody in position?"

"Everyone."

"Hand me the radio please Commander."

As Cmdr. Prosser was about to lean down and retrieve it from its cradle, the green walkie-talkie suddenly crackled to life.

"Rainbow six, rainbow six this is monty, this is monty, over." Jack quickly prized the radio out of the Commanders hand and responded in seconds.

"Monty, monty, this is rainbow six, rainbow six, receiving you loud and clear, report, over."

"There's movement on the bridge below rainbow six, two East German Kubelwagens and an ambulance have parked six yards due east of the main approach road, over."

"Do you have visual on the personnel? Over......"

"Standby........"

Five seconds later. Jack with the receiver still pressed hard against his ear listened as he heard the news he'd been dreading.

"Affirmative, rainbow six we have visual, three men in uniform are slowly walking towards the west side of the bridge waving a white pennant, walking a couple of yards behind them are two medics carrying a stretcher and what looks like an injured fourth person, over."

"Is it Salt? Monty, repeat is it Salt? Over."

"Stand by rainbow six, over."

The radio crackled again and hissed for a few seconds, before Sgt Steiner backed up by his spotter Corp Murphy who were hidden high above in the steel ramparts of the bridges structure confirmed Jack's worst fears.

"Confirmed rainbow six, the patient is Lieutenant Salt, we can just about make out his face from here, he doesn't look good though Captain… over and out."

Just before three that morning under the cover of darkness, Steiner and Murphy had scaled the iron bridge camouflaged in dark grey nylon smocks matching the painted ironwork.

They'd gotten straight to work removing two large steel bolts on the bridges central steel upright, and were using one hole to spot, and the other to shoot. Koralev, Medhev, and Black were all in their line of sight, and Steiner as professional as always would wait for Jack's coded order, *Blitz* before firing.

Jack was the first to move towards the centre of the bridge, his every step crunching the wet gravel surface underfoot as he was followed by Commander Prosser and two heavily armed Royal Marine Commandos, with a handcuffed Paddy O'Hare just behind.

On the east side, the stretcher bearers layed Salty's body down just shy of the thick white line that marked the official border between east and the west, as Medhev, Koralev, and the traitor, Black stood and waited. Jack stopped just short of the white line and looked down at the seemingly lifeless body and prayed it was his son. The coarse grey blanket betrayed his laboured breathing, in then out, in, then out, as his chest moved up and down and a seething Jack was sub-consciously imitating his son's movements.

"So, this is how you treat your prisoner's is it Koralev?" Jack asked, his face a mixture of loathing, hate, and revenge.

"My apologies Captain McPherson, this was carried out without my knowledge, Kapitan Medhev here got a little bit carried away, I'm sure he will surv…."

"He'd better Koralev, believe me for your sake, he'd better. Marines! Pick up Lieutenant Salt and take him to the ambulance."

At the same time as Salty was being stretchered away Commander Prosser unfastened O'Hare's handcuffs, and pushed him over the line with a shove, and said. "Our business here is concluded Koralev."
But it wasn't.

"No, it is not concluded yet Commander." Koralev replied as he pulled his Tokarev automatic pistol out and pointed it at the nape of Medhev's head who was standing just a foot in front of him.

"You see, McPherson I did tell Medhev here that I don't give third chances, or my reputation would be in ruins."

Medhev turned instinctively to face the barrel, and a second later the gun went off and the front of his face imploded in a mass of crimson flesh and tangled bone tissue, and his lifeless body collapsed onto the wet concrete.

And Koralev said; "Now we're even McPherson and this ends here Captain."

Koralev then carefully replaced the smoking Tokarev back into his brown leather holster without looking down towards the tangled bloody mess that had once been Kapitan Leonid Medhev, a decorated hero of the Soviet Union.

Commander Prosser and Jack then turned around and started to walk back towards the west end of the bridge and could see Salty's limp body being loaded into the ambulance at the far end. And it was about then that Jack's temper, like a lightning bolt from hell overwhelmed every other emotion he possessed, and he picked the radio up, keyed the mic, and shouted "Blitz!" into the green mouthpiece.

And almost instantaneously Sgt Steiner pulled the trigger releasing a 7.62mm stub nosed round that entered Lieutenant Black's forehead, and the ex-Royal Navy, a former Aristocrat and Soviet spy's body shook for a few seconds before it staggered forwards and he took a last glance towards the west then collapsed onto the pavement.

And Jack, without bothering to look around shouted out, in fluent Russian;

"Нет, теперь мы даже коралев...!!"

"No. Now we're even Koralev....!!"

The End

To Be Continued in:
Volume III – The Seven Dragon's
Third, in the Salt's War Series. Out Soon.

Hopefully you enjoyed "Blood and Country"
If you did please leave a review on Amazon.
Or contact the author by email at.
saltswar@yahoo.com

Printed in Great Britain
by Amazon